Prospero's Daughter

Prospero's Daughter

CONSTANCE
BERESFORD-HOWE

Stoddart

General Paperbacks edition published in 1989

Published in 1988 by Macmillan of Canada

Cover Design: Brant Cowie/ArtPlus Limited

ISBN 0-7736-1179-7

Printed and bound in USA

For my god-daughter
Constance Mary Turnbull
with love

"Everybody has his own theatre, in which he is manager, actor, prompter, playwright, scene-shifter, boxkeeper, doorkeeper, all in one, and audience into the bargain."

— *Augustus William Hare*

Contents

Prologue

By the time I recognized my father's back (he was looking into a window of Liberty's), it was too late to get away. Oblivious to the roar of London traffic and the glare and reek of a dusty April day, he stood there lost in critical survey of six mannequins holding up swags of fabric. Presumably he was early for an appointment or for lunch at his club, and had time to kill. The set of his spine and tilt of his head clearly indicated he had a low opinion of the window-dresser's talent and considered he could have done an incomparably better job himself. In short, he looked from the back exactly as he used to do when fiercely directing his children in those holiday Twelfth Night and Midsummer Eve productions we used to dread and love simultaneously. But I was not yet nimble enough on my two canes to move my reflection out of the window before he turned and spoke to me.

"Well, Paulina! What have you been doing to yourself?"

It was not, perhaps, the kind of greeting you might expect from a man who had not seen his youngest daughter for four years—that is, unless you knew my father. But then who, after all, really did know Pa? Certainly I was not wise enough a child for that.

When I say he was a novelist, I state a fact—though it

was, I used to think, the kind of fact that reveals nothing. Now, however, after all that happened from the moment of this encounter, I know this much: his being a writer of fiction was probably the most significant single thing about him.

Part of the reason for that, of course, was his success. The books Pa wrote were not only very popular but regarded as serious literature by the weightiest critics, and this gave him a self-confidence so immense it went far beyond mere arrogance. It also made him the most fiery and impatient of all possible parents. Unlike his fictional creations, all his children in their various ways resisted and eluded him. Not one of us ever proved malleable enough and so caused him the keenest exasperation and resentment. Except for Nan, perhaps, for whom his expectations were low, the rest of us all notably failed to give satisfaction.

Pa was now scanning me critically through the bottoms of his bifocals (new since I'd last seen him). And how familiar was that frowning and impatient yet affectionate stare. How completely did it peel away adulthood and expose the child who had brought home a zero in math, or knocked over the tea-urn, or failed to learn her lines.

"Well?" he demanded, indicating my canes with a manicured forefinger.

"Oh, it's nothing much—I was in a car accident."

And that, if I could possibly manage it, would be all I would ever tell him about that. But I knew only too well that if he really wanted to, he could and would get the whole story out of me. I shifted my weight to the less painful of my legs and tried to organize an escape.

"It's nice to see you, Pa, but I'm late for a—"

"I knew that fellow meant bad news for you, Polly. That's why I tried to warn you."

"Is it, Pa?"

I was proud of the shrewdness of this question, but no

sooner was it out than my eyes filled with tears that spilled over and ran down my cheeks with reckless abandon. It was one of the most awkward after-effects of the accident, and by far the one I hated most. But at once my father's bearded face became sweet with tenderness. He produced a clean handkerchief and with it gently mopped away my tears, ignoring the shoals of shoppers jostling past as if we were alone in total privacy. He'd always had an almost hypnotic ability to focus his attention so intently on one person that nothing and no one else seemed to exist. His concentrated attention created a sort of magnetic field inside which, fascinated, flattered, you softened; your personal boundaries melted, and you became utterly open to him and his power. These, at any rate, were some of the components of my long-standing love and resentment of him, a blend apparently as potent as ever. Now, before I could do anything about it, he had turned me around and guided me into a nearby small café. There he found a corner table and sat me carefully down, with my back to the room, before ordering tea.

"Now then," he said. "Let's have it. He's not with you now, is that right?"

"Right."

"So where are you living? And how?"

"The National Health is patching me up. I have a little room in Hampstead—it's not far from that house we had after Ma left, actually. In a couple of weeks the physio will be through with me and I'll start looking for a job."

Beyond a slight lift of his heavy eyebrows, Pa made no comment on this. None was necessary, of course. We both knew there are not many parts going for little-known, small, lame actresses. The strong tea, though, was putting some heart into me.

"And what about you, Father? That was great news about the Booker. I was in hospital then, in traction, or I'd have written." (Here, too late, I remembered it was the

Nobel he coveted, so far without success. Hastily I changed the subject.) "Olivia writes to me, but the boys don't. What do you hear from Alan and Bill? And how is Nan?"

"Your brothers—those princes of nonentity—are as far as I know quite well. They rarely trouble me with communication. Unless, of course, they want something." He paused, expelling his breath heavily through dilated nostrils, before adding, "Faugh."

"And Nan?"

"Oh, she's just as usual. P-perfectly well."

For the first time I noticed a faint, intermittent tremor in one of my father's long, beautiful hands, and detected an odd little occasional hesitancy in his speech that had not been there before. It was clear that he had aged, but I had changed too radically myself in the last few months to be sure just how, or how much, because my perceptions of everything, including myself, were now so different. But it was strange how easily Pa could still assert his old intimidating power over me.

"Where *is* Nan now?" I asked.

"With me, of course," he said, surprised.

"Still at home, then?"

"Where else would she be?"

"Well, I thought she might have—well, got married or something. People do, after all."

"You know perfectly well your sister is a special case. And retardation may be the kindest word for it."

"Poor Nan. She must be thirty-seven now."

He drew a heavy sigh. "In one sense, yes."

It's ironic, in view of all that happened later, to remember how clever I thought it was to focus the conversation on my half-sister, and thus deflect his attention from me. It was a strategy which I was actually a little surprised to find effective, because in herself poor old Nan was not a very interesting person. Or so I used to think.

"What does she do with herself these days?" I asked. "I

mean, does she still put in most of her time spinning that awful coarse wool and making itchy things for the family?"

"She runs the house now," my father said, frowning. "Mrs. Benchley became quite impossible. I had to get rid of her. Last year I sold the London house, you know, and bought a big old place down in Kent. Nan's happy there. She does all the cooking . . . shops . . . walks the dogs. Seven Oaks has a couple of acres of garden. Guests come down. There's plenty for her to do."

"I see. Just the same, it would be nice if Nan could have a life of her own, don't you think?"

He made an impatient gesture that nearly overturned the cream-jug.

"What a fatuous remark to make. You know what Nan is."

"Pa, she may be different, but she's not completely abnormal."

"Nonsense. Of course she is. Though just what the deficiency is, who the hell can say. None of those tests—except of course the I.Q.—ever turned up an answer. Of course her mother was, to put it mildly, peculiar, but still . . . In any case, you know as well as I do that Nan's not qualified to live a normal life. She'll always be my responsibility. One of my liabilities. Much as I care for her. And for all of you. In spite of everything."

He looked with such Lear-like gloom into the dregs of his tea that I felt an unwilling twinge of sympathy for him.

"Well, she's always adored you, Pa. And I'm sure she enjoys running this new house for you. It's just that it seems a pity she has no other—I mean, after all, you won't be around forever."

Too late, I realized this was hardly the kind of conversation likely to cheer him up. Nor did it help much to recognize this was the kind of fencing that had always given tension to my relationship with Pa. He was looking at me now with belligerence, feeling, without quite his old skill, for a weapon to counter with. As bravely as I could, I met his aggressive stare, telling myself, "He's got some broken veins in his cheeks, and his beard has gone quite white. And what's that queer little tremor—Parkinson's, maybe? He's seventy, after all."

"You seem very concerned about Nan," he remarked. "I mean, for anyone with your problems . . . "

"She's a good soul," I said quickly. "I'm fond of her."

"And so am I. In my fashion. Almost as fond as I am of you, Polly." And here, to my surprise, he leaned across the table and took my hand in his. "Look here," he went on hurriedly, "why don't you sublet your place, wherever it is, and come down to us for the summer—get on with your recovery in the country air? Nan would be so delighted. And when you're a bit stronger, you could maybe give her a hand with things. There's always a lot to do, running the place. I'm working on a new book, so Hamish—of course you remember him—is living in at present. And in a few weeks a Canadian crew from the National Film Board will descend on us to make a documentary. Ralph and Lally will be coming down to be interviewed for it, so it will be a pretty full house. You could really be useful. Nobody can make brioches like poor Nan, but for organizing anything complicated or coping socially, she is bloody hopeless, as you know. Yes, you'd better come down. It will be good for you. And helpful to me."

Just about the last thing in the world I wanted was to accept this invitation. It was bad enough to be a spectator of my own life, let alone his. And I might quite easily have found the nous to refuse, if he hadn't added, touching my cheek gently, "Do come, Pol. I haven't been . . . in the very topmost form lately. It would please me to have you home again for a while."

And so guilt and love joined hands in dubious fellowship, I said yes, and the whole thing began.

1
Charades

It amused me a good deal to discover that Seven Oaks was exactly the sort of baronial house of rosy old brick that Pa might have invented for the setting of one of his novels. Better yet, it was an extension of his persona, which was just as much a creation as any character in his fiction. Pa's actual and original personality had been generated in Kitchener, Ontario, by two middle-class schoolteachers. But quite early in life (how early, exactly, of course I don't know), he had already perfected the urbane, mannered, faintly Edwardian façade that was by now internationally celebrated. It was an image as carefully groomed as his well-shaped beard and his mid-Atlantic accent, and this house of his was simply a new extension of the old design. For one thing, it was as far as one could get, architecturally and every other way, from the cramped, drab conformity of small-town Ontario. Everything about it, from its tall, herringbone-brick chimneys down, had that air of time-worn, confident private beauty and eccentricity that is the British hallmark.

A tiled roof uneven with age rose against the pale English sky. One wing of the house was Jacobean, small-windowed and sagging a little on its oak beams. The rest was a pleasant muddle of later additions from Georgian to modern. Broad flower-borders offered roses, lupins, iris, and lilies to the soft air. The close-clipped lawns, mowed in a striped pattern, were starred with small daisies. Through a rose-trellis, croquet-hoops could be seen sunk in the green turf.

"No, it's almost too good," I said to Nan, grinning.

She glanced at me sidelong, but made no comment. I had almost forgotten how rare it was for Nan to volunteer any remark at all; now, for the first time, I felt a little self-conscious about my own tendency to verbalize everything. Just the same, it was her silence that more than anything else marked Nan as an oddity. When she did speak, it was always slowly. Her movements too were slow, and her calm, blunt-featured face was habitually without expression, except for her slow, lovely smile, and the way her light-blue, very clear eyes sometimes dwelt on things or people as if they saw more, not less, than everyone else.

Always a big woman, she had expanded a little in girth since I last saw her. Everything else about her, though, was pleasingly familiar, down to her shining, rosy skin and childishly straight fair hair caught back with an elastic band in an untidy knot. She had welcomed me at the door with one of her big, warm embraces, but we made a strangely ill-assorted pair of sisters standing there on the smooth grass, she so large and silent, I small, dark, and restlessly chatty.

"Can we sit down, Nan? My legs hurt. That bloody awful train. It must have been the oldest railway carriage outside a museum. Only sixty miles from London to Canterbury, but it felt like six hundred."

Nan dragged up a couple of garden chairs and I lowered myself cautiously into one of them. After a moment the pain eased off, and I turned my mind firmly away from those capsules in my bag which the doctor kept assuring me I didn't really need any more.

"Now tell me who's here," I said. "Besides you and Pa, of course. And where is he, by the way?—I'd have thought he'd be here to welcome the prodigal."

"With the dentist."

"Oh. Well, Hamish is living here, he says. Still the trusty right-hand man, is he? What staying power. And how are Ralph and Lally?"

"They come tonight."

"Oh, good. They're always fun. Maybe we'll have some charades. And what staff have you got to run this great barn of a place? Tell me what happened to Mrs. Benchley."

"She put salt in Pa's kedgeree." A slow smile widened Nan's lips.

"On purpose? Ah. Is it still breakfast porridge with grilled sausage and scrambled eggs in all those chafing-dishes? No wonder Pa's developed that little tum."

Nan didn't bother to answer these rather inane remarks. I lifted my face to the sky, where soft billows of cloud floated like ships of air on a calm blue pond. Somewhere in the holly hedge at our back, a small bird or animal rustled. A light breeze frilled the ivy on the old brick wall dividing off the kitchen-garden. Across the lawn a ginger-and-white cat crept toward us with histrionic stealth, rehearsing the stalk of some invisible prey. It was like that static moment after the curtain rises in a theatre, before the actors speak or move, except that I had no expectation of any drama at all evolving from this peaceful scene. The pain in my legs was ebbing. I was beginning to feel almost sleepy with com-fort when a square-built, crisply compact man with red hair emerged from French doors at the side of the house and began to cross the grass toward us. Though I'd not seen him for years, I had no trouble recognizing Hamish, Pa's long-time secretary. As he approached, I contemplated his limp with a professional eye. At the moment, mine was much the more impressive; but his was an irascible stump not without its effect. The sight of him reminded me that all injuries are abstract as well as concrete, and I made a grim resolve never to let my lameness become part of my personality as his had done. If it killed me, I would disguise my limp, keep my crippledom private; and if that meant playing a part for the rest of my days, so be it.

Hamish had lost a foot to a mine in the Mekong Delta, and not long after that, Pa plucked him out from behind a reference desk in a Halifax library and made him, as it were, his chief of staff. The sardonic twist of his mind for some reason amused Pa, who tolerated more from Hamish in the way of cynical comment and general eccentricity than he would from anyone else. For his part, Hamish, after his taciturn fashion, seemed quite devoted to Pa, and certainly got on better with him than either of my brothers ever had. I'd always liked Hamish myself, though at the moment looking at him was uncomfortably like looking into a mirror. He lowered himself with exactly my own wincing caution into a chair and we exchanged greetings. Nan got up and without speaking began to drift off slowly down the garden pathway.

So we have our exits and our entrances, I thought, as the two of us watched her move with dreamy deliberation toward the arched gateway to the kitchen-garden. There a figure carrying a rake appeared—a short, gnarled-looking man in an old cotton hat with a drooping brim. They both paused. Then he held out to her in one earth-stained hand a single trailing spray of sweet-pea that had been torn off clumsily, as if by a child. She accepted it gravely, and they parted. The whole encounter took place in silence, and Hamish and I watched it, sharing a vague, charmed pleasure. Both figures had vanished before I said, "The gardener, I presume."

"His name is Fisk," said Hamish. "But the locals call him Oldfisk—not because he's old, just because he's generally peculiar. He lives a hermit existence in a hovel somewhere in the woods west of here."

Whether because of some anatomical peculiarity or just intense self-protection, Hamish talked with almost no lip movement whatever. Perhaps, I thought idly, years ago he'd wired his own jaws together as a precaution against wasted language, for he never used an untimely or irrelevant word. On the other hand, he could, and often did, make quite commonplace remarks sound highly significant.

"Well, Fisk seems to have a vein of poetry in him none the less," I said, yawning.

He blew air out through his nostrils to dismiss this fancy. "You might not guess it from this perspective, but his mental age is about twelve. One sure thing is he hasn't had a bath for easily forty years. How true it is that distance lends enchantment."

Another thing I'd forgotten was the tart, enjoyable flavour of Hamish's commentaries on things in general. In my father's shifting ménage where wives and children restlessly came and went all through my growing years, Hamish was always more or less there, near enough to be reassuring, but never inconveniently close. It was a bit like having a youngish uncle about, I thought comfortably; someone you could relate to without the slightest sexual complication.

"You haven't changed, have you," I asked him warmly.

"Not at all. I'm still handsome, brilliant, and unsuccessful."

"Join the club."

He lowered one eyelid over a sarcastic blue eye. "This modesty becomes you. But you've survived, haven't you. Don't crowd your luck. And don't tell me anything about it."

"I won't."

There was a short silence.

"And how's Pa's work going?"

"It's not."

"Not?"

"No, not at all."

I looked at him sharply. "But wait, it must be over two years ago that I read somewhere he was near the end of a new book."

"That's right. He's still there. Near the middle, actually."

"Oh. I see." Not that I really did. Except that as a writer's child I knew this was truly bad news—so bad, in fact, as to be in a category all by itself. But I had no time to ask anything more, because Pa himself now came striding energetically round the corner of the house with two bounding black Labradors at his heels, and threw out both arms in welcome.

My bedroom was a chintzified affair with its own small fireplace, an embroidered bell-pull no longer connected to anything, and a four-poster bed of great charm that I suspected would be extremely uncomfortable. It was a third-floor room under slanting eaves wallpapered with garlands of violets. Matching print curtains hung at the little casement window. It was here, before dinner, that I had a short but nasty attack of panic—another legacy of the accident.

All my flesh pimpled in a chill that had nothing to do with the temperature. The room shrank around me to the dimensions of a coffin. There was no air to breathe. Gripping my canes I lurched to the window and wrenched it open wide. Below, in the gathering dusk, the standard roses glowed with dying colour in the cool air, and beyond the kitchen-garden wall, a pretty, neglected orchard could be seen. Diminished by distance, a woman in a white dress walked slowly under the fruit trees, through long grass thick with buttercups and daisies. It was Nan. The ginger cat followed her, his crooked, white-tipped tail just visible above the undergrowth. Whatever is she doing out there at this hour, all by herself? I wondered. What can there be to look at? She looks utterly absorbed—but in what?

By now, however, my heart rate had settled down.

Warmth began to creep back into my hands and feet. I changed into a dress for dinner, grasped the canes, and went downstairs to join the others.

Ralph, my father's agent, had just arrived with Lally as I reached the entrance hall. Their luggage was strewn extensively over the Persian rug and the polished floor. Lally's pug, leashed to the largest suitcase, was yapping crossly, his front paws lifting from the floor in spurts of indignation as Pa kissed Lally. Ralph at once came over to me and took my face into his hands. He was a very tall, lean man with the sort of beaky, bony face that at twenty must have made him look forty, and at eighty would no doubt make him still look forty. His actual age at this point must have been in the mid-fifties, but his flat, lithe body made him seem quite a lot younger than that. He was always most elegantly dressed, and scented with something expensive from Cardin or Saint-Laurent.

"Polly darling, what a joy to see you." With perfect tact he appeared not to notice the two canes supporting me. He gave me a lingering kiss on the mouth that I would much rather have done without. For some reason I had never liked him to touch me, perhaps because there seemed to me something essentially cold about his experienced sensuality. Still, it was a dutiful old reflex for us young ones to be polite to Ralph (though he forbade us to call him uncle). He so cleverly managed all the business details of our father's career that he had to be regarded almost as co-provider of the Daimler in the garage, the holidays on Cos, this house (no doubt), and many other good things.

"Go along in, all of you — go along in," Pa was saying, shooing us with little gestures into the sitting-room. Lally immediately sank gracefully into a velvet chaise longue, her eyes half closing in satisfaction, while I found a chair with a straight back. She was a deliciously pretty woman who had spent fifty-odd years raising total indolence to a fine art. No one I'd ever met could relax in so many dif-

ferent attitudes of picturesque abandon, all suggesting in
a genteel sort of way the languor of those French ladies of
pleasure known as *les grandes horizontales*. She had the
gift, too, of seeming to listen with close attention to anyone
who spoke to her, lowering mascaraed lashes as if in deep
concentration, while all the while she was in fact having a
refreshing little nap. She was practising these skills now
on Pa, while he clattered ice and glasses incompetently on
the drinks tray.

"Ah, there you are," he said with satisfaction as Hamish
stumped in, followed by the pug. "Take over here, there's
a good chap. You know what everybody likes."

"Come to Mother, darling," Lally murmured to the pug,
but he preferred to waddle over to me and wrinkle his soft
muzzle in a scornful inspection of my low-heeled shoes.
"Yes, I quite agree," I told him, smoothing his plush coat.

"But if anybody else called her a dog's mother" — Hamish muttered out of the side of his mouth as he handed me
a glass. Pleased to note that judging by its pungent smell
my drink was a double, I gave him a friendly wink. But
Ralph was pulling forward a wheeled tapestry armchair
and settling in, knee to knee, for a confidential chat.

"My poor dear. What on earth happened?"

"Car crash," I said.

"And Bard?"

"Killed."

"How terrible. I'm so sorry. Where did this happen,
love? And when?"

"I don't want to talk about it, Ralph." The panic was
threatening to descend again. I lifted my glass, swallowed,
and waited for the alcohol to do its kindly work. Nan had
at some point come into the room with a silver dish of hot
canapés which she was slowly offering around with her
vague smile.

Lally lifted an indolent hand and took one from the tray.
She tasted the mushrooms on their little triangle of toast

and gave a faint shriek of approval. "Nan, they are absolutely perfect. They may look like bird-droppings, but they're *quite* delicious."

"What a lucky thing it is you're so decorative, Lall," remarked my father indulgently. There had been a time when we young ones thought it possible that Lally might become our next stepmother, but nothing ever came of this. She and Ralph had now lived together for many years, in a sort of casual, tolerant coalition entirely free from the kinds of stress marriages are so often noted for. At first her Catholic husband would not agree to a divorce and the guilty lovers had the added pleasure of living in what was then thought of as sin. By the time he did finally agree, I suppose they saw no point in sanitizing the arrangement by getting married. In spite of all this, though, no one in our family—not even Nan—saw theirs as a romantic union. In fact I suspected they continued to share accommodation and a life together chiefly because Ralph might have been, and Lally certainly was, too lazy to make any change. She called all her pets Darling, she once told me, simply because she couldn't be bothered to think of any other name for them.

A tarty-looking maid in uniform, with a cigarette hidden in her cupped hand, now announced dinner, and we crossed the hall in procession to the panelled dining-room. Ralph solicitously held out a chair for me, murmuring, "I sit here, I hope," as he pulled out the one next to mine.

"No, Ralph, I want you up here beside me," Pa called down the table. "I want to talk to you about that BBC contract."

And they plunged into business talk and gossip while the rest of us concentrated on the avocado stuffed with shrimp that had been tossed in a garlicky vinaigrette. Nan's outstanding talent as a cook had evidently flowered in my absence. I wondered, though, why she served this course without sharing it, and disappeared again immediately after putting down the beef Wellington in its case of glossy pastry in front of Pa to carve.

"For heaven's sake, does she eat in the kitchen with the maids?" I asked Hamish.

He shrugged. "It's been like this ever since you—I mean for a long time. You know Nan. She prefers it this way."

"Faugh," I said, and Hamish's grim mouth twitched in a grin.

But I didn't pursue the subject. There was something seductively relaxing about the rich smell of the food and the warm air around the table into which the open bottle of Bordeaux near me diffused its delicate scent. The sweet appeared, a purée of strawberries spooned over slices of ripe melon. Outside the windows birds were sleepily settling into the dark shrubbery. A few small, bright stars had begun to wink out.

When I paid attention again to the conversation, it had taken a philosophical turn. They were all in the thick of an argument about illusion and reality. Ralph and Lally had recently seen Stoppard's *The Real Thing*, and been greatly impressed.

"Yes, but what was all that about swapping the dressing-gown around so all the characters had a go at wearing it?" Lally wanted to know. "After all, some of those characters were *imaginary*. Tacky old robe it was, too," she added, almost fully opening her eyes.

"That, my dear, was to illustrate the fact that illusion and reality are completely interchangeable," my father said, turning the stem of his wineglass in long fingers.

"What a dangerous theory," said Hamish. "Surely the artificial and the natural are dead opposites."

"Not at all. Art and life are the same thing. One is simply the distilled essence of the other."

"You're just playing with words, as usual."

"Well, that's my profession, after all."

"You mean that if this conversation and the people hav-

ing it were in a book, it would be more real than it actually
is now?"

"Exactly."

"Bollocks," put in Ralph. "How's that for reality?"

"Because we aren't *planning* what to say, it isn't real?
Of course nobody's editing, inventing, shaping, like a writer
orchestrating his material. We're talking at random—being
natural . . . being real. Nothing to do with art, and a good
thing too."

"That's right. There's all the difference in the world," I
said.

My father smiled. "Are you sure? Now I started this
topic ten minutes ago, and I've kept it in play ever since.
I made a bet with myself that Lally would hit (accidentally,
of course) on a relevant detail. I was sure Hamish would
disagree with me for intellectual reasons, and Polly for
emotional ones. And that's how it went. So you've had a
demonstration of how art becomes life, and life art. That
is, people illustrate themselves. At least they do when an
artist is around."

"This is just verbal sleight-of-hand," snorted Hamish.
"It's perversion to equate illusion with reality. Not even
Fowles in *The Magus* could make his puppet-master any-
thing but a monster."

Quite suddenly I felt almost dizzy with fatigue and pushed
back my chair.

"You'll have to excuse me, all," I muttered. "I have simply got to go to bed. Forgive the extemporized exit, Pa."

"Go in peace, child," he said blandly, and waved me
away. Trust the old wizard, I thought half-admiringly as I
toiled up the long staircase, to have the last word.

Next morning at breakfast, Pa announced that he was going
into Canterbury to have his hair cut, and asked whether
anyone wanted to come along. "No, thanks," Ralph said
from behind the *Telegraph*. I shook my head. (The four-

poster had fulfilled my worst fears.) Nan did not appear to hear the question. She was at the window gazing out across the garden toward the orchard where a fresh wind could be seen frisking in the tree-tops. Lally, of course, was still upstairs in bed.

"Oh, you come along, Pol," Pa urged me. "You don't want to stodge here all day. Do you good to move about."

"Will you want me to drive?" Hamish wanted to know. The question surprised me a little. It was new for him to double as chauffeur. Not for the first time I wondered why anyone so able and so doughtily independent should be apparently content to remain part of Pa's entourage.

"No, thanks, Hamish. A lot of mail came in the early post. Most of it's no doubt the usual stuff cadging money and free advice, but it will take you all morning to deal with it. Come on, Polly. You'll need a sweater or a jacket. You can have a nice prowl around the shops and then I'll buy you a fattening pub lunch. We'll be back in time for tea, Nan. Make some of those nice scones. No, dogs, you are *not* coming with us."

Minutes later we were in the Daimler spinning along the narrow road toward town. I was soon glad to learn it was only nine miles to Canterbury. Pa had a tendency to take the curves wide, and in the intervals he drove firmly in the middle of the road.

Traffic thickened around us as the ivory-coloured spires of the cathedral came in view. On the roundabout at the city's edge, huge container lorries swept past us, perilously close. Pa gripped the wheel doggedly. An oil tanker overtook us with a gushing roar, its driver mouthing something that was fortunately torn away in the slipstream.

"Pa, you really should keep left. This isn't Canada."

"Trust me," said my father calmly.

There followed some extended pother while we searched for space in one after another of the town's full car-parks. Finally, the car disposed of, Pa strode off toward a half-timbered shop labelled Gents Hair Styles, while I made a slower progress down the High Street. It had been turned into a pedestrian mall since my last visit, which meant that instead of being choked with traffic, the road was now densely congested with tourists. They all looked cross and crowded, but I liked the feeling of being part of an anonymous mass—uncommitted, all but invisible—just another casual sightseer.

"Buy fish for tonight," Nan had asked me, pushing a shopping-basket over my wrist. When I had finished queueing up at a fishmonger's, later adding a few lemons and a bunch of watercress on my own initiative, the basket began to feel very heavy. I was at the gate of the garden pub Pa had named ten minutes before opening-time.

There I sat on a weathered bench in fitful bursts of sunlight, occupying a corner of the garden haunted by a smell of beer and roses and old stone. Canterbury's old and new sounds lapped me gently round—a distant scuff of tourist feet, the pensive chime of the cathedral clock, the jingle of a milkman's float. The frontier between illusion and reality faded, and I felt safe. Gradually my eyes sank shut. Then Pa's voice with its rich grain jerked me awake. He set down two beaded glasses of lager and established himself with a thump on the other half of my bench.

"You're too young to be dozing off like this at noon, child. You must have inherited the tendency from your mother. She was always dropping off at the most ridiculous times. When the moon-landing was on TV, for instance. Or when the Duke of Gloucester came to dinner."

"Well, she was no doubt pregnant as usual. And he was probably a very dull man."

Pa never referred to my mother except to disparage her, and just as automatically I always came to her defence. This made much of our conversation absurdly predictable, and also highly irritating to both parties. Not one of Pa's four wives had proved satisfactory, and he never ceased to marvel at the fate that had dealt a blameless man such marital bad luck. His first had run away with the postman, leaving him saddled with one-year-old Nan. Soon after that the guilty couple emigrated to New Zealand and disappeared, he always maintained, in order to avoid having the child sent off to them. Number Two (mother to Olivia, Bill, Alan, and me) was an actress. He met her when she was cast in the lead of a dramatized version of one of his books. For a while everything seems to have been idyllic—at least for him. She gave up her career to have us four in rapid succession, but eventually she left him in order to go back on the stage. Not long after that she added insult to injury by marrying again—happily. A little of her wit, good looks, and brains had trickled down to the four of us, but because by agreement we spent most of every year with Pa, we felt (as he certainly did) that we were far more his sons and daughters than hers.

In due course he married again—one of his secretaries this time. She too failed to stay the course. Then, after only a brief interval, he chose yet another wife, a fan this time from Aberdeen; but this colourless, rather dim lady, after only a year or two, very inconsiderately died. He always counted this high among the many grievances heaped on him by these ungrateful spouses.

"Yes, taking it all round," I remarked, after taking a sip of my lager, "with luck like that on the home front, it's a mercy you haven't risked getting married again."

"No fear," he said, throwing in a quick, mischievous grin it was impossible not to return. "Though I often think, you know, Polly, now I'm getting on a bit, that I would truly like to have had more children." With unpredictable swiftness his mood, I saw, was beginning to darken. All of us knew only too well how to recognize the signs, though each of us had a different technique for dealing with them. Olivia, true to her Shakespearean namesake, used to plunge into melancholy with him. He found this kind of loyalty boring and would sometimes—though not often—cheer up to escape it. The boys used to try hearty, bracing remarks, a strategy that never worked. As a consequence the whole house could be enveloped in gloom for days on end. On the counter-irritant theory, my method was to annoy him. This sometimes produced an outbreak of temper, after which he felt much better. So now I poked my tongue out at him cheekily.

"No, Pa, you're much better off to quit while you're ahead. Five winners like us are more than you deserve."

He eyed me sardonically. "Would you call that an adequate description of your brother Bill, who when last heard of was teaching retarded children in Hackney? Or of Nan?"

This was hardly an accurate summary of poor Bill's successful crammer's school, but I let that pass. Pa also liked to describe my brother Alan's thriving catering business as a cake shop. As for Olivia and me, while he had no objection to acting as a career, it seemed to give him a glum sort of satisfaction that we'd never achieved stardom, to put it mildly.

"Anyhow, about Nan," I said stoutly, "she's happy, and she makes other people comfortable. What more can you want from her? You know the first thing in the world I can remember is her kindness. I was just learning to walk— you remember that polished parquetry floor in the London house—it looked as wide as an ocean to me. I was staggering along when it jumped up and banged me on the forehead, and Nan picked me up and just held me in a big warm hug till I stopped howling. She couldn't have been more than about eight herself."

"Ah, the poor wretch worries me," he muttered, pushing away the remains of his steak-and-kidney pie.

"Why, Pa? What's the problem? She's simply a good, innocent person that people like. I saw your old gardener give her a flower yesterday—it was such a nice little gesture—just like something she'd do herself."

"What, Oldfisk? Gave her a flower?"

"Yes."

For no reason I could fathom, his frown deepened. 'Well, it must be difficult to be you, Pa,' I thought. 'You have to come out of the private, ordered world of your own invention so often, and cope with the illogical, messy one the rest of us inhabit. It's no wonder all writers are so neurotic.'

We sat there for several minutes in gloomy silence, each wrapped in separate thoughts. Perhaps, for all I knew, he was feeling sorry for me. Then I became aware that a woman with her daughter at a nearby table who had been glancing our way for some time was now openly staring at Pa. When she caught my eye she got up abruptly and came over to us.

"Excuse me, but I just had to ask—aren't you the author Montague Weston?"

Pa eyed her warily. He loved being recognized, but experience had taught him how embarrassing some encounters of this kind could be. A woman once kissed his hand in Regent Street and told him she loved him, to the great joy of a passing band of street urchins. But this youngish American woman in a smart trouser-suit looked quite sane. "I absolutely adored your last," she told him. "I've read it three times and given a copy to everybody I know. Would you mind if I asked you to sign—Oh, my book-club back in Utah will simply *die* when they hear this." In a hand trembling slightly so her bangle bracelets tinkled together, she held out a pocket guide to Canterbury. While Pa splashed down his flamboyant signature, she went on eagerly, "I've always thought I'd like to write a book myself — some poetry, maybe — only somehow I never seem to find the time."

My father and I simultaneously gave her a brilliant smile. For years we'd kept count of the number of times people said this to him, until the total became so high it ceased to be really funny.

"Dear lady," said Pa, still broadly smiling as he replaced his pen in a vest pocket. "You *are* a poem. No need for you to write anything at all."

"How charming of you to say so. Thank you a million times for the autograph. And I can't *wait* for your next book."

She tinkled off then, to my relief. Pa's next book, according to Hamish, might well keep her waiting forever, and I was afraid mere mention of it might cause a return of gloom. But as we got up to go, I stole a look at him and found his face beaming with geniality. And his mood remained sunny all the rest of the day.

Until the camera crew from Ottawa arrived, the rhythm of the house went peacefully on its uneventful round. A watery English sun occasionally glanced out from the clouds long enough for us to have tea on the terrace, where the dogs lay at our feet and snapped at gnats, and wasps got into the jam. The part-time staff clocked in regularly. Oldfisk ground up the gravel path several times a week on his aged bicycle, and a queenly, white-haired char from the village arrived every Monday on a red moped. Nan got up at four in the morning to make croissants on a marble slab in the kitchen. Hamish fielded telephone calls and answered fan mail in a little library off the dining-room, while Pa closeted himself at intervals in his upstairs study, presumably getting on with the new novel, though nobody dared to ask. Lally spent most of her time on a sofa in the sitting-room, the garden being in her view too cold, hot, windy, or damp, depending on the day. She lay supine, looking lovely, with a book and the pug on her lap. I seldom saw her turn a page.

Every day I did my exercises faithfully and told myself that walking was getting easier. The day came when I made it from terrace to kitchen on only one cane. Clutching a jug we wanted refilled with cream, I looked triumphantly

at the staff collected around the big kitchen table polishing
silver. They all had mugs of mahogany-coloured tea. A cigarette drooped from the corner of the housemaid's purple
lips and she squinted through its smoke as she rubbed at
a tray. For some reason everyone in the house referred to
this lady with deference as Mrs. Pryde, and she made no
attempt to rise or be helpful now. It was the gardener who
said, removing a crusted pipe from his lips, "Fill up that
jug for the lady, young Eileen." A little scullery maid I'd
never seen before (and who looked exactly like a Beatrix
Potter mouse in a pink print apron) scrabbled to her feet
and took the jug away. I gazed at them all, leaning on my
one cane, still glowing with ridiculous satisfaction. And
when the little maid handed me the filled jug and held the
door open for me, she said, "That's roight, miss," as if she
agreed I really had achieved something significant.

It was that evening when, dressing for dinner, I saw Nan
from my bedroom window walking in the orchard as she
had on my first night, and suddenly I felt ambitious enough
to go down and join her there. Down the stairs I went,
across the lawn where long shadows pointed east, and into
the kitchen-garden. Oldfisk in his crumpled cotton hat was
pulling up weeds and tossing them onto a barrow. The place
smelled drowsily of sun-warm vegetation after the long,
bright day. "Good evening," I said. He nodded briefly.

My cane crunched on the gravel walk, then padded on
turf. The orchard proved to be rather farther away than
I'd expected: Nan's figure looked quite small in the distance. I paused a moment to catch my breath. The ginger
cat hopped off the wall where he had been sunning himself,
and ran to meet me. I knew his name now—Crackers. He
was so called because nervous tension or a bizarre sense
of humour sometimes made him leap high in the air for little
or no reason. He now twined himself affectionately but
inconveniently around my feet. Nan turned, saw me, and

after a moment slowly lifted her hand. She began to walk toward me through the long grass.

A feeling of rare and quite irrelevant happiness suddenly visited me. The quiet evening air fingered my skirt and the ends of my hair. The sky shone overhead, a flawless colour between silver and gold. As I looked up at it, the breeze freshened and there appeared first a drift, then a vast, thickening, golden procession of clouds. Driven by the wind they took on fantastic and beautiful shapes, like great winged creatures airborne with streaming robes and feathered wings. Fascinated I stared up at them. Nan stood beside me now in her crumpled white cotton dress, looking up with me. I glanced at her silent, lifted face. The wind fluttered her untidy fair hair. Something about her stillness or her silence for a moment gave me the absurd fancy that this stream of golden seraphim had materialized for her alone, or even that she had created it out of some alchemy of her own. A moment later, of course, it was only a fading sunset, and half an hour after that, Nan was serving sole véronique and slipping off to eat in the kitchen as usual.

I had been sleeping better recently, but that night I lay awake for a while thinking about Nan. My present mental and physical state seemed to bring me closer to her than we had ever been before. What could the future hold for two people so impaired, I wondered. Were we vulnerable or invulnerable, being so without desires or ambitions of any kind: so without any will to impose our identity on anyone or anything?

The next day the Film Board crew arrived, and any number of things began to change, without providing answers to any of these questions.

Interviews, of course, were no novelty to my father, who for so long had been the subject of countless magazine profiles, theses, TV appearances, and newspaper articles. By now I would have thought no question could be too silly or intrusive to surprise him, or no encounter with the media anything but routine. Yet when the Ottawa group appeared — late, because they'd lost their way trying to find the house—Pa suddenly became oddly negative and elusive.

The young people stood about the hall awkwardly shouldering what looked like tons of technical equipment; but Pa didn't ask them to come in or make them even slightly welcome. It was left to the leader, a good-looking young man with sharp, intelligent eyes, to introduce himself. "I'm Bruce Adams," he said, offering me a firm handshake. "Awfully sorry we're so late. My assistants, Joan . . . Michel . . . Patrick." He showed no signs of either awe or mateyness, both of which for different reasons Pa disliked, yet he stood in the background straightening a picture on the wall and offered them nothing but a rather distant nod.

"Make yourselves at home," he said vaguely. "Set up your gear if you like. Talk to my daughter Paulina here. Stay for dinner, you'd better, and perhaps we can begin tomorrow." And with that he turned away, making for his upstairs sanctuary on slippered feet that fumbled a little on the stairs. He had looked rather tired all day and the little tremor in his arm was noticeable; but this behaviour was a bit much. An awkward silence lingered after his disappearance.

"Well," said Bruce, "it's only Day One, after all. Maybe I could kick off by interviewing *you*," he added, turning hopefully to me.

"Only for background info," I warned him. "And only if you promise me not to ask what it's like to be the great novelist's daughter."

"I promise. Great. Joanie, will you set up the tape while I dig out my notes? Forgive us for getting on with this right away, but what with getting here late—you realize we have this truly minuscule budget, and every hour counts."

"Yes, I suppose it does. What got you into this, anyhow? You look like a student."

"Please," he said with a wink. "I got my Ph.D. from McGill last year." A freckled boy clipped a microphone to my cardigan while Joanie upended her large backside to fit a plug into the socket behind my chair. She then peered anxiously at the voice-level indicator as Bruce got under way. "Now you were born in Canada, right?"

"No, in London. All four of us were. But my sister Olivia and I spent quite a while at schools in Toronto and New York, to be near our mother. We feel completely Canadian —all of us. Until fairly recently Pa spent easily half his time over there, doing promotion tours and writer-in-residence stuff here and there. We lived in Calgary for a bit, and in Montreal for over a year."

"But he's not a Canadian citizen any more, is he?"

"Of course he is." This was boringly familiar ground. Pa had, it's true, lived mostly in England for the last ten years, and this, it always seemed to those who thought the English-speaking world consisted of Toronto, must necessarily mean the loss of his Canadian identity. But his essential nature with its streak of romantic, reckless energy (which I had regrettably inherited) was entirely North American.

Translating this view into politer terms, I added, "He's won the Governor General's Award three times, you no doubt remember, and he was given the Order of Canada, etcetera. He's still very much a Canadian."

"Point taken," said Bruce. "Now can you tell me . . . "

And so the interview went more or less predictably on. The light faded and rain began to patter lightly on the windows. The dogs, Boris and Ivan, wandered in and out, waving their tails hopefully. It was well past the time when Nan usually brought in tea, but there was no sign of her. Probably she was wrestling with the problem of stretching dinner to feed four extra mouths. Lally drifted in, was introduced, and sank onto the sofa. Eventually Mrs. Pryde appeared with the tea-tray and a sullen expression, and not long after that Ralph joined us, followed by Hamish and drinks. Pa, however, remained maddeningly invisible.

"Where the hell is he?" I hissed to Hamish.

"Incommunicado."

"Damn it, he's impossible."

Twilight came. I drew the curtains. The tall clock in the hall chimed eight. Finally I showed Joanie where the ground-floor loo was, left the lads to Hamish, and escaped to the kitchen to find Nan.

Tied into a large butcher's apron, she was basting a batch of guinea hens hissing hot from the oven.

"Nan, aren't we ready yet to eat? It's after eight."

"Pa said serve at eight-twenty. He'll be down later."

"Did he, damn it. What's he up to, anyhow? Why isn't he here?"

Nan didn't answer. She looked more than usually blank, as she always did when anything had happened to ruffle her. I wondered what that might be, until a drift of laughter and unfamiliar voices reached us from the sitting-room. Then I remembered. Strangers in the house always sent her into a private, controlled, but intense sort of solitude. She was decorating a large hors-d'oeuvre platter with parsley now, but I knew she would not bring it into the dining-room herself. As long as the film crew was in the house, Nan would not be seen. It would be tarty Mrs. Pryde, reeking of cigarettes, who would serve tonight's beautiful food.

By now feeling thoroughly cross with both my relatives, I went back to announce dinner. As I ushered them all through the double doors, a wave of amusement and surprise broke through the group. They were all looking at the head of the candle-lit table where a silver-bearded figure in evening dress lolled in Pa's chair as if drunk. For a shocked second I thought it was real and started forward before Hamish's hand took my shoulder. Then I recognized the figure: it was a life-sized doll my father had caused years ago to be dressed to represent him at a fund-raising banquet for indigent authors. Unable to attend himself, he sent the doll instead—a ploy that turned out to be worth its weight in gold, both literally and in publicity value. It was auctioned off at the dinner, bought at a high price by one of Pa's admirers, and then returned to him as a gift. The thing at a glance looked quite startlingly lifelike. I wondered, though, why Pa had chosen tonight to excavate it from some attic cupboard or other. Perhaps, I thought, it had some connection with the argument about illusion and reality we'd had in this room a week or so ago. Or perhaps it was simply a put-down of the young crew and their project. Either way, the doll in his chair, leering at us with its glassy eyes, did not amuse me.

Luckily, though, it seemed to tickle Bruce and his friends. When, just as the hors-d'oeuvres came around, Pa finally walked into the room, the four young people all got spontaneously to their feet and applauded him. His face, which had been austere, instantly broke into a beaming smile. Radiating goodwill and bonhomie, he made us all a little bow. With a flourish he plucked the doll from its place and tossed it ignominiously into a corner.

"What literary title, Pol? Eh? Quick."

"*Man and Superman*, I suppose," I said dryly.

"Clever wench. Pour the wine, Hamish. Have some of this brown bread, young Joan. It's made at home, like all the other good things you'll eat tonight. And after dinner we will play charades. That will be much more instructive and infinitely more fun than making your documentary film."

"Oh God," murmured Lally. She knew an evening of charades meant a lot of standing about in various poses wearing improvised costumes that might or might not be becoming. She also knew my father would allow no one to escape. Charades was his favourite game. And Lally herself was a surprisingly shrewd player. But the time was long past

when I was flattered always to be first chosen for Pa's side.
I would make my legs the excuse and go to bed early.

An hour later I was seated on a long-legged kitchen stool,
wearing a grand triple-caped opera cloak of Pa's, and pretending to blow a long coachman's horn that normally lived
over the fireplace. In front of me the dogs, grinning and
fidgeting on their leashes, did their best to represent horses.
Two spare tires from various cars had been propped up
broadside-on to the spectators to serve as wheels. Precar-
iously balanced beside me on a chair, Pa in a long muffler
and brimmed hat flourished a great whip from one of the
outbuildings.

"Coach," our audience chorused.

Pa smiled. "Last syllable."

After a frenzied scramble we erected an old tablecloth
lashed to two fishing-poles and blew it taut with an electric
fan. With some effort of the imagination it more or less
suggested a sail. Lally whistled "In the Bay of Biscay-o".
A blue blanket wrinkled underfoot represented the sea. To
heighten the effect, Ralph and Bruce, in ill-fitting oilskins,
swayed and staggered on the blanket as if on a heaving deck.

The audience appeared perplexed. "Sail," Hamish said.
"Storm" and "Sick" were also proposed. No consensus
emerged. They called for the whole word.

Pa took his place in a canvas chair of the kind used by
movie directors. A folding screen at his back depicting Robin
Hood in Sherwood Forest looked not unlike part of a stage
set. With a script in one hand he made commanding gestures
with the other at Lally and Bruce, who also had scripts.
Obediently they mimed grandiose movements and took up
positions as actors do at rehearsals. So compelling was Pa's
posture and the flash of his eye (he was well into the skin of
his part) that I was transported straight back to my fifth
year when I made my stage début as Little Bo-Peep in a
skit he'd written for someone's birthday. The years between

then and now vanished like a dream. I smelled the make-up on my own lips and felt my joy in the pink-and-white shepherdess costume conflicting with terror lest I fluff my lines and call down Pa's wrath. The audience of weekend houseguests swam before me as I bleated my first line, "Where are my sheep?", to a wave of kindly applause. I think it was in that same production that one of my brothers dried up. From behind the canvas backdrop Pa delivered a hard kick to his backside, and, like an engine jump-started, Alan at once began to gabble his lines.

Pa was in such good form tonight I would not have been much surprised to find him using similar tactics on Bruce, who at the outset had been a clumsy performer; but luckily he improved as the evening went on. Indeed, by now Pa seemed to have developed something close to affection for him. It increased his good humour even more when the other side, after several wrong guesses, had to give up and ask for the answer: "Stagecraft".

From the corner of my eye I caught sight of Nan, or a segment of her, at the hall door, which she'd been holding on the crack. After many tearful failures she had not been required to take part in these nursery productions, but Pa's performances in charades invariably magnetized her, even when strangers were in the house. He had noticed her too, I perceived with some trepidation. Generally he preferred her to keep out of sight when outsiders were around. But now instead of scowling he beckoned her jovially to come in. She instantly vanished, yet his good humour remained high. Indeed, he seemed quite euphoric as he slung an arm across Bruce's shoulders and urged whisky nightcaps on everyone.

Well, why not, I thought. The old boy's illusions had been a success. His riddle had intrigued and baffled his audience. It seemed likely he had spent most of the afternoon behind his study door concocting this game of charades instead of writing, and, if so, I wondered why it gave him such unclouded satisfaction. 'You are indeed a very strange old man,' I thought, just as he further proved it by saying out of the blue, "Now you youngsters will stay the night. It's late — we'll make an early start tomorrow on your video. And tomorrow night we'll play another round of the game. How's that, eh? How's that?"

Without pausing to tell him how I thought that was, I hobbled off to make hasty arrangements about bed linen and morning tea for four unexpected guests. No wonder, I told myself, none of his wives could put up with him for very long, one of them even taking refuge in death from this kind of exasperation.

"Yes," said Ralph. "What with steady paperback sales to college bookstores and the like, plus various things like film rights and translations, Monty's income from writing alone runs to well over fifty thousand a year. That's in pounds, you understand. In fact, this year with the Booker prize-money, it jumped to over double that."

"Surely that's a lot for a fiction writer," said Bruce, trying not to look amazed.

"Remember we're talking here about a distinguished literary career that goes back over forty years. Monty had some very lean times there at the start, like everybody else. Not," Ralph added austerely, "that I agree in any way with people who think an author can't be truly first rate if he makes real money at it."

Bruce made a chopping gesture at the lad shouldering the heavy camera. "Thanks, sir. That was great."

Ralph got up, looking slightly chagrined. It was not hard to see that he would have liked to be asked more about his own arts — for example the skill with which he negotiated contracts and gave advice about taxes and investments. Oddly enough, though, his own financial affairs were often in disorder. To my knowledge Pa had several times actually had to lend him money to clear off his debts. In fact, without these rescue operations and Lally's small private income, I don't know how they would have survived these occasional crises.

Pa was now settling into an armchair by the hearth where we'd lighted a fire of apple logs to counteract the rain outside. Joanie, frowning in a pair of oversize headphones, stepped over a tangle of cables to train a hot bank of white lights on him. A mike was clipped to the lapel of his velvet house-jacket. Last night's late hours and extra drinks seemed to have done him nothing but good. His little beard (freshly trimmed by me after breakfast) set off the good colour in his cheeks and his eyes had a twinkle of amusement in them, though the young people, deeply into their project, had been extremely solemn all day.

Bruce was now leaning forward in a chair facing Pa with an air of earnest inquiry.

"Right. (Roll it, Pat.) Now can we talk, sir, about what the critics agree is your special gift — creating character."

"Why not?" Pa asked genially.

"That's what most readers see as almost a form of magic — to make people who never existed seem so alive they make flesh-and-blood readers laugh and cry. How do you do it?"

"It takes a bloody great talent," said Pa, grinning. But Bruce remained grave.

"Can you tell us how much is sheer invention and how much is observation of actual people you know? Your women, for instance — they're specially vivid. How can a man portray them with so much insight?"

"Oh, writers are an androgynous breed, you know. And quite shameless voyeurs. We're everlastingly taking notes on human behaviour, even at moments of private intimacy or crisis. This is one of the things that create great loneliness for us." He stared penetratingly at Bruce, who shifted a little in his chair.

"So objectivity is the essence of it, would you say?"

"Oh, my dear young man, I don't know. It's not my job to know. I just conjure up the illusion, and it seems to work."

"Your old woman, Gertrude, in *Some Farewells*, for instance, she's so real with her hats and that crazy laugh —how did you manage to make her so vivid and at the same time so complex?"

"Ah well. One cheats. Nobody human is ever so simple as a character in fiction, even the greatest of them. All the muddle and complications are cleared away so the writer can expose a central conflict of the sort we all have but seldom can define. In you, Bruce, for instance, I see the scholar and the artist locked in some kind of enormously complex struggle for dominance. Did you know that about yourself? You're a highly analytical person. But last night in the charades a romantic—a dreamer—actually began to show itself in your body language and the expressions on your face. A quite different man played that game than the one who's conducting this rather ridiculous interview."

Bruce blinked. His face was caught wide open in a look of naive surprise. My father smiled faintly as he caught my eye. 'Yes, I know *you* are the one conducting this interview,' I thought. 'What I don't know is why you are deliberately putting a kind of spell on this boy.' And sooner than stand there in the doorway and watch him doing it, I moved quietly away and went to see if Nan could use some help. Though he was probably only a couple of years younger than I was, something about Bruce made me feel protective, and with his usual damned penetration I was sure Pa had noticed this. I even wondered uneasily whether Pa had it in mind to involve me in some design or other of his own, and, if so, what it could be. Then I told myself briskly not to be morbid, and took along a colander of new peas to shell in the larder. Crackers abandoned the kitchen table, where Mrs. Pryde and her cohorts were as usual sitting over tea, and trotted after me out of curiosity.

The slate shelves and flagstone floor of the larder had a smell of cream and mould, and a chill that was not agreeable. Rain was rattling down steadily on the low roof. From the kitchen came a raucous gust of laughter, and without warning a great wave of desolation swept over me. Blindly I fumbled for Crackers and picked him up to have something warm to hold; but he soon kicked himself free and stalked off with a fastidious twitch of his long tail. I went on shelling peas. When the bowl was nearly full, Pa suddenly appeared. He had approached so quietly in his velvet slippers, and my mind was so far away, that I gave a great start.

"Where is Nan?" he demanded.

"She was in the kitchen a minute ago, making pastry."

"Well, she isn't there now. I wish she wouldn't disappear like this. I wanted to tell her—look, run her to earth, will you, and tell her to chill a couple of bottles of champagne to go with the sweet. And Pol, get her to tidy her hair and put on a clean apron. After all, she's a comely woman. She doesn't have to go around looking as if we'd kept her in the cinders all her life. Smarten her up a bit, will you? There's my puss." He gave my chin a caressing little pinch and had only just vanished when Nan herself came into the larder with a big bowl of whipped cream in her crooked arm. Jam stained her crumpled apron. Much of her fine hair had escaped its knot and floated in tendrils around her face, which was pink from the oven.

"Come here and let me fix your hair. Pa wants you to look decent."

"Why?" she asked simply.

"Why does he do anything he does? Hold still. You have nice hair, you know. In fact, you're good to look at all round. Just the kind men go for, if you'd only realize it. There, that's better." Swiftly pinning and tucking I tidied her up while she stood, head bowed obediently, like a large child bullied by a small parent. "He says change your apron too,"

I added as she escaped toward the kitchen. She would do it, I knew, because Pa had told her to. Unlike me, she had never rebelled against him in anything, either because she loved him more or herself less than I did.

Later, at the table, when the sweet had been served and we were washing it down with champagne, Pa disappeared from his place. Seconds later he was back, tugging Nan after him by the hand. Her hair was smooth and her apron almost clean.

"Ladies and gentlemen, I want you to charge your glasses and drink a toast with me," he said. "To the author of the excellent meal you have just consumed. My daughter is in her way a great artist. Isn't that so, Bruce? All of you — I'm sure you agree. To Nan."

Thumped forks and raised glasses answered him. Nan blushed a painful, hot pink and, averting her face, tried to pull away, but he held her fast a moment longer. Out of pity, and to comfort and calm her, Ralph took her free hand and murmured, "Dear Nan." He had known her since she was ten, and one of the nicest things about him was his gentleness with her. She shot him a hunted look of gratitude before Pa released her and she could bolt from the room.

"As you see, she's extremely shy," Pa said, addressing himself to Bruce. "But Nan's a person of very rare quality. You should try to get to know her."

Bruce mumbled something inaudible but no doubt polite.

"You looked bemused, Pol," said Ralph, smiling at me as he topped up my glass.

"Well, it's rare, you must admit, to hear Pa actually speak well of one of his children. What can the old gorilla be up to?"

"Why should he be up to anything?"

"Because he always is. One way or another."

"Oh, tut, Polly. You're such a little pepper-pot. Why can't you give him credit for being an affectionate father — and a good one. Because he is, you know."

"Up to a point, yes. Only as a parent he has a tendency to confuse himself with Almighty God from time to time."

Ralph laughed, but the exchange was broken off here because arrangements had been made for the crew to film a re-enactment of last night's charade. As Pa shepherded us all out to dress for our parts, I heard him say to Bruce, "Yes, I know. But before you fly back, come down to us for the weekend. You too, Joan. It's agreed, then. We'll really enjoy that."

Perhaps it had been too long or full a day, but for whatever reason I struggled up that night out of a bad dream soon after falling asleep. Bard, strapped into the seat beside me, was snoring. Eyes closed, lips relaxed, he looked perfectly intact except for the cracked lens in one side of his glasses that caught the red light of the police van outside. An agonizing weight pinned me by both legs. The workmen cursed as they wrestled with their hydraulic equipment to free us from our metal cage. Between bursts from a pneumatic drill, the dry whirr of Provençal cicadas piped tranquilly in the fields. Gasping, I sat up in bed. Hugging my own knees I tried to reassemble myself in the present time and place, a setting that seemed so much less convincing than it should.

After a few minutes I crept out of bed and went to the window to look out at the night. A high, bright moon glanced out from an attendant rack of cloud, bathing the garden below in a cold white light. Something dark crept alongside the flower-border — it was Lally's pug, which from this angle appeared to have no legs whatever. Idling along behind him was a tall, elegant figure in the blazer he had worn at dinner. Its metal buttons glimmered, as did his white shirt-front. He carried a light stick or switch and swung it idly to and fro. It was Ralph, overseeing the final airing of Darling.

I was just about to call down to him, not because I had anything particular to say, but just to prove that I did, in spite of everything, still exist, when the moon darkened, then swiftly reappeared. Before I could speak, I saw — or thought I saw in that tricky light — Ralph's arm lift high in a quick gesture. He brought down his stick on the innocently waddling pug in a single, sharp cut that made me gasp. But did I hear, or just imagine I heard, an agonized yelp? When the moon emerged again, Ralph was strolling calmly along behind the dog. He carried no stick. The pug lifted its stumpy leg and sneezed placidly at the floral scents that rose to me on the quiet night air.

A hundred times I had seen Ralph fondle that dog—even kiss its petulant velvet face. There was no question about it, what I imagined I'd seen was nothing but a projection of my own neurotic sense of the arbitrariness and cruelty of happenstance. But God knows *that* was real enough. Shivering, I went back to bed, turned on the light, and read till the sun finally rose.

The removal next morning of all the lights, cameras, coiled flex, and extra people from the house allowed us to get back to something like a normal routine. The centre leaf came out of the dining-room table. Spare trays were put away in the butler's pantry. Sighing luxuriously, Lally repossessed her favourite sofa in the sitting-room. Nan's spinning-wheel hummed once more in her small ground-floor crafts room. Now that we were alone again, she left this door ajar so the long skeins of wool she dyed blue, yellow, and red could be seen hanging on the wall, with Crackers sitting on the rag rug gazing with unblinking green eyes at the wheel, which fascinated him.

Yet a sort of undissipated electric charge of some kind seemed to linger in the house for days after the film crew had gone. Perhaps the continuous rain had something to do with a sense of unfinished business that hung over us all. Pa went up to London with Ralph to sign a BBC contract that could perfectly well have been sent down to him, and they said they might stay up to do a theatre or two. Pa also spoke of being measured for a new suit, though he already had more clothes than he could conceivably live long enough to wear out.

"You don't suppose, do you, that he fancies young Joan?" I asked Hamish idly. As if he also felt the unsettled atmosphere, he had wandered out of his office, ostensibly to read me a letter from a fan in Regina wishing to carve Pa's bust in chocolate for part of a series of Canadian writers in candy meant to educate schoolchildren in our cultural heritage.

"Joan? Not at all likely. He's never gone much for big bottoms."

"He's asked her down here, you know."

"Only because she was there when he asked Bruce. Besides, she's his girl, you know."

"Oh, is she?"

"His room was next to mine, remember."

"So it was. Not like Pa to miss a detail like that."

We had wandered out to the little conservatory some former owner had tacked on to the side of the house. Here through the wet glass a steady rain could be seen not so much falling as hanging static in the saturated air. A grapevine had been romantically trained over the roof, but instead of providing a flowery sanctuary for lovers, this room had become a repository for old rubber boots, clay pots, discarded magazines, and broken canvas chairs. The cushions in the wicker furniture smelled of must, and the green vine overhead gave our faces a wan, drowned look. I poked with my cane at a torn edge of the floor-matting, dislodging after some effort half of a cardboard moustache on elastic thread of the sort children wear at costume parties.

"I rather thought you fancied Bruce yourself," Hamish said casually.

"What a bizarre notion."

"Is it?"

"Of course it is. My fancying days are over. As far as all that's concerned I might as well be a hundred and six, whereas Bruce and his pals are their normal age, so you see how—"

Here Hamish plucked the cardboard moustache impatiently out of my hands and threw it out into the rain. His reddish eyebrows were knitted into a frown. "Who's ever really their 'normal' age, Polly? Do you think I am? Stuck fast in the fantasy stage, that's my status, and a damn ridiculous place to be. Or maybe it's that I'm in some kind of crazy time-warp — a displaced Launcelot with twentieth-century bridgework. . . . " There was a short silence. Then he added briskly, "Anyhow, I think Monty's virile days may be over. He hasn't married anybody for years."

"Well, no, but . . . in that case, why the new suit?"

"Something to do, isn't it? Instead of writing, that is."

"Really stalled, is he?"

"Completely."

"That's grim for him. Like being dead."

"Well, perhaps not quite. He keeps on tinkering with little changes. Rearranging the sequence — that kind of thing. But it's stalled, all right. I'm not too hopeful the thing will ever — I don't know why he keeps me hanging around here, in fact."

"Poor old Pa."

"Oh, he'll be all right as long as he doesn't realize or admit . . . just as he's never admitted what happened to him with that queer turn he had a few months ago. You've noticed his left arm shakes a bit sometimes?"

"Yes—what *is* that? What happened?"

"Well, it turned out to be nothing very dire, but still. He was at the table, house full of guests as usual. Somebody asked him a question and he didn't answer. For maybe five minutes he was right out of it, with his eyes wide open. When he came round he was a bit confused, needed help to get up . . . you can imagine we were all in a tizz. But the doctor told me later it was just something called a transient ischemic attack, not a stroke. Anyhow, next day Monty was laughing it all off. Told everybody he'd had too much port. By then most of it had worn off, and he's been insisting ever since that nothing happened to him at all. But the fact is—I looked it up later—about a third of the people who get these attacks later on have a stroke."

My eyes were stinging. One of these days, then, something similar might happen to my father again, perhaps leaving him paralysed or, if he was lucky, dead.

"Damn it, Pol, I'm sorry. I shouldn't have told you."

"It's nothing," I said, angrily rubbing my eyes. "Pay no attention—I *do* this nowadays for no reason. Certainly I'm the last person to get sentimental about Pa. He's had a good long run, and more fun than most people ever get. Only I know what it's like to have the Grim Reaper come along and give you a portentous bloody great whack with the scythe—and then just go away. The anticlimax—it's so embarrassing."

Hamish looked at me, his high-coloured face without expression. Then he uttered his short, angry bark of a laugh.

"Exactly," he said. "Let's have a drink."

"A bit early, isn't it?"

"There are some days when it's never too early."

"True."

In the kitchen-garden one sunny afternoon I came on Fisk the gardener, hoeing vegetables. Though it was very warm, he was evidently much too British to take off his shirt, but he had rolled his faded blue sleeves as high as they would go. Between his sun-browned neck and his collar a band of very white skin showed. Several butterflies of the same whiteness were fluttering in a dilatory way over the cabbages near by. It gave me a mild surprise to discover that Oldfisk was neither ugly nor old; in fact, with his muscular, gypsy arms and his eyes of the same milky blue as his shirt, he was as pleasant to look at as the garden's greenery and the butterflies swimming in the sunny air.

He straightened then, and surprised me even further. Without speaking he held out one arm at full length, a faint smile on his face. He stood there a full minute quite motionless, and one of the butterflies danced close, hovered indecisively, then lighted on his outstretched hand. It perched there, slightly flexing its delicate wings, while one could have counted to twelve, before it fluttered off. Fisk bent over his hoe again without comment, and I went away smiling.

Next morning Pa phoned down from London to announce that he and Ralph would get home on Friday in time to receive Bruce and Joan for their weekend visit. He would drive down, he said, with his publishers, James and John Harris, as added guests. "Marguerite can't come — her arthritis is playing her up—so Nan will have to sit at table with us to make an even number. See that she looks presentable, will you."

"All right, Pa."

"And I want it to be a rather special dinner."

"Good Lord, Pa, it will be special enough with ten of us to sit down. I can't think why you want so much activity and complication."

"Those are the sentiments of a slug, child—a slow-belly —shame on you. Get Mrs. Pryde's daughter to come in and help if you can't cope. I want smoked salmon for the starter, tell Nan. Make sure the hock is well chilled. And stuffed shoulder of lamb to follow. Burgundy with that. Then any sweet she likes."

"—stuffed shoulder—"

He breathed heavily and impatiently down the line while I scribbled down these instructions. "And I *think* a bottle of Château d'Yquem to finish off with. It will be Midsummer Eve, you know."

Until that moment I didn't know, and didn't care; but Pa always liked to seize on calendar dates and make occasions of them. Even in alien environments like Ottawa or Calgary, on Guy Fawkes Day a huge bonfire always blazed in our garden. Similarly on St. George's Day, Twelfth Night, and May Day, festivities were held which were often quite shamelessly pagan in character. He continued to enjoy these celebrations long after we children became bored with them, as if for all his sophistication and subtlety he had never quite grown up. Now he rang off full of cheerful anticipation of a good party, saying, "Love to all." It never seemed to occur to him that these affairs always meant a great deal of work for everybody but himself, and he would have been not only offended but hurt to have this pointed out to him. With a sigh I got up and went to find Nan.

Generally at that hour she was working at her loom or rolling pastry in the kitchen, but I could find her in neither of these places. The sitting-room was occupied only by Lally, who was on the sofa asleep while listening to Haydn on Radio Four. Eventually, however, I found Nan in the utility room at the back of the house, with the dogs wagging expectantly around her as she buttoned on a raincoat. Glancing outside, I saw that though it had been raining, the overcast was breaking to show a patch or two of blue.

"Walkies, is it? Look, I'll come with you, part of the way anyhow. The exercise has to be good for me, I hate it so much. Pa's phoned with a long list of orders."

As usual she didn't answer, but reached down an old mac and held it out for me, giving my shoulders an affectionate little squeeze once I got my arms into the sleeves. She was so pleased to have my company that she actually volunteered a remark.

"I'll show you the old pond."

"All right, if it isn't too far."

So we set off, our wellies squelching over the sodden lawn, while the dogs bounded joyfully ahead. After a few minutes she adapted her long stride to my slow pace, and we went comfortably enough along a muddy lane skirting the orchard. Overhead masses of cloud rolled and shifted, but the rain had stopped. Occasionally the sun even glanced out, lighting up the drenched grass, the hedgerows, and the tree foliage with a bright glitter.

As we walked along I relayed all Pa's instructions to Nan, who received them calmly and without comment. Boris and Ivan kept plunging ahead out of sight, then galloping back, grinning and panting, to thrust cold noses into our hands. From time to time I paused, leaning on the cane, to rest my legs. The air smelled deliciously of rainwater, clean stone, and soaked earth. Our path ran for a time alongside an old, rusted railway line; then it cut across a field where some damp cattle stared at us curiously with their stupid, beautiful eyes. Long tendrils of vine and weeds brushed our legs wetly and trees showered cold drops on our heads. Our boots grew heavy with mud, but Nan strode on vigorously.

"Not so fast—wait for me. Oh, and Pa wants you to sit at table with us for the Midsummer Eve dinner."

She gave her shoulders a hitch, but the message didn't seem to disturb her as much as I expected it would. To please her, I added, "I'll do your hair for you. We'll make you look smashing, how about that?"

At this she glanced back at me and smiled. There was something so amused, wise, and lovingly indulgent in her face that it both touched and surprised me. Not for the first time I wondered whether Pa's remark about her quality hadn't been truer than he knew.

Here we topped a little rise of land, and Nan stopped. She pointed ahead to a hollow in which a small, dark pond lurked. Several gnarled old trees leaned over the water as if to hide it from the casual eye. Overhead the rain clouds had thickened again, dimming the light so the little pool looked almost black. A gust of wind brought a squall of rain with it, and I shivered. My legs were aching now.

"If that's your pond, it's a hell of a gloomy place," I said. "Let's get home."

Someone had roped a child's swing to one of the stouter apple boughs in the orchard, and on a still, bright afternoon, idling along there to escape preparations for the weekend, I sat down on its warm board seat, first propping my cane carefully against the tree-trunk. Soon the little swaying motion lulled me into a child's total, mindless pleasure. The sun twinkled through gaps in the leafy umbrella overhead. To and fro I swung, to and fro my own shadow floated under me across the rough grass. The white of daisies and the varnished yellow of buttercups flowed into one bright colour.

How perfect this was, I thought, this solitude and silence. How good it was to be entirely suspended, swinging idly between heaven and earth, between past and future, a transient. This kind of contentment, I knew, was a result of the disaster I'd survived, and consequently to be deplored; but I hugged it to me like a treasure. To be without either memory or plans seemed the ultimate pleasure. To and fro I swung, closing my eyes in bliss. Then the sun abruptly vanished behind a vast cloud, and it began to rain hard. Cursing, I seized my stick and hobbled rapidly back to the house.

Pa's arrival on Friday with his guests luckily coincided with a dramatic improvement in the weather. Midsummer Eve was warm, cloudless, and serene. The light coming through the dining-room windows as we sat over dessert was a thick, golden colour. Too lazy to move, we lingered at the table over our coffee. Dinner with its various courses, ending with the sweet white wine, had left us all feeling rather flushed and heavy. The candles burned steadily in their crystal cups, adding to the languid warmth of the air. Most of us had been content for some time to contribute little or nothing to an argument Pa was having with James Harris about Shakespeare.

"People are always admiring the Bard for the wrong reasons," my father said, rolling a long cigar between his fingers. "They forgive him, for one thing, the many atrocious lines of nonsense he wrote. And they seem to think his range and variety were enormous, whereas in fact most of the plays are monotonously centred on one theme only."

"Monotonously?" inquired James, lifting his eyebrows mildly. "And that theme would be—?"

"Why, that's obvious. The function and nature of the creative imagination," said Pa.

"My dear fellow, Shakespeare died a rich man. Nobody ever made a fortune harping away about the creative imagination." James was a very short, completely bald man with thick glasses shielding a pair of small, amused eyes. His insignificant appearance was one of his most notable business assets—that and his extreme tact. He had been Pa's publisher, without any serious friction, for the last twelve years.

"Nonsense," insisted Pa. "You find him at it all the time. How many of the histories, tragedies, comedies — how many of them, I say, focus on some kind of masque or performance or disguise. Plots and deceptions, his work is full of them, from *Midsummer Night's Dream* on. Just look at that interplay of the real and the surreal in the woods . . . Oberon and Puck making magic. And he's at it again with Prospero and Ariel at the end. It's a monomania."

"'Pass the bottle,'" said Hamish. "This being a literary discussion, I hope you all recognize the quotation."

Pa ignored this and swept on. "In nearly every play some kind of creative artist is seen spinning his web. What else, I ask you, is Richard III up to—or Hamlet? He used the theatre as his central metaphor because he knew it best, but what obsessed him was the power of language to create illusion."

Across the table Bruce struggled to maintain a look of alert interest. Nan sat beside him with her hair smooth and wearing a dress made of tawny wool woven by herself. She looked quite civilized, but she yawned now as openly as a child. Her jaws tightening against the contagion, Lally toyed with the rings on her fingers.

"What about the farcical interludes then, like Quince's marvellous 'Pyramus and Thisbe'?" James wanted to know. "Half the time, if you ask me, Shakespeare was sending up the whole business of illusion-making. Perhaps he thought the creative imagination was just as absurd as anything else, if it's taken too seriously."

"You need to read the plays again, James, this time with your eyes open."

But James only smiled tolerantly. "My eyes are open in this house to only two things, my dear chap. One is the beauty of your daughters. The other is your next novel. Is there any sporting chance I might be allowed to see even a few pages of it this weekend?"

Bruce leaned a little forward to get a better view of Pa's face. Weeks ago he had begged in vain for a glimpse of the unfinished MS. There was an expectant pause. Then Pa flashed an impish grin around the table before turning to James with a ceremonious little bow. "Not," he said with great distinctness, "on your nelly."

With this he pushed back his chair and went to the French doors, which he flung open wide. "It's much too warm in here," he said. "Let's all wander outside. It's a lovely night. Look at it — ten o'clock and not nearly dark yet."

Willingly enough we drifted out onto the terrace and lawn. Behind me I saw Pa wait for Nan to snuff the candles and then draw her out to join us. It was indeed a lovely night. The clear twilight seemed to distil a richer colour out of the pink standard roses, the frilled lavender hollyhocks, and the tall yellow lilies with their spotted throats.

The air was perfectly still. The oaks, elms, and tall shrubs stood as motionless as painted trees. In the pale sky a paler moon was just beginning to rise.

Singly and in groups we wandered about on the soft grass, breathing in the heavy scent of night-stock. Perhaps it was the brightening moon, or this perfume mounting to our heads like an extra glass of wine, that soon began to make us all feel a little giddy. Pa struck a grandiloquent pose and proclaimed to Joan, "Ill met by moonlight, proud Titania", remembering perhaps that years ago he had produced an abridged *Midsummer Night* for my sister Olivia's fifteenth birthday, with eight-year-old me cast as Puck. Most of the play's lines were consequently part of our mental furniture. I piped up, "Help me, Lysander, help me—"

But Pa had now seized Nan's hand to declaim,
"Hipollyta, I woo'd thee with my sword,
And won thy love doing thee injuries,
But I will woo thee in another key,
With pomp, with triumph, and with revelling."

"Do thy best," I went on shrilly, clutching the rose-trellis and shaking it, "to pluck this crawling serpent from my breast."

Joan now darted into the shrubbery and Bruce plunged after her into the shadows, where a squeal soon proclaimed he had caught her. The dogs, inspired by this foolery, lumbered about barking. Even Lally felt the contagion and lifted a languid white hand to the sky, murmuring, "Well shone, Moon."

Unable to resist, I darted behind the holly hedge as nimbly as my cane would allow, calling back as I did so, "Fairies, skip hence—" But before the last word was quite out, I had come into sudden collision with someone whom I couldn't identify even as I was seized and roughly kissed. He held me in such a hard, insistent grip that for a few seconds I couldn't get my breath. His hard facial bones and teeth hurt my mouth and conveyed a sort of horror. It was like being kissed by a skull. Violently I wrenched myself free. Hamish stood there, the milky light of the moon showing every grim line etched into his face. From his expression it was clear that what he had done to me was not nearly as destructive as what I had done to him. We stood there a moment looking at each other without speaking. Then simultaneously we said, "Sorry." I turned and moved awkwardly away, leaving him alone.

Murmurs, scuffling, and laughter could still be heard in various corners of the garden. When I neared the house again, Bruce, his arm around Joan, was leading her up to the terrace, where my father now lay extended in a long chair.

"Give us your blessing, sir," he said. "We're going to get married. For real," he added with a wide smile.

Pa looked up, first at him, then at her. Then he muttered as if to himself, "'Nor hath love's mind of any judgement taste.'" As speedily as I could, I went over and, taking his arm, urged him to his feet, saying, "Pa, let's go in. It's getting chilly out here." He turned on me a face darkening with one of those onsets of gloom I knew so well. The young couple looked at each other, puzzled and uneasy. Lally slipped past us and went into the house. Hamish had already disappeared. The moon, quite small and high by now, looked down on us with its ambiguous white disc of a face. Nan stood by soberly, one big hand on each of the dogs' necks. We all stood there without moving as if under some kind of spell.

Just then a white owl out hunting swooped down without a sound onto the lawn near by in pursuit of some little vole or shrew he'd spotted there. As he rose, his soft, broad wings made a faint creak in the still air. We all watched him fly off, white and wild, into the black trees. Nan's face all at once shone with delight. She turned to Ralph as if to share it with him, and he said gently, "Yes. Lovely."

When Pa sent down word next morning that he was starting a cold and intended to stay in bed for the day, we all
felt a certain sense of relief. Even if he had not been difficult the night before, we would have shared this reaction,
because it was undeniably true that even when at his best,
Pa's undiluted presence over a long period of time imposed
a degree of strain on everyone. As it was, Bruce and Joan
were quite openly glad to get into their taxi for the station
and escape without encountering him again. Even James
and John received news of the cold without undue distress,
and drove away together before lunch.

Instead of sitting down to a hot meal, the rest of us seized
the opportunity to nibble at a collection of leftovers on the
buffet, eating out of our fingers standing up, in a way Pa
was well known to despise. Hamish didn't bother to appear
in the dining-room at all. As for me, as soon as I'd helped
Nan clear away the scrappy meal, I went up to my attic
room and lay on the bed, intending to enjoy an uninter-
rupted read of the new Burgess novel I had stowed away
there like contraband. I knew better than to leave it anywhere around the house where Pa might see it. The more
brilliant his rivals were, the more scathingly he reviled
them and their admirers. On the other hand, he would often
go out of his way to heap praise on some little-known, third-
rate author. This syndrome never embarrassed him in the
least, but it made me, for one, very uncomfortable. Soon
after stretching out on the bed, however, I felt last night's
fatigues and follies catching up with me, and dropped into
a heavy sleep.

Unfortunately I forgot until it was too late how clogged
with (generally unpleasant) dreams a daytime nap often is.
An hour or so later, yawning, my mouth thick and eyes
heavy, I shook off a jumble of images that slid and tumbled
in my brain like the contents of a spilled bureau drawer.
Nurses were wheeling me in my bed down a wide, polished
corridor. We paused by the open door of the room I knew

to be Bard's. A woman in black sat by the bed. One of my attendants remarked to the other, "La légitime," and it was indeed his wife Doris, whole and blameless, whose eyes met mine.

I sat up now and got my legs clumsily over the bedside. Burgess had slipped to the carpet. A westerly wind was driving squalls of rain against the window. The light was wan. It was four-thirty, and Bard was dead. Somewhere below I heard a cough.

'Right,' I thought. 'Here and now exist, no matter how much you might prefer some other arrangement. Get up on that cane, sister. Go and take your poor old pa a cup of tea.'

Even before I set the tray across his lap, I could see that, just as I'd suspected from the first, Pa's cold was not so much a virus as a frame of mind.

"Oh, I don't want that," he said heavily from the pillows I'd briskly plumped up and wedged behind him.

"Yes, you do. Tea is well known to improve pretty well any condition. Except maybe AIDS. And you haven't got that, I trust."

"You're in an antic mood, aren't you, miss. It must be nice to be young and soulless. Faugh," he added, looking gloomily at the tray.

"Yes, it must."

"Well, you might as well go. I feel completely ill. Completely. And take this stuff with you—I don't want it."

I lifted the lid of the muffin dish just enough to let the aroma of Nan's new-baked cinnamon buns escape. Then I saw by his face it would be reasonably safe to pour his tea and sit down near by with a cup for myself. Dear, ridiculous Pa. He did, after all, look rather seedy. The cup trembled in his hand, slopping a little tea into the saucer. Difficult as he often made it, I was fond of him, and felt the impulse to let him know it.

"How wise you are to stay in bed. That cold may be completely gone in the morning. You've been working too hard, that's what it is. Or living too high up in London. Or perhaps you got a little chill last night out there under the moon."

His only answer was a grunt. With a noisy slurp he took in some tea.

"Try one of the buns," I urged him. "Nan made them specially to tempt you."

He nibbled at one, frowning, then munched down the rest of it in two bites before reaching another one out of the dish.

"Admit you're glad now you let her quit school and study Cordon Bleu instead."

"My poor Nan. They all but asked me to take her away, you know. She couldn't learn. Geometry—sports—it made no difference what, she just couldn't cope. Something terribly wrong. By the time she was fourteen it was painfully obvious. What could I do but let her stay home? I've looked after her as well as I can, but—"

"Of course you have. She's all right, Pa. Quite happy."

"But as you said that day in London, what would happen if I weren't here to look after her? Eh? Of course she's all right now. Protected. Nothing to worry her as long as she's sheltered here. But what about afterwards, Pol? What about then?"

His urgency disturbed me. He thrust the tray down to the foot of the bed and sat forward, clasping his bony knees as he stared at me through the room's dim light. "For God's sake switch on a lamp," he said irritably.

"Well, as far as money goes, you can set up a trust fund for her, Pa. You know none of us would object to that, no matter how much of your estate—"

"No, no, no," he said fiercely. "That's not what I mean. Money won't meet the need. Not for someone like that. She needs *care*. You and Olivia have your lovers and your own lives—the boys are married—but she'll be so alone."

I looked at him. It was clear he was truly and deeply concerned, for once, about someone other than himself, and I thought uneasily that he must indeed feel ill to have such thoughts. 'Tomorrow,' I thought, 'I'll maybe ask the doctor just to drop by casually and have a look at him. This kind of concern worries me.'

"She really ought to marry, you know," he muttered, as if to himself.

"Good Lord, Pa, who would marry Nan?"

"Surely it's a perfectly reasonable idea. She's quite beautiful, in her way. And I can see to it she has money. It should be quite feasible to find somebody who'd be damn glad to have her. And I mean to find him as soon as I can."

"But Pa—"

"Now don't be obstructive, Pol."

"I only meant what if she doesn't want to marry."

"She will want what I want for her."

This was exactly what I meant, though I didn't have the courage to say so. In any case, the opportunity was gone.

"Listen to me, Polly, and carefully. I want your help. I'm going to need you here. Stay with me at least till next spring."

"Oh, but I couldn't do that," I said, alarmed.

"And why not? You know quite well you're not fit yet to be on your own. If you don't, I do."

"But look, Pa, I can't—"

"Polly, I think you owe this much to me. And to Nan, come to that, if you're as fond of her as you seem to be. You can do so much for her. Take her to a dressmaker—a hairdresser—build up her self-confidence. She loves you; she'll take your advice. Talk to her . . . you know . . . woman to woman . . . make her more aware—"He broke off here and shifted his legs restlessly under the bedclothes. "Don't you see, that's what she's been lacking. Your influence and all that could make her more—more normal. After that it should be quite easy to get her married. To somebody suitable, of course."

What took me so off guard about this proposition was that I found it tempting. Independence had subtly over the last weeks become less and less attractive. The comfort, the security, of my father's house were things I couldn't, when it came to the choice, easily refuse. Still, perversely enough, I couldn't accept them easily either.

"But Pa, there aren't that many eligible men who—"

"Blarney," he said, flashing me a smile.

"Well, you aren't planning to advertise, are you? Come on—can you think of anybody we know that would qualify?"

There was a brief pause. Then, turning his head aside, he said, "Well, for a while there, I thought of Bruce."

"What! There must be almost twelve years' difference—" But all the pieces of the Bruce puzzle had now fallen into place.

"No problem," he said calmly. "That wouldn't have mattered at all, you know. He's the sort to be comfortable with an older woman. No, one must not let little things interfere."

I bit my tongue. Here, as so often, I had to admit he was probably right.

"But of course," he went on, "the timing was unfortunately wrong. He'd already fallen for that cow in the jeans. So that's that. But the idea's perfectly sound. We just keep looking, and one day—"

"Oh Pa, I don't know."

"You do know. You said yourself in London that Nan might marry."

"Oh God, did I?"

"You did. And I think I have a right to your support now, Pol."

There drifted uneasily across my mind the possibility

that not Nan but I was the daughter he was seeking to manipulate. But it was too late now to extricate myself. All I could say was, "Well, I'm not promising anything. I'll think about it—but no promises."

"That's my good girl," he said warmly, as if this were a wholehearted commitment. 'But it isn't,' I told myself stoutly. 'It's nothing of the kind.'

Rather to everyone's surprise, including perhaps his own, Pa next day produced all the symptoms of a true and heavy cold. He huddled under the blankets alternately shivering and coughing, and raised no objection when we suggested a visit from the doctor. Hamish had gone out somewhere —nobody seemed to know where or why—so Ralph went to the phone and rang Dr. Bagshot, the local medic. Nan set out for the village with her shopping-basket to buy the ingredients for a jugged hare. She knew that when ill Pa would have nothing to do with invalid slops, but required the consolation of an even richer gourmet menu than usual.

His illness and the doctor's impending arrival produced a series of dislocations in the household. All of us found ourselves scurrying here and there on unfamiliar chores. Mrs. Pryde hulled strawberries for lunch in the kitchen while the scullery-maid dusted the sitting-room, and the char set up a steam-kettle in the sick-room. Perhaps it was all this unconventional activity that inspired Lally to say to me, "I'll fix some flowers for Monty's room. Come and help me choose them, Polly."

So I collected an old pair of gloves and the secateurs and we went out to the garden. It was a fresh day with wind making sheets on the line behind the brick wall balloon and struggle like captive whales. The pug trailed after us, wheezing cynically at the abundance of fresh air. Helping Lally to choose, of course, meant that I cut the flowers and laid them in the trug while she pointed out what she wanted with a graceful hand. We were doing these things when we glimpsed Hamish in the archway of the kitchen-garden. At once he vanished.

"Why does Hamish dart away from everybody these days?" Lally asked idly. "Do you think he might be turning into a nipper with a secret bottle somewhere? With men as buttoned-down as that, you never know."

"I doubt that. Probably he's just feeling a bit awkward. He made a pass at me that night we were out here in the moonlight. Silly, really. We were all a bit tiddly, I think. It didn't mean anything."

"Not to you, maybe," Lally said.

"Or to him." ('Now why am I playing a part here?' I wondered uneasily. 'And not even as well as Lally always plays the role of herself.')

"Ah," she was saying lightly now, "you know these Scots Calvinists. They feel guilty about absolutely *everything*. And your Maritime ones are the worst, Monty says."

"Are they?"

"Get me that yellow rose—the one in bud. And a couple of those nice fringey daisies."

I looked over my shoulder at her. "You can't be serious, Lall. He's forgotten the whole thing by now. It was only a crazy passing impulse. To him I'm just the brat with braces on her teeth he used to play dominoes with."

"You know I'm never serious, darling—what would be the point, when life's so ridiculous? But Hamish is a dead-earnest chap, you must know that. When we heard you'd gone off with Bard, Monty flew into the most colossal rage, but Hamish's face . . . "

The rest of her sentence faded out, because I wasn't really listening. A sharp memoryflash had brought back that moment of pure and reckless joy when Bard and I threw the suitcases into the back of his car (on which, I later learned, a number of payments were still due), slammed the door shut, and shot off down the road toward France. Behind us trailed a discarded litter of responsibilities no longer of any significance, like my bit part in *Private Lives*, and his wife.

"Just because you have no feelings like that for poor old Hamish doesn't mean he has none for you," Lally went on, drawing her cashmere sweater more closely around her shoulders. "Rotten luck, isn't it, when desires just don't mesh. So lovely, though, when they do."

"Yes." Carefully I cut a long stem to the yellow rosebud. Lally's face was lifted to the wind that blew back her curly white fluff of hair, and her eyes as usual were half-closed in lazy pleasure. Something about her tranquil indifference to nearly everything soothed me into confession.

"I haven't got the faintest interest in sex any more, you know. Not since the accident. Not a flicker. Never will have again, either, is my guess."

"That I doubt. You're only twenty-eight, aren't you, Pol? It will change. If worst comes to worst you can always fake it, and in time you'll convince yourself."

"I was pregnant, you know."

"Well, that probably has something to do with it. Hormones or something. But not to worry. Some gorgeous man will come along, and hey presto. You just never know when it will happen. Or where. I met Ralph at a dog show. Or *why* it happens. He's not actually a nice man at all. But when he sits down his knees fold over each other in this madly aristocratic way ... quite irresistible. Like those blue, blue eyes your Bard had."

A long thorn here luckily barbed my forearm, and I could pretend it was that pain that made my tears pour down.

"Poor lamb," said Lally cheerfully. "But just remember this, Pol—the world is full of compensations. The only one to avoid is food, because of getting fat. That really *is* fatal."

Without wanting to I broke into a watery giggle, and we went back into the house, the pug waddling after us. Once Lally had been established with two water-filled jugs in the scullery, I went off to put a bit of plaster on my arm; but part way up the stairs I turned back on impulse and went instead to the door of Hamish's workroom. Before my resolution could weaken I rapped and opened it.

He was standing at the desk slitting open mail and his face instantly stiffened at the sight of me. Yes, I should have known, without any help from Lally's light, random chatter, that he was vulnerable, like everybody else. I had behaved too long like my father's daughter, treating this man like a piece of furniture or one of the dogs. Though I had no interest in him as a lover, I didn't want to lose him as a friend. I recognized this kind of thrift with a certain ruefulness as part of my new self, but wasn't sure yet whether I admired or hated it.

"Hamish, I want you to forget all about that silly business in the bushes the other night. Let's just agree it never happened. All right?"

He shrugged. "Oh, that. Of course." His face was so expressionless I thought with relief, "Lally's mad."

"It's forgotten," he said. "I had a drop too much wine."

"We all had. Anyhow—"

"And the truth is, I'm bored. Bored bloody stiff. There's nothing for me to do here, really. Dog's-body stuff—routine mail—I've been thinking for some time of suggesting to Monty that he let me go. He could get in a part-time typist to look after this. He only needs me as a court dwarf or something of that kind—"

"But you're never thinking of leaving Pa! Good God, Hamish, don't do that." The thought of the rage and frustration this would inflict on Pa (and consequently on Nan and me), with all the subsequent domestic upheaval, was enough to make my mouth go dry. "Look, I know it's selfish of us, but we honestly do need you here. With Pa in this writing block, it would just about finish him."

He thrust both hands deep into his pockets and shrugged. "Oh, you don't need to appeal to my better nature. I don't suppose I'll ever actually go anywhere.

Unfortunately, I like it here. I've got used to my creature comforts. My status as Friday . . . he was quite happy to call Crusoe Master, for pretty much the same reasons."

"Well, I don't really care what your reasons are. I'm just glad you're around."

"Thanks," he said dryly. "That's honest, at any rate."

"We are friends, aren't we? I mean, that's a pretty grim expression you're wearing."

But suddenly his sandy-lashed eyes, which were the hard blue of slate, grew more prominent. He had noticed the streak of dried blood on my forearm. He pointed to it in silence with a look almost of horror.

"Oh, does that bit of blood bother you? I'm just off to clean it up." At that moment, glancing through the window, I saw the doctor's Morris Minor coming down the drive. Hamish then found his tongue again. "I'll let him in. You go and bandage that up. You look like the Bloody Child."

"Will do. Thanks, Hamish." And we went our separate ways. I felt quite cheerful now.

Pa was recovering nicely from his cold when he woke one morning with a foot so inflamed and swollen he could not put it to the floor. At 5 a.m. he roused the whole house with a loud bellow of pain, and once more all of us scattered in various directions—Nan to borrow a Red Cross bedpan, Ralph to call Dr. Bagshot—others just anywhere out of range of his temper. He actually slapped my hand when I tried to arrange the bedclothes to take their weight off his foot.

"Now, Pa, it just looks like a little sprain," I told him. "It can't be anything much."

"Imbecile," he snorted, glaring at me. "How could I sprain my foot in *bed*? Oh, Christ on a crutch, leave it alone!"

Before the morning was over, Ralph and Lally set out

for Canterbury in the teeming rain to look at the spot where Becket was martyred, a locale where they felt more secure than at home. The rest of us tiptoed around and waited for the doctor, who, however, didn't put in an appearance till noon. He had barely brought the Morris to a halt before I had the front door open.

"Sorry to be troubling you so soon again," I said. With maddening deliberation he pocketed his keys, groped for his bag, and extricated himself from behind the wheel. He even paused a moment, with rain pouring off his hat-brim, to look up in admiration at the ivy-covered façade of the house.

"It's good of you to turn out in this filthy weather."

"Not at all, Miss Weston. My job, after all, isn't it."

He was a pleasant-looking, youngish man, with receding hair plastered down with some kind of sweet-smelling pomade over an egg-shaped skull. His mild eyes widened slightly as we stood at the foot of the stairs where my father's voice could be clearly heard raised in blasphemous protest. It was embarrassingly obvious that Nan was trying to help him use the bedpan, and that he was not grateful for the aid. Bagshot and I waited tactfully on the landing, looking out at the rain with all the interest we could muster. Finally the bedroom door opened and Nan moved off down the hall with the offending object under a towel. The doctor caught my eye and gave a tittering little laugh, in which I joined him out of politeness. His face, however, was professionally grave when we went into Pa's room.

After one glance at the foot, he said, "Gout."

"Ridiculous!" shouted Pa. "How would I get gout?"

"Heredity will do it sometimes, sir. Or diet. Luckily, we're pretty sure to put you right in a few days. Quite. I think we'll try colchicine — it's still the best medication — the Romans used it. Modern drugs like indomethacin are all very well; but they reduce all inflammation, whereas colchicine relieves only gout. We'll start you with .6 milligrams every two hours, and the symptoms should abate quite soon."

"*Faugh!*" said Pa with passion. "Never mind the goddamn symptoms! Do something about the *pain.*"

The doctor opened his bag and produced a pill which Pa snatched from his hand and swallowed without either water or thanks.

"Sorry about this," I muttered to Bagshot.

"Irritability is one of the symptoms of the disease," he said tolerantly. "Now I'll leave you this supply of codeine just to see you over the weekend — one every four hours — and the colchicine as well. Drink plenty of liquids, but absolutely no wine or spirits, of course. Also avoid all fats, red meats, or nitrogenous vegetables like asparagus —"

Here Pa groaned loudly.

The doctor permitted himself a prim little smile. "That's a hardship, is it? I'm a bachelor myself; that kind of fare doesn't come my way very often. Now keep the foot raised and warm, and in a few days you should be able to walk fairly comfortably. Phone me on Monday, Miss Weston, and if there's no improvement I'll come round again." He checked Pa's pulse and lungs, then snapped shut the clasp of his bag. By now the pain-killer had begun to take effect, and Pa's black scowl was easing slightly.

"I may have been a bit noisy," he admitted. "But the pain — it's like being shot. Slowly. With red-hot slugs. God, nobody would believe it. But thanks for coming out, Bagshot. Good of you. You'll stay for a bit of lunch, of course. Have Nan lay a place, Polly. My daughters will look after you." With this he closed his eyes and dismissed us both from his mind.

"Well, I'm not due at the hospital till two, but perhaps I really should get along . . . " the doctor murmured as we went downstairs.

"No, no; we'd be glad to have you stay," I said, forcing sincerity into my voice. "My sister Nan is a good cook. And we like having guests."

But I barely needed to tap my acting skills. Bagshot had already stowed his bag in a corner of the hall and, rubbing his large, clean hands, had walked into the sitting-room and hopefully eyed the sherry decanter.

"Do sit down. Let me give you a glass of sherry."

"Thank you so much. Quite. Very nice."

Here the conversation stalled so totally that I was forced in desperation to mention the weather again. We agreed it was horrid, and another silence fell. I refilled his glass. He kept rearranging his feet in their highly polished brogues as if his limbs belonged to someone else. However, halfway through his second glass of sherry, a little cowlick of his hair sprang free of its pomade. This went some way to offset the stiff collar and three-piece dark suit, in which garb it seemed he might have been born.

"I often see your sister with her dogs in the village," he said, leaning a little forward and looking at me earnestly.

"Yes. She . . . er . . . goes there. To the shops."

"But I've never had the opportunity to speak to her."

"I'm afraid she's very shy."

"Quite."

"The quiet life down here suits her. Away from London. And all Pa's fame. She loves the countryside."

"Very pretty county, Kent."

"Qui—I mean yes. Very."

"A country practice suits me. I'm a very quiet sort of chap myself. Don't even play bridge."

Another silence yawned.

"The other day," I said brightly, "Nan showed me how to find sloe berries in the hedgerows. We spent all day picking them. She's going to make gin. But perhaps you disapprove of that."

"Well, as long as your father has none of it—" he said,

and this time smiled quite naturally. His glass was empty. I refilled it.

"Perhaps one day you and your sister will come and have tea with me. Fox Cottage in the High Street. I have a nice little herb garden you might enjoy looking at. Perhaps we could fix a day now. Though I imagine that two such—such—er, ladies must have a very busy social calendar."

"Oh, no, we haven't at all. You see—it's very kind of you, but—the fact is my sister's a bit of a recluse. It's hard to explain, but she never goes out. I mean socially. She's really terribly shy."

"Well, so am I," he said. "As you can no doubt tell. But I'd like so much to have you both drop in. No formality, just a quiet—it would be so pleasant. Let's hope it can be arranged some time soon." With a pink rose in each cheek planted there by the sherry, and the tuft of his cowlick jutting up, he looked more human every minute, and sitting beside him through lunch turned out to be less of an ordeal than I expected. Nan didn't appear at the table except fleetingly to serve coffee; but when he talked about his herbs with their haunting names — tansy, valerian, rosemary, and fennel—I noticed her listening.

It was about a week later when, after putting out my light, I heard a series of unusual and rather furtive little sounds from my father's room below. The luminous hands of my bedside clock indicated a quarter after midnight. I was due to go up to London later that day for X-rays that would show whether or not my femur had healed enough to allow removal of a metal bar. The prospect did nothing to encourage sleep. From below came a faint clink and a smothered laugh. Then I heard the unmistakable squeak and pop of a drawn cork.

Seconds later, gowned and slippered, I appeared like Nemesis in Pa's doorway. By his bedside Nan in a white terry robe was prying the lid off a pot of Dijon mustard.

Pa was propped up, a large tray on his lap, a forkful of rare steak halfway to his mouth.

"Father, you are a bad, bad man."

"My dear, I am, and enjoying it enormously. Come on in. Nan, why don't you grill one of these for Polly? She's got no flesh on her bones at all. Join me in sin, my dear. Let's make a night of it. *No*, Ivan. This is all for me."

Nan gave me a questioning look and, when I nodded, slipped away down the back stairs to the kitchen, taking the dogs with her.

"Give me a kiss," demanded Pa, lifting a jovial face to me. He reached his free arm down the side of the bed and drew up an open bottle of wine. "Get yourself a glass out of the bathroom," he told me, "and then sit down. Entertain me with sparkling conversation."

"But this is so naughty, Pa. What would Dr. Bagshot say?"

"Who cares? It's a damn sight better to die of gout than boredom, isn't it?"

"Quite."

We both giggled shamelessly. I drank up the wine he sloshed generously into my glass, and held it out for more. When Nan appeared with a tray for me, the little steak sizzling in its own juices smelled delicious. I cut into it greedily as Pa demolished the last of his. Nan stood by, hands in the patch pockets of her gown, gazing at us kindly.

"Ah, this is the life," said Pa, laying down his fork. He looked fondly from one to the other of us. "What girls you are, the pair of you. Matrimony may have been unkind to me—not to say brutal—but at least it gave me a couple of fine daughters."

"Pa, I believe you're a bit drunk."

"Nothing of the kind. Having children is what it's all about. Remember that, you two. What marriage is about, that is. You're in your prime, both of you. Pol will have better luck next time"—here I caught him in the very act of censoring the words "and better judgement" — "and what a mother this big wench here will make, eh Nan?"

She smiled at him but made no answer. As usual it was hard to tell whether or not she actually heard him. She seemed to be looking at or listening to something else that absorbed most of her attention.

"'With pomp, with triumph, and with revelling,'" pursued Pa, crossing his arms behind his head and stretching out luxuriously. "Ah yes, that will be a day and a half. Quite. By the way, Dr. Bagshot dropped in this afternoon to look me over. Said he was in the neighbourhood, and so — Nice of him, eh? He seemed very disappointed to find you were both out."

I yawned. "Was he."

"He said something about having you round to see his garden. Nan and you, that is."

"Mm. I'm off to bed now, Pa."

"Good night, my dear."

Was I imagining it, or was Nan a little flushed as I gave her the stacked trays? No, I was not, because Pa noticed it too, and closed one eye in a swift wink on my side as I bent to retrieve the empty wine-bottle from the floor. As he settled down, eyes heavy, he looked like a large, benevolent cat too sleepy at the moment to have any plans regarding mice. Before I closed the door, he said drowsily, "Don't worry about the X-ray tomorrow, Pol. It's going to be all right." Immediately I felt as warmly, deliciously relaxed and reassured as a child tucked into bed. "I love you too, Pa," I said.

2
"The Hue and Cry after Cupid"

T en days later I was discharged from hospital, and Ralph met me at Canterbury East Station. He looked wonderfully elegant in his grey slacks and white cable-knit sweater, with a silk scarf knotted at his throat. Several housewives dragging tired children and bags of shopping off the train looked at him with undisguised greed.

It was a windy day with high-piled towers of cloud overhead. A faint, salt tang of the sea blew in from the Channel, and I breathed it up eagerly after the stuffy air of the train. The platform seemed to heave slightly under my feet as it used to do after long journeys in my childhood.

"All right?" Ralph asked, taking my case. "It isn't far to the car—can you manage? Bad luck about the infection. But they've put you right again now, I hope. That's the girl. Take your time."

The car doors clunked shut, we belted ourselves in, and soon we were bowling smoothly along the road toward home. Cloud-shadows sailed over the downs, which had been nibbled smooth as yellow plush by the flocks of sheep grazing there. The wind streamed like green water through trees and hedges, with a cool, rushing sound. It felt unexpectedly good to look at Ralph's familiar, bony profile.

"Tell me how everything's been at home. Is Pa mobile again?"

"Well, after that little relapse, the gout seems to have disappeared. Monty's become rather attached to it, though. He's acquired an ebony cane with a silver handle. The doctor still comes round occasionally, but last time he did that, I found the two of them in the library playing cribbage."

I savoured the mental picture of Pa with his stick before remarking, "Cribbage?"

"Yes. A piddling sort of game—not Monty's style at all, is it. Any more than Bagshot is his kind of man. But there it is. Your father's always full of surprises." Ralph glanced sidelong at me. "He seems to want people around him much more nowadays than he ever used to. Have you noticed that?"

"Well . . . it's part of getting older, maybe."

"Could be, I suppose. But the fact is, Pol, Lally and I have been at Seven Oaks for nearly six weeks now, and to be perfectly honest, I find it very inconvenient trying to conduct my business this far from London. Of course Monty's always had a tendency to forget he's not my only client. But it seemed to upset him so much a few weeks ago— after those Canadians left—when I suggested it was time for us to get back to town . . . and then when he got ill, and you had to go into hospital, I didn't have the heart to leave. He really seemed to need us, and of course he's a dear old friend. But now you're home again, Polly—"

"Of course. You've been very good. But you and Lally must go whenever you like."

"We thought tomorrow, actually."

"Just when it suits you, Ralph."

A blue Morris was approaching us at a sedate pace. At closer range, it proved to have the neat, pinstriped form of Dr. Bagshot at the wheel. I waved to him as we shot past and his face broke into a broad smile. Ralph glanced at me again, this time rather sourly.

"I seem to be the only one around to find that young man a complete twit. Did you know his first name is Crispin? I mean really."

"Faugh," I said, and laughed. Ralph did not join me. But I was thinking with satisfaction of the blue box striped in silver we had just stowed away carefully in the car's boot. Earlier in the day a tweed jacket and a skirt of soft blue wool had caught my eye in a smart shop-window in Oxford Street, and with the aid of Pa's credit card I had bought them (together with a white silk blouse) as a present for Nan. The outfit with its simple lines would suit her perfectly. It would also be the ideal thing to wear for a tea-time visit to the garden of a country doctor.

"Come on, Ralph, step on it. Let's get home and I'll play you a rousing game of cribbage."

"Ha ha," he said. Clearly he was not amused.

Immaculately clean and tidy, my little room under the eaves was waiting for me. A blue mug crammed with the flowers children pick — field poppies, clover, and Queen Anne's lace—sat on the bureau. Nan's work, of course. A small handful of mail had been put on the night-table. When I opened the casement window wide, it was to let in the clean rural air, not because I felt the old claustrophobic urge to escape. The garlanded wallpaper and low ceiling in fact now seemed quite cosy, and this must surely mean, I thought with satisfaction, that I was much healthier now both in mind and in body. If only this peaceful equilibrium could last, it would be all I'd ever ask from the Fates.

After unpacking and stowing away the contents of my small case, I sat down to look at my mail. There was a postcard from Walt, an old RADA classmate with whom I used to rehearse being in love. A letter from a dull old schoolmate in Toronto who for some reason wanted to keep in touch. And a plump envelope in my sister Olivia's large, round hand. The postmark was Stratford, Ontario, and I opened the letter eager to hear all about her roles — Nerissa in *The Merchant of Venice*, and Miss Neville in *She Stoops to Conquer*. But, to my disappointment, most of her six pages were devoted to a nuclear-protest group she had recently joined. She described her part in one of their demonstrations with a passion I found both naive and inexplicable — perhaps because it was so long since I had cared that much about anything. Did she really imagine she could have the slightest influence on world affairs? If so, surely she could only be heading for disenchantment. At least playing a part on the stage you could move people to tears or laughter. How much better, I thought, tossing the letter on the bed, to accept a sphere of influence as narrow as one house — a world horizon no wider than the orchard framed by my window. Let poor deluded Olivia carry her placards and try to influence governments. I would go and find Nan, try the new suit on her, and see if she could be coaxed to go with me into Canterbury tomorrow to have her hair done.

The result of these manoeuvres, unfortunately, was almost nil. With much reluctance Nan did allow herself to be taken to a hairdresser, who back-combed and sprayed her fine, fair hair into a stylish coiffure. But an hour after everyone at home had loudly praised it ("A masterpiece!" Pa cried, lifting both hands), she went away and brushed the whole creation back into its old untidy knot. As for the suit, which did look very well on her, she simply hung it away in a cupboard and continued to wear her shabby old cords and bulky home-made sweater on trips to the village.

She was in this outfit, a few days later, her hair windtorn, when we met Dr. Bagshot outside the butcher's shop. In one chapped hand she clutched a basket containing two limp rabbits wrapped in newspaper. The dogs, leashed to her other hand, had recently been through a mud-puddle.

"*Damn*," I thought, while simultaneously crying out, "Hullo! How nice to run into you."

"Yes. Yes, indeed," he said. He had flushed up quite brightly at the sight of us. "A delightful surprise. Do tell me how your father is getting on." He patted the dogs somewhat gingerly as people do when trying to conceal the fact they actually dislike dogs.

"Pa is very well, thanks to you. He's as spry as can be these days."

"Excellent. Quite. Splendid. Now, ladies, do let me offer you a cup of tea. My house is just down there—the cottage with the yew hedge. It would be an honour."

"What a good idea. We'd love a cup of tea. Come on, Nan." And before she could back off, I hustled her along the narrow pavement, where our basket and the dogs jostled Bagshot embarrassingly often. But he soon nipped ahead of us to open and hold a gate and then usher us with ceremony into the house. Gently he persuaded Nan to release the handle of her basket, at the same time pretending not to mind the muddy paw-prints of the dogs.

"There we are now; the basket will be quite safe there by the—do both of you come in, and welcome. Welcome to my little home. *Parva sed apta*, ladies, as you see—just a modest bachelor pad, as they say, but adequate for my needs. Now do sit down. Miss Paulina, you must have this comfortable chair, and here's a little footstool for your—so glad, by the way, to see you're walking more easily now—fractured femur, was it?—that's excellent—now tea—I'll just—the kettle's filled, it won't take a minute." He darted off as if afraid we might disappear in his absence, and indeed Nan was so stiffly perched on the edge of the chair nearest the door I thought she might actually make a bolt for freedom.

"Smooth your hair," I hissed at her. "And relax. He'll show us his herbs in a few minutes, if you're good."

Sooner than one would have thought possible our host

was back with cups jingling on a tray, though he kept plunging back to the kitchen regions for forgotten items like sugar, or plates to hold the cake. The cups, clearly his best, each had a little dust in the bottom, and the sugar-tongs were tarnished. Something about his flustered air suggested that, like me, he welcomed this encounter, but much deplored its timing.

"Now would you be mother, Miss Nan?" he proposed, setting the tray in front of her. This was a happy sugges-tion, because pouring tea and cutting cake gave her some-thing familiar to do while not requiring her to say anything. After popping up and down several more times to fetch extra hot water and provide bowls of milk for the dogs, he settled down more quietly and smiled at us both with satisfaction.

"Now this is extremely nice. Delightful to have you here. Do have another slice of this cake, Miss—Miss—or Polly, if I may call you that. It's just from the shop down the road —I'm not a fine cook like some people not a thousand miles away, but I daresay it's eatable—and by the way, do call me Crispin. Won't anyone have more tea? A little more cake? Well, if you're quite sure—not even a drop?—then maybe you'd like to glance around my little garden. Let me just help you with that jacket. Mind that little step there. Yes. Not too chilly out here for you, is it? You see, my property runs right back to that wall—the lot is narrow but quite deep. Borders here, a few shrubs, and down here at the end, my little herb garden."

Silently, but with a little smile of pleasure, Nan squatted down to inspect the low-growing pennyroyal and thyme. With chagrin I noted two bald patches on the seat of her disgraceful old cords. But Bagshot continued to chat away happily, as if he noticed nothing eccentric about her at all. It was easy to see she was genuinely interested in the herbs. He broke off a little sprig of rosemary and offered it to her. Smiling, but still without a word, she rolled it in her fingers to release its clean herbal scent. He moved me a little further along the cinder path.

"I dry this camomile for tea, and I may say there's no better medicine at any chemist's for a disordered tummy. Such a versatile plant as well. Did you know it brings down fevers, and can also be used as a rinse for ladies' hair?"

"And it has these nice little daisies into the bargain. What more can you ask when a thing is both useful and ornamental."

"Quite. Quite," he agreed eagerly. "Very well put. Useful and—oh, very good. You have a way with words, most certainly. No doubt inherited from your gifted father. Dear me, I was quite astonished to discover what a famous man my patient at Seven Oaks is. Quite an honour to treat him. And then later on to find him so—so very friendly. Quite charming."

"Well, I'm glad you've forgiven him for his awful rudeness at the start."

"Oh, that's quite forgotten, I assure you. Quite. I do so hope that now I can be considered a friend. Of the whole family, that is."

"Yes, of course you can." As unobtrusively as possible I edged us back to where Nan was kneeling to inspect a clump of basil. As I did this she raised her face and beckoned us closer. Without speaking, and touching a finger to her lips to silence us, she held the small, scented leaves apart to reveal a little earth-coloured toad sitting there. He looked at us quietly, his large eyes bright, his throat gently throbbing. He and my sister contemplated each other with a kind of friendly mutual curiosity, neither one dismayed by the other's strangeness. The yellow evening sky overhead shone in her calm eyes. With a little lift of triumph, I thought, 'I believe she's happy.'

Once the household had shrunk with the departure of

Ralph and Lally, Pa became notably restless. A prolonged spell of wet and windy weather added to his fretfulness. He spent a great deal of time on the phone exhorting various friends and connections in London to come down for the day or for a weekend, to cheer us up. Unfortunately, for one reason or another, no one seemed free to oblige him, and he had to content himself with booking up numbers of them ahead for a party to celebrate Nan's birthday at the end of September. Plans for this affair grew and elaborated themselves every time Pa turned his mind to them. By now they included a band and a marquee in the garden, and mere mention of the whole thing made poor Nan look miserable in advance.

"We'll maybe lay on a bit of a pageant," Pa suggested, gesturing largely over the remains of his breakfast kipper. "Harvest Festival. Nan as Ceres, eh? She'd look glorious all in gold. Or a masquerade ball is fun. Have you started a guest-list, Hamish? The boys and their families, of course; you'd better book half a dozen rooms at the County Hotel for the overflow. And be sure you ask Bagshot. Haven't seen him for—what is it—must be a couple of weeks now. Why haven't you girls asked him round for dinner?"

"Pa, I told you. He's gone to Australia for his sister's wedding." He'd already seen it, but I tossed him the little hand-written note that had been dropped into our mailbox days ago. Pa reread it with disapproval, though it was a pleasant little letter. In it he hoped to have the pleasure of our company — all three of us — to Sunday lunch, the week of his return. Meanwhile, he was ours faithfully, Crispin.

"Didn't know he had a sister," grumbled Pa. "Much less one in Australia."

"Tiresome of him," I agreed. Outside, sagging grey clouds like leaky canvas sacks dribbled copious rain over the discouraged-looking trees and the bepuddled lawn.

With an impatient flip Pa tossed Bagshot's note back to me. It fell short and Boris pounced on, worried, and killed it.

"Heigh," said Pa, throwing himself back in his chair. "This bloody weather does get me down. What time is it — only ten? Why have wet Sundays got twice as many hours in them? That's the trouble with country life—it so often closely resembles death. Come on, let's for God's sake go somewhere in the car. I've got it—we'll all go to church in the village. That will be a nice little surprise for the Vicar. Then we'll have lunch somewhere, maybe at that nice pub in Chilham. You're coming too, Nan" (as he spotted her drifting out of the room). "Put on that nice blue suit and fix yourself up. And you too, Polly. If you don't move around more, my girl, you'll take root like a weed. You'll drive us, Hamish, there's a good chap."

"All right. But I'll wait for you outside. Psalm-singing makes me want to heave. It's one thing for Polly to pray for salvation, but church is hardly your scene, is it, Monty? Why this sudden fit of respectability?"

Pa ignored this question, to which Hamish probably didn't expect or even want an answer. We were all so bored by the long rainy spell that even a mile's ride to the village made a welcome diversion. It was positively exciting to pass Oldfisk swathed in a black waterproof, splashing along on his aged bicycle, and to discover that the village newsagent's shop had a broken window.

Outside the church Hamish parked the car, firmly donned a pair of Walkman headphones, and opened a book. The rest of us climbed out and ducked under already streaming umbrellas for the wet walk through a churchyard full of leaning, ancient gravestones.

Through the open church door came the wheezing drone of a harmonium in inexpert hands. Only about a third of the boxed oak pews were occupied, and the congregation turned with one accord to stare as we walked in. The music—if it could be called that — broke off sharply in mid-note, then hurriedly recommenced. The organist was Mrs. Pryde's daughter, who occasionally helped us in the kitchen. She bobbed her hat at us before bending to the massacre of the opening hymn.

Pa knelt on a hassock embroidered with the text "Fear God" and plunged his face into his hands. The Vicar, a diminutive man in early middle age, with rosy cheeks and a pair of golf brogues visible under his cassock, herded three scuffling choirboys ahead of him up the aisle and we all rose to sing.

In the course of the sermon, during which the Vicar contrived to speak for twenty minutes without saying anything whatsoever, I gazed around at the medieval font carved with cherubs, and the chancel with its brass pots crammed too full of dahlias and chrysanthemums. The odour of sanctity was there in good measure, in this case consisting of candlewax, damp, brass polish, and a suspicion of mouse. Pa, head slightly on one side, was studying the Vicar's habit of rising on his toes at the end of each sentence. Slyly catching my eye, he wagged one of his own long feet up and down. I pulled out a handkerchief and coughed into it.

'What a pair of heathens we are,' I thought, a little shamefaced after this performance. 'This is more likely than most places are to be God's house, if He has a house. We have no business sitting here like ticket-holders in a third-rate theatre.' Only Nan retained some kind of personal dignity, sitting quietly beside Pa, eyes fixed on the folded hands in her lap. She only raised her head once, when a small bird, startled by a shriek from the organ, flew down from the overhead beams and flustered its indignant way out into the rain.

A few minutes later the Vicar was at the door to shake hands with his flock. When our turn came, he held out both hands and gave the three of us a charming glance of welcome from flax-blue, very round eyes. "I'm pleased indeed to see you here," he said. "I don't think I've had the—"

"Montague Weston's my name. These are my daughters. A very interesting sermon, sir."

"Not the celebrated writer? Ah, I'd heard you were settled among us — well, I'm honoured that you should approve of my little sermon."

"Yes, very nice indeed," said Pa, preparing to move on. But the Vicar had him by the elbow.

"I'm sure you agree with me that 'In the beginning was the Word' is the most fascinating of all possible texts. The implications of that phrase 'the Word' have been the subject of speculation for centuries, of course; but what I take it to mean is a summary of the divine intention, a sort of compendium of the whole creative purpose of the Almighty — unless, indeed, as Thomas Aquinas suggested, He invented the universe merely as a sort of game, and that is hardly—"

"No doubt," put in Pa. "Very interesting indeed."

"The Word, you might say, expresses not only—"

"Yes," said Pa. "Quite. You might like to come to dinner — with your wife, of course — and tell us more about—"

The Vicar blinked his blue eyes. "I am a widower, sir. But you are most kind, I'm sure. It's a rare treat to find someone interested in shades of verbal meaning. Now, the etymological root of—"

"My daughter will ring you one day soon," Pa said, raising his voice slightly. "I should also like to make a small contribution to your Restoration Fund. Perhaps you could call round at Seven Oaks — on the Preston Road — at your convenience, and discuss it with my secretary."

And with that he made his escape. We retreated demurely down the gravel path, resisting the temptation to break into a run. Once in the car, Pa threw himself into a corner of the back seat and burst into guffaws of laughter. Remembering the innocent kindness of the little Vicar's eyes deterred me for only a minute before I began to laugh too.

Hamish stared at us in astonishment. "You're both insane," he said. Nan, lost in who knew what thoughts of her own, paid no attention to any of us. It had stopped raining and the sun broke out in sudden radiance.

Oldfisk was burning leaves and garden refuse behind the kitchen-garden wall, and a blue column of smoke spiced the air as we sat on the terrace over tea. Nan and I, armed with crooked sticks and gauntlet gloves, had been blackberrying all afternoon, and my arms ached pleasantly. The sun, a hazy saffron ball, shed its faint autumnal warmth over us, and drew a rich smell from the nearby bed of dahlias. Our cups were empty, and nothing was left of Nan's walnut cake but a few crumbs.

In the chaise longue that Lally used to occupy, Crackers lolled, belly uppermost, a smile on his three-cornered mouth. Nan was knitting with a steady, rhythmic click of steel needles. Pa dozed lightly, his silver head lowered. Hamish's eyes too were closed. His brick-coloured face sealed up thus looked more impenetrable than ever.

A sneeze from one of the dogs abruptly woke Pa, and as if it had just occurred to him, he said, "By the way, we are all invited to a coffee morning at the Vicarage tomorrow."

"Thanks anyway," remarked Hamish.

"Well, that's all right," I said comfortably. "We don't actually have to go to it. All you need to do, Pa, is send along a donation to their Organ Fund or whatever it is. It's a good enough cause, God knows, remembering that organ."

"We are all going to the coffee morning," said Pa distinctly.

"But what on earth *for*?"

Pa stared at me. "You've become terribly anti-social, Pol, do you realize that? You never want to see anyone or go anywhere. It's unhealthy. It's downright abnormal."

I stared back at him. My heart had begun to thump. There rose in my gorge all the sour dregs of many past conflicts with Pa, culminating in the devastating row years ago about Bard. Before I could stop myself, I struck back.

"It's a lot healthier than going some place you don't really want to be, just to make an impression, or to play some kind of squire-of-the-manor role you fancy yourself in at the moment."

"That is an insolent remark, Paulina."

"So was yours to me. Being a parent doesn't entitle any-one to be insulting."

Hamish's eyes had snapped open. He now struggled to his feet. "I'm getting out of here," he said to the air between us. "It's no place for an innocent bystander." And he stumped off into the house. The click of Nan's needles had stopped. She looked frightened and bundled away her knitting as if to protect it.

"If you'd listened to your parent a few years ago, instead of flying up in the air like a wildcat," said Pa quietly, "you wouldn't be in the shape you're in now. It's maybe time you had the decency to admit that."

"I've never denied it, Pa."

But Pa went on, swept along by the momentum of his self-pity and what appeared to be genuine moral indigna-tion. "How you could do it I've never been able to under-stand. That poor Doris — what Bard put her through all those years — you *knew* all that, and yet — An irresponsible man without principle or conscience — "

"You were jealous."

"Of course I was. But that wasn't why I warned you. I was trying to protect you. The man was a disaster looking for somewhere to happen. What became of him — and you — was completely predictable."

"I know that."

"You actually admit it? That I was right?"

"Oh yes. You were perfectly right."

He threw himself back so angrily in his chair that its legs gritted on the flagstones.

"Well, it's damn late in the day to tell me that."

"No doubt."

"Then why wouldn't you listen to me at the time?"

"Because, Pa, it made no difference. What's more, I would do it all again, you know. All of it. And I know much more about his character now than you ever will. That night it happened, for instance, we were skipping out on a hotel bill. To punish them, Bard said, for the lounge furniture. Driving too fast, Bard a bit squiffed. That whole last year—well, why go on. Of course I'm neurotic. If I had the choice I'd do it all again. That's how it was with me. And still is."

There was a long silence. Then he said gently, "My poor child."

I waited. In a minute or two I could see and hear normally again. The spire of blue smoke still rose in the windless air. Crackers leaped up and over the wall in one fluid motion. A bee droned over the dahlias. Nan had disappeared. The sound of my own dry, strained voice telling the fearless truth had left behind a clean, medicinal silence. Pa's stertorous breathing quieted. After a moment I said, "You're right; I made my own catastrophe. And the great thing about that is it can't happen twice. Now all I want in the world is just to be neutral, do you see what I mean. I'll go with you to the coffee thing, as long as you understand it doesn't matter to me, one way or the other."

After a moment he said tenderly, "Don't come if you'd rather not."

"Well, maybe I am a bit of a hermit. And the Vicar is a nice little man."

"Also we must give him points. He hasn't come around cadging funds, even though I gave him the chance."

"Or expounding the Word."

He gave a snuffling little laugh. "You'll see, love. We'll get entertainment out of the damn thing, if nothing else."

"Dear Olivia,

"I meant to answer your letter ages ago, but country life is quite dangerously relaxing, while at the same time it can lure you into some surprising kinds of action. Life as a spectator sport with yours truly in a box seat — that's my thing nowadays; but would you believe I recently went to a fund-raising affair in aid of the village church-tower, and met all the local gentry for miles around? Or that the village doctor laid on a Sunday lunch for us the week after that? Most surprising of all, both these affairs were quite amusing. After the Vicar's coffee morning, Pa said to me, opening his eyes wide with something like amazement, 'And Pol, I was not bored.' What's more, neither was I. The V's Aunt, an old dear of eighty-two with dyed red hair and a faint smell of gin, took me hostage in the shrubbery and actually charmed me into agreeing to help her with a jumble sale for the church. I *know*. But Pa's taken a great fancy to both of them (they're bidden to dinner here soon), so I'll have to be careful or I'll wake up to find myself in charge of some horrible Brownie pack.

"One thing that specially interests Pa is the Vicar's library of rare books. He has a big collection of Elizabethan and Jacobean drama, masques, etc., and old books on witchcraft and folklore generally. Pa's borrowed some Ben Jonson and Samuel Daniel things with titles like *The Masque of Queens* and *The Hue and Cry after Cupid* for inspiration, because his latest scheme is to stage a masque to celebrate Nan's birthday at the end of the month.

"This is going to be quite a bash, and Pa will expect you to be here for it, no matter how wildly inconvenient this may be. The guest list is over fifty now, and growing all the time. He's actually mustering performers and musicians, mostly professional, from London to take part; Alan has been booked to cater, and so on. I've managed to convince him that Nan must be allowed just to be an observer of the whole extravaganza, so she's actually quite easy about it all—even, I think, just a bit excited.

"You may find this hard to believe, but Nan not only came with Pa and me to lunch at the doctor's house, but put on her best outfit for it with hardly any nagging. Of course, she didn't make any social chitchat once there, but you can't expect miracles, can you. The doc. is a rather nice little man, kind and very shy—lives by himself. He was greatly chuffed to have us, and had gone to no end of trouble—but, poor thing, everything went disastrously wrong for him in the kitchen. We were offered nettle beer on arrival, and he may have been into it himself before we got there, to calm his nerves. Anyhow, he miscalculated the roasting-time for the chicken, so when he plunged in the carving-knife, the bird bled horribly all over the platter. The poor man's face was a study in pure horror. But our Nan was marvellous. You'd have been amazed. While I tried not to have the giggles, and Pa covered up the crisis with a lot of jolly chat, Nan just slipped out to the kitchen with the wretched fowl and cut it up. Then she devilled the pieces with some mustard and cayenne, and brought the whole thing back a few minutes later all grilled and delicious. So the lunch was a success after all, and the little doctor was so grateful I thought he might actually kiss her.

"So you see life down here hasn't been at all dull. Of course I miss London and all that, and there are times when I think it isn't very good career strategy to be out of touch with agents and casting gossip and that scene generally, but in the spring when I've finished mending"

Here my ballpoint abruptly lifted from the page. I reread

the letter. It struck me as unutterably trivial and I crumpled it into the wastebasket. Some other day, when I felt more in the mood, I would write to Olivia.

"Miss, the doctor is here with some greens."

Mrs. Pryde, complete with cigarette, and wearing a pink gauze turban bound around her hair-curlers like a bandage, stood in the door of Hamish's study. I was trying to help him assign sleeping-space among the flock of guests expected down for the weekend of Nan's birthday. True, Seven Oaks had nine bedrooms, but four of these were occupied, and one was a sort of windowless cupboard under the back stairs, where no doubt some wretched knife-and-boot boy had had to lay his head in the good old days. It was all very well for Pa to book some of his grander guests into the County Hotel and airily mention sleeping-bags for the rest, but arrangements like that were not going to be adequate for, say, Lally and Ralph. The very thought of Lally confronted with a sleeping-bag was enough to make me throw down my pencil crossly.

"Greens?"

"Yes, miss. Plants, like. E's in the lounge. Askin to see you."

"All right, I'm coming. Where's my sister, Mrs. Pryde? Fetch her right away, will you."

"Went out, she did, just round eleven. Couldn't say where."

I sighed and got up, trying on my way across the hall to smooth my face into an amiable expression. To some extent I must have been successful, because Crispin bounded to his feet, all smiles, the moment I appeared. A long, rectangular box about the size of a coffin rested on a sheet of newspaper spread near his chair.

"Ah, Polly, good morning. You'll forgive my dropping in like this—but I was called to this part of the world earlier for a—for a confinement, and so I took the opportunity to

— just this little offering — a small, very small token of regard . . . your sister's great kindness in rescuing my little luncheon party the other day — I was so — it was so — I mean such a—"

"Oh, that was nothing. But how nice of you." I looked as politely as I could at the coffin, in which a variety of rather insignificant-looking herbs had been planted. Chives, rosemary, and lemon balm I could identify; others, drooping in a defeated sort of way, I could not. "Nan will be so pleased. Unfortunately at the moment she isn't in, but as soon as she—"

"Quite. Yes. I thought, you see, it would make a useful window-box for the kitchen. So handy to be able to cut, say, a few chives when she's cooking for the family, without going outdoors. An inspired chef, your sister, truly."

"Yes, I think she is. Well, it's a lovely gift. I know she'll want to thank you herself, but—"

"Oh, not at all. No thanks necessary. Not at all." Here, however, instead of going, he sat down again with a sort of enthusiastic bounce, and out of courtesy I had to sit down too.

"Perhaps." he began, lowering his voice confidentially, "you'll allow me just to say a word about your sister."

I glanced toward the open door. "Oh, by all means."

"She is indeed a charming person."

"Yes," I said warmly. "Not everyone's got the discrimination to see that. In fact the general tendency is to undervalue her. I'm glad you don't."

I wondered whether to get up and close the door by way of encouragement, but decided against it. For one thing, Nan herself might drift in at any time. Of course Mrs. Pryde had a way of lurking, motionless, duster in hand, in odd corners of the hall, but after all, what was there here to hide?

"Quite. If I may say so, Polly, I notice a—a distinct, shall we say improvement in—a slight increase of—a less withdrawn . . . that is, since I've known you both, she has, so to speak, developed quite distinctly, and it's obvious you have been the cause of—in other words, you're to be congratulated on—"

"Oh no, I've had little or nothing to do with it, truly. But you're right this far—she has come out of her shell just a bit lately. In fact, it's been your tact and patience as much as anything . . . anyhow, I've been very pleased to see it."

"But the credit is most certainly due to you. That's quite clear. Yes. Most encouraging. A very fine person, Nan. And she is lucky in having so devoted, and—if I may say it— such an excellent sister as yourself. Quite."

His colour had come up brightly, but after this, though he cleared his throat elaborately, he said nothing more. A gaping hole of silence widened between us, and I couldn't think how to fill it. He seemed for some reason quite paralysed with shyness or embarrassment. Finally I said lamely, "You're very kind. It's nice to know you appreciate her."

"Appreciate—oh yes. Quite." Once more he dried up, as if something were stuck in his throat.

"She'll be sorry to have missed your call."

"Yes. Yes."

"Well, thanks again, Crispin, for the—"

"Not at all. My pleasure."

Again a ponderous silence fell. Somewhere in the house a door banged, but I knew it did not announce Nan's arrival. She never banged doors. One of the dogs whined to get in, or out. Hamish's old typewriter rattled dimly in his office. A delivery-boy whistled in the driveway. I was beginning to feel slightly desperate when at last he muttered, just audibly, "I'll say no more just at present."

'Why the devil not?' I longed to ask. Instead I arranged the pleats in my skirt and hoped that silence would for once be golden. What a nice little man he was, after all. And he really seemed sincerely to care about Nan. But it was plain that, for the moment at least, he'd lost his nerve. The clock in the hall ticked away steadily. His eyes were fixed intently on his own toe-caps. It seemed quite possible we might sit there forever in this impasse, so at last I got up and went over to the long box at his feet.

"This is so nice of you—a perfect present for her. Could we take it out to the kitchen now, do you think? I can give you a hand, and between us we'll manage it nicely, I'm sure. It will be a pleasant surprise for Nan to find it there."

For a second he looked distractedly at the box as if he had forgotten what it was. Then he scrambled up, looking for some reason rather harassed. With difficulty, one at each end of the heavy container, we lugged it through the hall and the butler's pantry into the kitchen, where Mrs. Pryde, the char, and the mouse in the print apron all eyed it without enthusiasm. We cleared the broadest windowsill of its china cats, betting-slips, copies of the *Daily Mirror*, chipped tea-mugs, and a battery radio belting out "Top of the Pops". This manoeuvre was not popular either. No one helped. The awkward box was finally heaved and shoved into position by the two of us alone. In the process poor Crispin painfully scraped the knuckles of one hand. But he stopped only long enough to run a little cold water over the graze before making a hurried exit, his back stiff and smile forced.

It was a relief to hear his Morris grind off down the drive, though why it should have been I couldn't quite say. Nothing was wrong, after all. He was just shy. It was clear, in fact, that he was on the point of some kind of declaration. Everything actually looked quite promising. It was going to be all right, I assured myself. Just the same, when I mentioned this visit to Pa later that day, I didn't go into any of the details.

" 'The fat of young children,' " quoted the Vicar, deftly peeling a pear with the silver blade of his fruit-knife.

"'They put hereunto *eleoselinum, aconitum, frondes populeus,* and soot. They stamp all these together, and then they rub all parts of their bodies exceedingly, till they look red and be very hot, so as the pores may be opened, and their flesh soluble and loose. By this means in a moonlight night they seem to be carried in the air, to feasting, singing, dancing, kissing, culling, and other acts of venery.'"

Raising his face from the open book by his plate, he looked round the table at us with satisfaction and popped a slice of pear into his mouth.

"Fascinating," said Pa.

"That kind of thing never went on in Antigonish, even in the dark ages," said Hamish. "Deplorable, I call it."

"But obviously the most *immense* fun," remarked Hermione, the Vicar's aunt. She sat on Pa's right, wearing a black velvet evening gown rubbed bald with age on the bosom and the seat. A number of chains and ropes of pearls were slung about her in a haphazard fashion. On one arm she carried a beaded bag with a silver-mounted rabbit's-foot clasp.

"And Scot's significant word here, you observe, is 'seem'," the Vicar went on, opening his blue eyes at us in admonishment. "*The Discoverie of Witchcraft* is surprisingly modern in its perceptions. Of course in the sixteenth century the sedative properties of aconite were well known. But it's remarkable he should have been so clearly aware of the contagion of hysteria in so-called witches. He goes on to say about these orgies, 'The force of their imagination is so vehement that almost all that part of the brain, wherein the memory consisteth, is full of such conceits. And whereas they are naturally prone to believe anything, so do they receive such impressions into their minds, as even their spirits are altered thereby.' Oh yes, Scot's a much sharper commentator on this subject than even a well-educated man of letters like James I."

"Is he the one who thought witches could cross the sea in a sieve?" I asked.

"He is. They told him they could, so he believed it. And we're told it put him in 'a wonderful admiration' — which is to say he was horrified. But the point is, the witches believed in their powers. Therefore, in a sense, they had those powers."

"What a pity witchcraft as it were went out of style after Salem," said Pa, sliding the decanter of port down the table.

"Oh, it's still practised here and there in these islands, you know. White *and* black magic. In fact, in a more general sense, it's spread rather than vanished. You'll find it today in the rhetoric of demagogues. In revivalist meetings. Also in the lyrics of hard rock. Everywhere, in fact, where power is invoked. Any man — or, of course, woman — who uses, or rather, abuses, power over a crowd or just another individual is a sort of witch. Evil. Mr. Grant is quite right." Here he sent Hamish a clerical look of approval.

"But what interests me," put in Pa, "is the part language plays in all this. Chants, charms, incantations — verbal spells. It goes right back, obviously, to primitive ritual. The exorcist still functions today, doesn't he, Richard? And he's not just splashing the holy water about, but using words."

"Oh yes, my dear fellow. Few people know better than you do that words are a great vehicle of power."

"*The* greatest, I'd say," added Hermione, helping herself generously to port. "Next, of course, to sex."

"Not for nothing has the word 'charm' got two meanings," agreed the Vicar.

More to head off an etymological lecture than because I really believed it, I said (thinking of Nan and her quietness), "But there are so many things words can never do. They're no good at all for describing the joys of music, for instance. Or, come to that, sex. In fact, silence may be a lot more powerful than words, don't you think, no matter how magic the words may be."

"Never," asserted Pa.

"Doubtful," the Vicar said.

"How can anybody be sure of that?" Hamish demanded.

At this point the tray of coffee things came in, with Nan doing her best to appear invisible behind it. The dinner had extended itself to a late hour, and Mrs. Pryde, a strong believer in her rights, had evidently gone home. Nan looked flushed and put about. She made no attempt to reply when Richard and his aunt murmured polite greetings, but, keeping her back to us, pushed things about on the buffet to make room for the big tray. Pa, however, perhaps encouraged by the port, turned to her and, rolling his tongue richly over the words, said

"'What thou seest (Nan dear) when thou dost wake
Do it for thy true love take.
Love and languish for his sake,
Be it ounce or cat or bear—'"

Nan gave him one vivid glance of annoyance, set down her tray, and strode out of the room. Pa, his mouth still open, was left abandoned in mid-spell. The rest of us burst out laughing.

As preparations for the birthday celebration mounted, so, unfortunately, did Nan's tendency to retreat, withdraw, and even disappear from view altogether. I began to worry that all her recent progress might be undone by the affair, in spite of all the effort and good intentions Pa and I had invested in it. The afternoon before the party itself, while Pa was in the garden supervising the erection of a gaily striped marquee, Nan was supposed to have a final fitting of the gold silk dress that had been made for her as a birthday present. Instead she was nowhere to be found, and the dressmaker had to go away, disgruntled, leaving the gown still shrouded in its white muslin bag. Tea-time came and went. Nan remained absent. Pa was too busy directing the placement of folding chairs and strips of carpet to pay attention to anything else, and this irritated me even further.

Leaving my cup half full, I heaved myself out of my chair and set out once more to look for her. As I left the garden Pa was embarking on orders to two men on ladders preparing to string fairy lights in the trees. "Don't wear yourself out," I told him. He ignored me.

Crackers, who was enjoying a doze on top of the sunny wall, opened one lazy green eye as I limped into the kitchen-garden, where Nan could sometimes be found in wordless communion with Fisk over the young carrots or the ripe raspberries. No one was there now, though, except a few thieving birds who flew off at my approach. Then I caught sight of something white at the far end of the orchard, and somewhat grimly set out toward it. Through the archway I went, and across the deep grass. In the distance a ladder was propped against one of the trees, with Nan just visible on top of it, picking apples into a basket. The tangled boughs, heavy with foliage and fruit, all but hid her, except for the betraying piece of white shirt-tail that had pulled out of her trousers.

"Nan, you really are tiresome. Where were you when the dressmaker came? That lovely dress cost a fortune, you know. Don't you care whether it fits or not?"

The leaves overhead rustled. Nan's face looked down at me. She said nothing, but the answer was so clearly "no" that I gave a great sigh of exasperation. Apparently quite unperturbed, she went on picking the fruit.

The sun warmed my back as I stood there with the lush long grass enveloping me to the knees. Ripe apples, fallen all around the tree, had split and softened on the ground. They sent up a heady, wine-like fragrance, and wasps hovered and droned around them in the warm grass as if drunk.

Unwillingly I felt my irritation easing away. The low orange globe of the sun seemed not so much to irradiate as to suck light out of everything it touched, even the rough tree-bark and the tangle of dark boughs where Nan was working. After a moment I took up a basket and began to pluck fruit into it from the lowest branches that leaned into the yellowing grass. Even the firm red cheeks of the apples felt warm.

"Pa is going to enormous trouble over this party, you know," I grumbled. But I no longer really wanted to scold her. "You'll simply have to play up a bit, or he'll be terribly hurt."

There was no reply. One of the dogs galumphed through the archway and humped his way toward us, black ears, back, and tail surfacing at intervals as he waded through the long grass.

"Ralph and Lally will be here early. So will Alan and Co. I've put their little girls in that tiny room under the stairs — it's so unhygienic and awful they'll be thrilled. It's a mercy, really, that Olivia can't make it, because there's not an inch of room for her. You won't mind my bunking in with you, just for two nights, I hope. Mrs. Pryde swears the folding cot won't let me down, and I hope to hell she's right. Crispin's lent us a couple of tents, did you know, so Bill's boys can camp out here, or in the garden. Nice of him, I thought. He's been very helpful all round, don't you think?"

I didn't really expect any answer to this and was rather surprised when she said, "Yes." Then I remembered her wordless but evident delight when she first saw his gift of the window-box. "He's a very nice chap," I added. "I like him a lot."

A moment later she began to extricate herself from the top of the tree, and back clumsily down the ladder, careful to hold the full basket free of entanglement. Boris, now at the foot of the trunk, waited for her, his black muzzle raised in a grin of welcome that exposed his white teeth and long pink tongue. She sat down on one of the ladder's lower rungs and dropped the basket into the soft grass. The dog laid his glossy head on her knees and she began dreamily to pick burrs out of his neck and ears. In that rich light there was something very lovely about her bent head with its fair hair, her round arms and full breast. She was almost certainly a virgin, yet there was a serene ripeness in her soft flesh covered with what looked like a peach's golden down.

"Tell me something, Nan," I said, unable to check my sudden curiosity. "Do you ever think of men—I mean, as lovers?"

She glanced at me sidelong and shrugged.

"But you must sometimes think about sex."

"No. Why?" she said.

"*Why*? Because everybody does, that's why. It's basic. Everybody has those feelings, so naturally they think about them. It is the ultimate pleasure, after all, you know. Nothing else comes near it. Haven't you ever—"

She lifted her head then and met my eyes so directly that I couldn't go on. My curiosity embarrassed not her, but myself. What applied to all those I so glibly called "everybody" might well have no relevance to her. Indeed, it didn't even apply to me any more. Quite possibly Nan had no need at all to think about such things as sex. And perhaps she was right: they were not meant to be thought about. In any case, it was clear she needed no instruction or advice—not from me, of all people. I was sorry I'd ever opened the subject, and promised myself not to do it again.

The sun hung low now, a smouldering, tawny ball sinking as if of its own weight to burn low on the horizon. Without further words we collected the baskets of fruit and, leaving the ladder for Fisk to retrieve later, made our way back to the house. Under the tall garden trees, Pa and the workmen were now testing the strings of fairy lights. In the rich glow of the sunset the little globes shone out feebly. To me they looked insignificant, even ridiculous. Nan did not appear to notice them at all, though she raised a hand to greet Pa.

"Well done! Splendid!" Pa called to the men.

But next night at twilight as the trees darkened into a feathery mass against the sky, I had to admit the little strings of light did add a certain charm to the garden. Our guests, too, gave a festive air by standing about on the terrace and the trim lawns looking decorative in their long dresses and white ties. A pleasant buzz of talk and laughter rose as they waited for the entertainment to begin. From the dining-room's open French doors there floated faint, reminiscent scents of the buffet meal they had just eaten. Devastated casseroles and the remains of a vast trifle in a crystal bowl had not yet been removed from the lace table-cloth. The scrape and flutter of stringed instruments could be heard in the distance. Behind the yew hedge the procession of actors was forming. Alan's five-year-old daughter Jill, excited as a flea, dragged heavily on my hand as she hopped from foot to foot in new party shoes.

"Don't pull Polly about like that," Ralph said from behind me. "You're almost knocking her over." He laid a steadying hand on my bare shoulder, adding in a lower voice, "You look quite ravishing in that dress, love." It was a pretty dress of dark-green watered silk, but my cane made management of its long, full skirt rather awkward. I was a little tired, too, after a couple of hours on my feet making conversation with people and seeing they had plenty to eat and drink. I envied Nan, who was already enthroned in a seat of honour banked with tubs of flowers in the marquee.

"Here they are!" piped Jill, bearing down again powerfully on my hand. And the procession came into view, with Pa leading the file. He walked down the garden at a steady pace while the rest of us fell back to make way for him. His evening clothes were hidden by a long black opera cloak lined with satin. In one hand he carried a gold-painted wand upright like a staff of office. I wondered as I often had before how it was that a man of only average height could contrive to look so tall. Flaming torches carried by the actors following behind cast a dramatic light over his silver hair and on their own glittering, multicoloured tunics, capes, caps, and gowns. They were all masked, and their costumes winked with spangles, sequins, gold thread, and stage jewels. The effect, even at close quarters, was quite dazzling. One of the actors raised his silk mask slightly as he passed, to wink a bright eye at me, and I recognized my old friend and pseudo-lover Walt Baker, from RADA days. Laughter broke through the spectators as the next part of the procession wound into view. This consisted of capering and mowing dancers wearing grotesque papier-mâché heads of tigers, bears, apes, and goats. Some of their antics prompted Jill to say disapprovingly, "They're quite rude, aren't they?" But when a dancing lion tickled her neck with the bush of his plush tail, she backed against me squealing with delight. Last of all came the players of a string quartet, filling the cool evening dusk with the formalized gaiety of baroque music.

We all closed in behind the musicians and poured into the marquee, where rows of folding chairs had been set up. One end of the tent had been fitted with a raised platform and stage lighting. Pa, after hesitating over earlier works like "Lady of the May" and "The Twelve Goddesses", had finally chosen Milton's *Comus*, with some of its windier sermonizing abbreviated. He now took his place and with a dramatic flourish reversed his cloak to expose a black lining sewn all over with gold stars. This, with a crystal goblet and the gold wand, transformed him into the enchanter Comus — but a much more benign kind of wizard than Milton surely intended. His face, his whole posture, radiated a sort of paternal and generous joy. He was the host alluring us all to sensual pleasures of only the most harmless sort. His voice was full of tenderness as he stepped forward, eyes on Nan, to speak a brief prologue. It was clear that whatever the masque held in store for Comus, Pa himself was going to triumph by sheer force of personality.

"Ladies and gentlemen," he said. "This lovely masque was first performed exactly three hundred and fifty years ago tonight. We offer it now in honour of my daughter, Anne Isabel Weston, as a tribute on her birthday."

He then waved his wand, the lights went down, and the performance began with a song from the Attendant Spirit, none other than my old friend Walt decked out in filmy green wings appropriate to the woodland setting. Pa had wisely chosen to avoid using any elaborate backdrops or stage effects. A simple arrangement of dark-green drapery suggested the nocturnal forest glade where the chaste Lady wanders lost, and is bewitched. A trapdoor in the platform provided entry for the bearers of the cardboard feast which was to tempt her into sensuality, and later for the singer in shimmering blue who represented Sabrina, the river-goddess rising from the water to break Comus's spell.

The whole performance was so deft and well-paced that we were all quite entranced by it. Even Nan, who earlier in the evening had been wretchedly ill at ease, now sat watching intently, her face a little flushed with pleasure. She leaned forward slightly in the draped gold dress in which she no longer looked at all awkward. Her eyes never left Pa. The masque ended after the rout of Comus with a whirl of stomping country-dances and a final song from Walt, but she continued to gaze at Pa where he stood to one side, his magician's cloak folded over his arm. To loud applause and a lively musical postlude, he then led Nan ceremonially down the aisle and out into the garden, where the rest of us spilled out after them. It was quite dark now, but the garden was gay with coloured Chinese lanterns in the shrubbery, and blazing torches planted at the edges of the flower-beds. Caterers' men circulated with trays of champagne, and soon everyone was sipping and chattering as they flocked around the players to congratulate them.

A huge harvest moon slowly rode up as if on cue and cleared the dark tree-tops. It looked close enough to touch, and soft as a blood orange, but the multitude of thick-strewn stars in remoter space shone hard, bright, and white, like chips of mica. A few bats flickered in and out of the trees, bewildered by the artificial lights. After the marquee warmed by so many bodies, the night air fell damp and chill on my bare neck and shoulders. I was thinking of making my way inside for a wrap when Walt appeared with a champagne flute in each hand. He embraced me, managing to combine grace with enthusiasm, and all without spilling a drop. He had been the undoubted star of our class, but his charm was such that we all liked him anyway.

"Polly, me old duck. What fun to see you. It's been ages."

"Hasn't it. A very good performance, Walt."

"It was superb," he agreed cheerfully. "And your papa did a really nice job, for an amateur. He projects well. But you notice he has that wide space between the eyes and the long upper lip actors have. Hardly fair, is it, sir, to have two sets of talents?" he said as Pa moved slowly past us through the crowd. My father rewarded him with a courtly inclination of the head, and then vanished. Walt then waved over my shoulder to attract the attention of a passing tiger, and darted off toward him saying, "See you later, ducky— I must just have a word with Kevin. He owes me a fiver."

The champagne tickled the roof of my mouth but did nothing to warm me. I began to move toward the house, encumbered by the crowd and by my voluminous skirts. Hamish detained me a moment to mutter that Bill's three boys were playing Star Wars in the orchard with Fisk's weed-killer spray, and he was on his way there to murder them. He had just disappeared on this mission when

Crispin stepped out of the crowd and stood in my path. Like Walt he had a glass of champagne in each hand, but the wine had slopped out and now ran in a bright dribble from each of his wrists. None the less he offered me the fuller glass and an anxious smile.

"I'm afraid it's a little—such a crush—let me give you a handkerchief just in case — to protect your beautiful gown. Quite. Most becoming. Yes, indeed. And what a dazzling entertainment your father has given us—truly magnificent. A memorable night. And the garden is looking—"

"Yes, it's a bit of luck the fine weather's held. Have you seen Nan? She was over there by the trellis a minute ago. Let's go and find her, shall we?"

"Ah, now, Polly, I saw you shiver just now. You are not warm enough, you must not stay out here and catch a chill. Let me take you inside. As a medical man as well as—yes, I must insist—we can't have you catching cold, now. Certainly not."

And he tossed down his champagne, returning the glass with a masterful air to a passing waiter before putting a hand under my elbow to steer me into the house.

The dining-room was thick with people sampling pastries, meringues, and sherbet from the buffet. Hermione, in an extraordinary tam of squashed blue velvet that looked like one of Rembrandt's hats, waved an éclair at me gaily. Mrs. Pryde in a lawn apron and cap presided with an air of hauteur over a huge coffee-urn. Lally, looking exquisite in rose chiffon, was pretending to listen to one of the Vicar's discourses on medieval mummings and disguisings. Without bothering to ask permission, Crispin plucked somebody's abandoned mohair stole off the back of a chair and put it around my shoulders. He then intercepted a waiter on his way outside and took two more glasses off his tray.

"Now," he said to me, "shall we just—if you'll follow me

—we'll find a quieter corner and—warmer now, are you? Excellent. Quite. Ah, here we are."

With this he ushered me into the sitting-room, which had been lighted up and decorated with flowers but for some reason, as one room at a party often does, remained completely deserted. He closed the double doors behind us triumphantly.

"That's better, isn't it. Yes. Now let me suggest—this little table here for your glass— are you sure you're warmer now? Quite comfortable? This is most excellent champagne, I must say. Not that I'm any connoisseur, of course. But it seems to me very good indeed. Quite delicious, in fact."

'Yes,' I thought, glancing at him sharply. His cheeks were heavily flushed and his forehead shone as if someone had lacquered it.

"I'm so very happy to have this opportunity—if I may call it that—just for a quiet moment with you," he went on, dragging a footstool up inconveniently close to my chair. Once he was seated there, the top of his slicked-down hair was level with my collarbone and close enough for me to catch the cloying smell of the pomade he used. One of his knees firmly pressed my leg, but he made no apology for this; in fact he did not seem to notice it. Unquestionably he'd had a drop too much of the champagne. I tried unobtrusively to shift my leg away from his knee.

"Polly, I don't think you realize how—how your whole family has—how my life has changed since you came here —the difference, I mean . . . You see, to a retiring sort of chap like me, an occasion like tonight, for instance, has simply been—well, the fact is, I can't wait any longer to tell you how much you mean to me."

I was sure his "you" was plural, not singular, but just the same a twinge of alarm darted through my mind. It escalated when he took my hand and pressed it gently, like the filling of a sandwich, between both of his warm, moist palms.

"Er—Crispin, I'm sure you know we all think the world of you—"

"I'm delighted to hear it. Delighted. And so, my dear Polly, I have your permission to speak? To offer, as it were, my heart and hand?"

"Speak about Nan, you mean. Of course you can."

"About Nan!" There was consternation in his voice, but it was nothing to my now total chagrin.

"I'm afraid there's been some awful misunderstanding," I said, trying to struggle to my feet. But he was sitting so close to me as to make this impossible, and furthermore one leg of his stool was pinning down my skirt. His hands, however, now cold and damp, were already releasing mine.

"What an unfortunate muddle," I went on, trying to keep my voice from cracking into ridiculous nervous laughter. "You see I—we thought—I assumed it was Nan you—"

"Oh no no no. It's been you all along. Surely you knew —how could anyone suppose—"

"Oh dear. Because you see, I'm not at all—I like you so much, Crispin, but I'm simply not—"

"Quite. Of course. I see."

He jumped stiffly to his feet and with one distraught hand smoothed his impeccably smooth hair. There was a painful silence. I tried again to get up, but the stool was still enveloped in my skirts, and its weight made me totter clumsily to one knee. At this juncture the sitting-room door opened and the Vicar's head popped in. We both turned our faces to him in heartfelt relief.

"The actors are forming up now to process out—will you come out and see them off?" His blue eyes beamed at us kindly. "You won't want to miss it, I'm sure."

"Oh no—certainly not."

"Quite."

"Come along, then," he said, and bustled off. We hastened after him, careful to avoid each other's eyes. I had only time to think miserably, 'How in the devil's name am I ever going to tell Pa about this?' before we were out again in the night air. Careful to avoid even the slightest body contact, we joined the guests who had gathered to watch the ceremonial exit of the actors.

"How nice the costumes look, don't they," I said, in order to say something. He nodded, his eyes firmly fixed ahead. There was a cross, sulky droop to his mouth that might have been funny in different circumstances, but was not at all funny now.

This time the orchestra led the parade, and the clownish dancers in their grotesque animal heads brought up the rear. The tiger pranced inventively, wagging his striped and painted countenance up and down. Suddenly he pounced on Nan, who was standing near us. She gave a scream of real terror and Jill, now thoroughly overtired, threw back her head, exposed the broad gap in her milk teeth, and began to howl in sympathy.

It was the little Vicar who coped best with this situation. Without a word he simply put both arms around Nan and held her in a firm embrace, soothing her bodily as one would a frightened horse or dog. Though he barely came to her shoulder, he emanated a sort of calm authority mingled with gentleness, and she grew quiet at once, even breaking into a faint smile before he released her. The transformation made me think for some reason about his mention of exorcism weeks ago. Meanwhile Pa had swung Jill up to his shoulder and Ralph plugged her wailing mouth with a piece of cake. The procession retreated serenely, to fading music and a scatter of applause.

Most of the guests then followed Pa to thank the players and see them into their minibus, while those who were left drifted around finishing off the champagne, and Crispin seized the opportunity to disappear. The garden had a jaded look now. Many of the torches had guttered out. Crumpled paper napkins, corks, and cigarette-ends littered the grass. I found a full glass of wine among the empties on a terrace table, and tossed it down in one gulp. When I lowered the glass it was to find Walt beside me.

"Just time to kiss you good night, my sweet," he said. "What a pity we had no time for a nice gossip. Where did you disappear to? Be sure to let me know when you're next up in town. God, you really are dishy, you know." And with this he took me in his arms and began half playfully to kiss my cheeks and neck. By now, however, I was so tired that without his support I felt I might well melt helplessly to the ground, or even sink right into it and disappear. As for his kisses, I was as limp and indifferent to them as Pa's life-size doll would have been. When somewhere on the stone flags of the terrace a glass broke, and I glimpsed Hamish's tight-lipped face, these details had the inconsequence of a dream. So did Ralph and Lally strolling past, her chiffon skirt drifting against his long black leg, and Boris slinking off as he gulped down a clandestine pastry. I hardly noticed Walt running lightly away to board the bus, blowing me a kiss as he disappeared.

"So there we are," said Pa, appearing beside me on the terrace. With satisfaction he tucked both hands under the tails of his dress-coat and took a deep breath of the night air. "A completely successful evening, wouldn't you say, Pol? Couldn't have been better, if I say so myself."

"Well, yes. In its fashion." But I was careful not to add this out loud.

With the aid of a little ingenuity I was able to avoid any but brief contact with Pa for several days after the party. On Sunday, however, he drafted me into attending the Harvest Festival service with him. Hamish had gone off on holiday to Scotland, and Nan, busy at her loom, shook her head at the mention of church. So the two of us drove off alone to the village and sat through the Vicar's discourse, its fruitful text taken from one of Donne's sermons—"How different are the wayes of God, from the ways of Man!" We were halfway through the lych-gate and making for the car to drive home when to my dismay we came face to face with Crispin Bagshot taking a short-cut through the grave-yard. He carried his professional bag, but he had been saun-tering along in a leisurely way until the moment when he caught sight of us. He then began to step out briskly with an air of stern preoccupation.

"Ah, my dear fellow, how are you?" cried Pa, stopping short on the path.

"Well, thank you," he said, with a curt nod. He paused, but was obviously anxious to escape. He kept his head turned aside to avoid any eye contact with me.

"Off to some bed of pain, are you?" Pa asked. "If not, do come home with us for lunch. We're very dull these days, after all our festivities."

"Thank you, no. Good of you, but—extremely busy."

"Dinner tomorrow, then, perhaps," pressed Pa, sliding a glance at me.

"So sorry. Quite impossible, I'm afraid. You'll excuse me now—I must be off—" And without further ceremony he hurried on his way.

Pa looked quizzical, but unlocked the car and opened the door on my side without further comment. I waited unhap-pily. As soon as he had negotiated the turn onto the main road for home, he said, "All right, Polly, what was all that about?"

I mumbled something only half audible.

"What's that you say? Do speak up. No more nods and becks and wrethèd smiles—what ails the man? Have you had some sort of tiff with him?"

"Yes, well—yes. That's about it."

Pa gave me a suspicious stare. "Come on, then. Let's have it. What happened?"

I took a deep breath. "Well, the fact is—it's quite ridiculous, of course, but he seemed to think—he got it all wrong somehow, or we did, or something, and so he—"

"Paulina, will you please make yourself coherent."

"Well, if you must know, the night of the masque he proposed to me."

"*What!*"

"It was the champagne, that's all, or at least that's what I hoped, but—well, today he didn't actually want to speak to us at all, did he? It's obvious he's offended."

"What a cock-up," groaned Pa. "Oh Pol, how could you possibly get things so wrong?"

"I'm not the only one," I said, nettled.

His reply to that was, "Pshaw. Women are supposed to know how to cope in such matters."

"Well, he'll get over it, I daresay."

"He's not the type to get over a thing like that. Not easily, anyhow."

"Maybe not."

"I wouldn't have had this happen for the world."

"Neither would I, Pa."

"*Faugh.*"

"Anyhow, there it is."

"What a shame. Because, quite apart from—from anything else, I quite liked him. He's a nice little chap."

"I'm not so sure about that. He didn't behave at all well today, did he? It could be that Nan's had a lucky escape."

"But how the devil did it happen? How could you let the situation get to such a point? I mean, you're not an inexperienced schoolgirl."

"Pa, I told you he was a bit flown with wine. He just *pounced*. And by the time he understood his mistake, his vanity had got injured. That's why today he—The fact is, he obviously fancies himself, like so many people who come on all timid and modest."

Once more Pa glanced at me. "Possibly."

"Anyhow, the whole thing was very embarrassing."

"No doubt. Did he fall to his knees?"

"No, I was the one who did that."

"I wish I'd been there."

"So do I." An unwilling little snort of amusement escaped me.

"Swept off your feet, were you?"

"After a fashion."

Suddenly, as if his imagination had plucked the whole absurd scene wholesale out of my memory, Pa threw back his head and began to laugh. He wheezed. His face grew pink. He patted one hand on the steering-wheel. A tear rolled down the cheek nearest me. But for the life of me I couldn't laugh with him, because I was thinking about Nan. How could this ever possibly be explained to her? It never could be, of course, and there was nothing really funny about the implications of that.

A couple of weeks later I stood at the Vicarage door waiting for someone to answer the bell. It was a cold day with an easterly half-gale piling heavy cloud into tumultuous masses and tearing leaves both yellow and green off the trees with a sort of reckless, random destructiveness. The evergreens shrouding the Victorian-Gothic windows twisted and writhed, their boughs creaking as if in pain. I turned up my coat collar before ringing again. At last, just as I was about to turn away, the door opened. Richard had the slightly crumpled and foggy appearance of a man wakened from a nap, but he smiled at me kindly.

"Why hello, Polly. What a nice surprise. Do come in."

"Thank you."

"Let me have your coat. Shocking weather, isn't it. Walked all this way, have you? Then you'll want a spot of tea. Hermione's making tomato chutney, but she'll be brewing up any time now."

"Richard, please don't bother—this isn't really a social

call. I'd just like to talk to you. It's—I have a problem—
and Pa's away. He's up at Cambridge giving the Fielding
Lectures, and he won't be back for another week. Even
Hamish is off on holiday, so—"

"I see. Come along to my study. You'll forgive its disorder, but I find it impossible to think in neat surroundings.
Luckily Hermione is like-minded, so we live in happy
squalor."

He ushered me along a hallway decorated several generations ago in chocolate-coloured woodwork and flock wallpaper patterned in yellow Grecian urns. In his study the
air was heavy with the sweetish, dry smell of old books.
He cleared several large tomes, together with an old
sweater and a black kitten, off a cracked leather armchair
for my use. Then he took his place in a swivel chair behind
the desk and peered at me inquiringly over its heaps of
books and papers. I took a deep breath.

"It's about Nan."

"Yes? She's not ill, I hope."

"Well, not—not exactly ill. But yesterday I found her
cutting up a scarf, one she'd woven for . . . for somebody
as a gift. Cut it all up with shears, and put the bits into an
envelope and addressed it . . . all pretty disturbing. I took
it away from her, of course. But since then . . . it's hard to
explain. She just sits at her loom and never moves. Or at
the window looking out at nothing. The dog sits there too,
with his face on her knee. They just sit there, the two of
them, by the hour—" Here my voice began to waver, and
I stopped.

After a pause he asked mildly, "What's upset her, then?"

"Well, she must have run into him, in the village, probably—a few days ago, it must have been—not that she'll
tell me anything about it—and he maybe snubbed her, perhaps passed her without speaking — anyhow, the whole
thing is my fault. Ours, that is. If we hadn't—"

"Polly, my dear, I think you'd better start at the beginning. Using nouns, not pronouns. Take your time. I'm listening."

He swung his chair around so as to give himself a view of the thrashing Vicarage laurels and allow me the comfort of being unobserved. So I told him the whole story, very awkwardly and with much halting and repetition. He listened attentively, chin a little lifted, making and unmaking a steeple with his ten short fingers. The kitten jumped into his lap and curled up there without his appearing to notice it. Finally, when my voice petered out, he said, "I see."

"I hope you also see that this is a sort of confession. I mean there is honest-to-God guilt involved here. The nicest word you could find for what Pa and I have done is maybe mischief. And there are lots of nastier ones."

"Yes, there are."

"Well, I feel totally lousy about my share of it."

"I'm glad of that, at any rate."

"But of course this kind of damage is the last thing we ever—"

"No excuse, though, is it."

"No."

He waited, swinging one foot gently.

"Richard, tell me what to do. How can I—"

"Ah. If only that were easy."

"Because I'll do anything, if only she—"

"Well, my dear, you've made a start. Cleansed the bosom and so on. Remorse is also good. And reform should follow."

"It's going to, I promise you."

"Promise yourself, child, not me."

"All right. But in the meantime, what can I do?"

"We'll go to Seven Oaks straight away, and you'll leave me alone with her for a bit. I'm not bad at Visitation of the Sick."

"Oh, would you? She likes you, I know. I saw how you comforted her, the night of the masque."

"Get into your coat, then." He pulled on a disreputable

old mac and went a few steps down the hall to call into the back regions that he was going out for a while. A dim reply and a spicy smell of tomato chutney drifted back. He then, after patting all his pockets in succession, found his keys and put me into his muddy little car. The wind blew storms of leaves against the windscreen as soon as we began to move. When we turned out onto the road, the car rocked under threatening gusts from the gale, but I felt almost warm with relief and reassurance. The Vicar was so small a man he had to sit on two cushions to see over the steering-wheel, but this in no way lessened his dignity.

"I'm truly grateful for this, Richard," I told him, and meant it.

"Not at all, my dear. All part of my job." Not long ago, Bagshot had made much the same remark to me when he came to the house to treat a physical illness, and the recollection with its attendant ironies silenced me.

When we got home, we found Nan sitting at her loom, the dog's head on her knee. Boris rolled up his eyes at us but did not shift his position. Richard went in and quietly closed the workroom door behind him.

For half an hour the murmur of his voice could be heard. Then there was a long silence. Some time after that, he came out with Boris wagging at his heels. I never knew what he said or did while he was with her, but when I looked cautiously in a few minutes later, I saw her pick up the shuttle and begin slowly to thread it into the work on the loom.

3
The Lord of Misrule

The first thing Pa said when he got back from Cambridge was, "They gave me a standing ovation." He stood in the hall with his hat still on and repeated, "A standing ovation."

"That's lovely, Pa. We figured your train would be this late, so dinner's just ready. Come and sit down. Nan's cooked partridge."

"You'll have to excuse me a minute first. We are all mortal men with mortal kidneys, you know."

A moment later he walked into the dining-room, escorted by the exuberantly capering dogs. He unfurled his big table-napkin and tucked it into his vest buttons, but before sitting down he bent over the centrepiece of late yellow roses to draw up a noisy sniff of their sweet, peppery scent.

"Yes, if I say it myself, the lectures were a success. Even the undergraduates told me so, and nobody knows more about boredom than they do. One of the old profs—he looked about a hundred—told me the Fieldings were never better done. And there was a chap there on faculty exchange from Johns Hopkins who wants me to do a lecture series over there next year. Furthermore, I might just go. Not only is the money a bit of a temptation, but contact with the young can actually be quite stimulating. Keeps one awake."

He spooned in a generous amount of Nan's vichyssoise before appearing to notice that there were only three of us at the table.

"Where the devil is Hamish, then?" he wanted to know. Like the philosopher with the tree in the quad, it seemed he could not seriously believe Hamish existed if he were not looking at him.

"He phoned to say he was extending his holiday for a bit. Apparently the salmon are biting up there in the Trossachs, or whatever it is that salmon do."

"Well, he'll have to get out of those waders at once. Call him first thing tomorrow, Pol. I want him here."

"Do you really need to drag him back, Pa? True, the mail has piled up a bit, but—"

"I tell you, get him back here." Pa paused briefly to gaze with affection at the little game bird steaming on his plate. Then he attacked it energetically. "And not next week," he went on. "Immediately. On the train coming home, I suddenly realized what's been the damn obstacle all this time with the new book. The point of *view* is wrong. Totally wrong. A different angle of vision—that's what it needs, and that's what it's going to get. (This is excellent, Nan.) I can't think why it didn't occur to me before. Been a confounded nuisance. But now we can go straight ahead. James will be delighted, for one. Of course he wouldn't dream of saying anything, but I could tell he was getting a trifle restive. We'll have him down for the weekend soon, eh? Pass me some more of those glazed carrots. Yes, and another thing. One of the Masters with some sort of pipeline to the Palace hinted to me that my name would probably be canvassed for the next Birthday Honours List. Well, girls, how does that grab you, as they say? Sir Montague—eh? Of course I shall politely refuse, news of which will have an even better effect, specially in North America, where they so dearly love to hate a lord."

"Apple tart, Pa?"

"Certainly. Is this the cream? Excellent."

After sweeping his dessert plate clean he sat back, unbuttoned his vest, and lovingly rolled a cigar in his fingers while Nan poured the coffee.

"Ah, that was first-rate. And what have you girls been up to? Breaking any hearts?"

I sent Pa a warning glance which he did not seem to notice. "No, we haven't been doing anything at all. It's been very dull here, actually. No social life at all. Between that and the weather, we've—we've moped, rather. Except for the Vicar, we haven't seen a soul, really, since you left."

"You don't say. Oh, and you'll never guess what happened after the Founders Banquet — fellow from Quebec approached me — tall, tall chap built like a stick-insect — can't think of his name. Anyhow he made a fortune in cement and is now on the Board of Governors at McGill; and *he* tells me they're planning to offer me an honorary degree. That will make my eleventh. Not bad, eh?"

"That's nice, Pa."

He threw back his head and drew luxuriously on the cigar. "Ah, but it's good to be home. Been a bit dull for you, then, has it? Well, we'll soon put that right. You've had nobody over?"

"Only Richard. He just came along once or twice to be helpful . . . he cheered us up."

Once more I tried to communicate subliminally with Pa, who this time did appear to pick up the signal. He rolled a speculative eye at me over the cigar.

"Did he now."

"As I said, Pa."

"Nice of him. An excellent fellow, Richard. Now you two mustn't let this book consume me completely . . . we'll have him and Hermione round to dinner soon. Call them tomorrow, Pol. No more dull times for you girls, now I'm back. And I'll tell you what, we're going to have a really tremendous Christmas this year—stockings, mistletoe, carols

— all the children must come to us — we'll make Jill the
Lord of Misrule — have a rousing good time. Eh, Nan?"

She gave him a fleeting smile as she backed out through
the swing door with the coffee things.

"Don't forget to get hold of Hamish first thing tomorrow,
Pol," he said, pushing back his chair. "And then call
Richard."

"Pa."

"Eh? What is it?"

"Look," I said, lowering my voice and keeping one eye
on the door, "after that Bagshot fiasco, Nan was really
depressed. I was quite worried. That's why Richard came
over here. She's all right now, but I have taken a solemn
pledge. Absolutely no more matchmaking. Got it? I'm serious, Pa."

"Matchmaking?" he repeated, as if puzzled to find any
connection between the word and the rest of my remarks.
"But of course you're serious, Polly. That's always been
your chief problem, my love. Now I'm going to look
through the mail and make a few calls to London before
bedtime. Perhaps Ralph and Lally will come down for the
weekend. You run along to bed, dear; you look a bit tired."

"Have you been listening to me, Pa?"

"Of course I have, my dear."

"All right, then."

It seemed to me the least we could we could do to make
up for curtailing Hamish's holiday was to meet him at Canterbury. "His train gets in at five," I said pointedly to Pa.
But he was on his way upstairs for a fresh encounter with
his manuscript, and irritably waved me away.

"I see no need; there are plenty of taxis about. But you
can go if you like — take the Daimler. The keys are on the
hall table."

The prospect of driving a heavy car without an automatic
shift was not appealing; nor did I really want to meet Ham-

ish by myself. But Nan was busy in the kitchen making meringues, and paused only long enough to ask me to bring home a dozen eggs. When I went back to Pa, I found him involved in a phone call from Italy. So I pulled on a coat, took the keys, and set out alone.

My reward (or penalty) for all this self-righteousness was the unguarded smile that broke over Hamish's face when he came through the gate and saw me in the grimy, draught-swept waiting-room.

"Well, this is nice of you, Pol." Luckily he was too encumbered by luggage and his own reserve for any embrace to be offered or received. We went out into a twilight smelling of tar and decaying leaves, making the sort of small talk people use to bridge separations.

"You won't mind driving us back, I hope. This car is too much for me, really."

"Of course I don't mind."

"We have to stop at the Dawson farm for eggs."

"Right."

He slung his bags and rod-case into the back seat and heaved himself under the wheel, crumpling his heavy tweed jacket in the process.

"Good fishing?" I asked as we pulled away.

"It was great. I've got three beauties back there in dry ice."

"Nan will be pleased. We've got Ralph and Lally coming down for the weekend. It will be rather nice to have the house full again."

"Bored, were you, then, on your own?" His glance at me was sharp. "What about the lovelorn medic?"

I hunched my shoulders. "Don't be silly. If he ever was, he isn't now." The edge in my voice sent his red eyebrows up, and I went on in a more mollifying vein, "No, that place of Pa's is too isolated. I'm a city person, after all. Stuck out there these last weeks in the middle of nowhere, with nobody but Nan—oh, I don't know, it all led to a sort of morbid, broody state of mind. Molehills into mountains — you know. Once Pa is settled in and his book is ticking over again, I'll be off, back to my little cubbyhole in Hampstead."

"Will you."

"As for Nan, even she prefers to have people around the house. People she knows, of course, and can trust to leave her alone. That way she can melt into the background where she likes it best, and where she's safe."

How much, if any, of the unspoken part of all this Hamish could perceive I didn't know or much care. He listened to it all with his usual air of impassive detachment, which I found reassuring.

"So your holiday was a success."

"Well, if that's the word for two weeks with a couple of aged remote cousins, both of them deaf. Our evenings went something like this: 'Ian, I had to pay forty pound for these shoes.' 'What's wrong with your shoes, wumman.' 'Eh? What d'ye say?' 'They look all right tae me.' 'No, not fifty. *Forty pun.*' 'Don't shout, wumman, I'm not deaf.' '*What?*'"

"God, no wonder you went fishing a lot. There's the egg place, on the left. Just hang on a minute and I'll collect them." A moment later I was back with my basket full of freckled brown eggs, some with a curl of feather or a bit of straw clinging to the shell, and some still faintly warm as blood is warm. Hamish let in the clutch and we moved off again through the dusk.

"Things could have been a lot worse, though. Another relative of mine was there too — from Inverness. Jean's a lot of fun. And a damn good fly-caster."

"Really?"

There was a pause. Then he gave his hard bark of a laugh. "Come on," he said. "I can *read* you, Polly. You thought of saying, 'How come you've never married, Hamish?' and then you decided it would be better policy not to ask. Well, I'll tell you why. It's because I understand women so well that none of them can stand me. And my cousin Jean weighs two hundred pounds and is the same shape all the way up, front *and* back. All right?"

"If you say so."

"Not funny, then?"

"Why don't we step on it a bit. It's getting late."

Again he glanced at me sidelong. "Now I could ask why you haven't married, but I know why, so there's no point. The thing is, though, Pol, you should do it anyway. You've got a sharp, peaky sort of look about you lately that I don't like at all. An old-maid look. Your nose is getting longer. Your collarbone sticks out. These are warning signs, you know. The hell with romance ought to be your motto. The hell with charm and glamour. A restful, friendly, old-shoe marriage is what you need. Other things you also need I won't mention at the moment."

"Oh, do shut up, Hamish." Not only did these comments annoy me, they—or something else—had suddenly created a tension between us as palpable as glass.

"I speak for your own good, you know," he said coldly. "And I speak the truth."

"That is very rarely a good idea."

"It's very rarely successful, if that's what you mean."

'He's picked up some of Pa's fondness for having the last word,' I thought, 'no matter how unattractive that might be. Well, this will teach me to go meeting people at railway stations.'

The car's headlights threaded the curving gleam of cat's-eyes in the dark road. A chilly silence maintained itself between us until we drew up to the house. In getting out of the car, I clumsily rapped the edge of my basket on the door handle and broke one of the eggs.

"Stupid," I hissed.

"Yes, I was," said Hamish, his jaws locked even closer than usual. "And I apologize."

"Oh, don't be silly. I didn't mean you."

I turned away, but he caught the cuff of my coat in one hand.

"'I will not let thee go except thou bless me,'" he said.

"Oh, do stop being an ass."

"Spoken like the gracious lady you are," he said, and made me a burlesque curtsey. I bit back a grin.

"Idiot."

"That's better."

And, oddly enough, it was.

With Ralph and Lally (complete with Darling) in residence again, and Richard and his aunt bidden to dinner as well, the house felt pleasantly full again. We all sat around the fire after the meal, warming ourselves with Irish coffee, and I looked with something like affection at Hermione's Rembrandt hat and Lally's bejewelled, useless little hand stroking the pug. Hamish had chosen a wing armchair, its back to us, on the outskirts of the group, as if to assert his detachment. All that could be seen of him was the tip of one well-polished shoe. He had remained silent, with unusual tact, through a number of provocative remarks from Pa on the subject of ghosts. "This being All Souls Night," he was saying now, "no right-minded person can possibly deny they're abroad all around us."

"Of course souls exist," the Vicar remarked mildly, as if there could be no possible debate about that. "But to believe they walk the earth after being separated from the body is contrary, you know, to the Word of God."

"Pah," said my father, dismissing the Word of God as a thing of no account. "There has to be truth in these persistent legends. The souls of the dead do wander. Listen to that wind—they swarm in the air tonight."

"Oh, surely most of us get along quite nicely, day or night, without a soul," I said. Pa, ignoring this, went on, "It's a fact, isn't it, Richard, that the church in its wisdom has appointed Ember Days four times a year, for fasting and prayer? And why? Because those are the seasons when ghosts most often walk."

"Your views, I'm afraid, rather smack of popery," said Richard, shaking his head with a smile.

"The Vicarage is haunted, you know," put in Hermione in a matter-of-fact way. "Several times I've seen a little boy of about six at the foot of the stairs. He seems to be playing. Richard claims I simply need new glasses, of course."

"'Ghosts wandering here and there,'" quoted Pa with relish, "'Troop home to churchyards: damned spirits all/ That in cross-ways and floods have burial,/Already to their wormy beds have gone—'"

"Please. I loathe worms," said Lally.

"You ladies will not be offended if I remark that according to legend it is largely the ignorant and females who believe in ghosts," Richard went on.

"On the contrary," said Pa vigorously, "all intelligent and imaginative people believe in them. Shakespeare, for instance. Henry James. That great pragmatist Daniel Defoe. None of them either ignorant or female. Now you've already conceded, Richard, that the soul is a separate entity from the body. So it has to follow that after death the soul continues to exist somewhere, right? And where more likely than here on earth, where most of us would like to stay? Where, I say—"

"And what is wrong with the Kingdom of Heaven?" asked Richard with some asperity.

"Even though I grant you," Pa swept on, "that not everyone has the capacity, spiritual and otherwise, to see and hear these disembodied creatures—"

Here Nan appeared among us, silently holding up in turn the coffee-pot and the whisky bottle. Most of us passed her our cups for a refill.

"A timely reminder that spirits may come in several different forms," said Richard, smiling at her.

"You're right this far," said Hamish, putting his red head and grim smile round the corner of his chair. "Not everyone suffers from a neurotic imagination. I'm with Scrooge, who put the whole thing down to indigestion."

"And lived to change his mind," retorted Pa. "Deny if you can, Richard, that in time past priests in full regalia were sent to the burial-place of those restless dead who gave trouble with their wailings and wanderings. The exorcist kicked the tomb and ordered the ghost, 'Get thee packing back to hell.' This rite was said to be very effective, what's more."

"A disordered conscience or a sick mind, my dear fellow — what they may, in quotes, see, is purely subjective."

"You mean only the guilty or the diseased can see visions?" Ralph asked. "That rules out people like Blake, doesn't it? Not to mention all those saints like Joan who seem to have been great on paranormal experiences."

"Let me just remind you that the great majority of saints were first of all notorious sinners."

"Very neat, Richard, but not convincing," said Pa.

"There's nothing neat at all about the co-existence of purity and corruption," he said, and something in his voice made me glance at him curiously. With surprise, and hoping I was misled by the flickering firelight, I saw a look of something almost like torment cross his kindly, ordinary face. "Who can say," he went on, as if speaking more to himself than to us, "where evil, greed, or lust may not corrode the purest of intentions? Who among us can claim to be innocent — which, as you know means harmless, not ignorant or unaware? I tell you, no one is harmless. Except perhaps for that rarest of all beings, the true saint. And we poor wretches may be in the presence of one such without being worthy enough even to know it."

This odd and obscure commentary left a rather embarrassed silence in its wake. No one protested when a little later Hermione told Richard he was tired and wanted to go home. Still, all the farewells were cheerful, and once they had gone, the rest of us, yawning comfortably, turned out the lights and wished each other prosaic good nights. I seemed to be the only one to feel that the evening had ended on a curious, even eerie, sort of note that had nothing to do with ghosts in white shrouds. Later on, in bed, I found it hard to relax. When, in a lull of the wind, I heard the Who—who—who of the white owl that lived in the nearby trees, I shivered.

All this talk about souls may well have had something to do with the subject and spirit of my next encounter with my father.

"Book coming along well now, is it, Pa?"

"Of course. But I've only just begun the new draft."

"Still, it's a start. And you have lots of company these days. Even after Ralph and Lally go back Monday . . . well, it's nice you and Richard are such friends now."

"Very nice. What's all this leading up to, girl?"

"Just that it's time I got back to my own life, Pa."

"And by that grand phrase I take it you mean unemployment benefits in some tacky bed-sit?"

"There's no need to be hostile. I simply feel that—"

"You promised to stay here till the spring."

"But Pa, that was when—that was before—oh, why do you have to make this so awkward? Why do you have to put me on the defensive? Surely it's natural for me to want to get back to my own place and my own—I mean, you must see that being a daughter at home—I'm really past all that now. Besides, it's an obsolete way of life altogether."

Pa took off his glasses and turned his face to me. Without them he looked vulnerable, frail and older. Probably he was well aware of that, but as he thumbed his eyes wearily I couldn't help feeling an unwilling pang of compunction.

"It's not that I'm ungrateful, Pa. You know that. Only

I have to go sooner or later, and the longer I put it off—"

"Of course you must do what you like," he said heavily. "I shall miss you terribly—and so will Nan—terribly—but all that's neither here nor there. Except that surely you've noticed that she . . . well, never mind. Do as you wish. You always were an independent little cat. Maybe that's why I—But these are just the maunderings of an old man. Fond and foolish, no doubt. Fatherhood may be, as you say, obsolete."

"Pa, of course I'll stay for Christmas," I said, though this had not been my intention at all.

"Well, well, I suppose that's something. I'll say no more, my dear. Give me a kiss."

I did that and made my escape before he could win any further points. After all, I thought, Christmas at home could be fun. And the New Year was an appropriate time for a new start.

It had been a keen annoyance to Pa that persistent heavy rains earlier in the month made it impossible for him to stage his usual spectacular Guy Fawkes bonfire. But near the end of November, a spell of dry, mellow weather set in, and he hastily organized us all for a delayed but extravagant celebration.

"I'll just get on with typing those new pages," said Hamish.

"No, you will not. I want you to go out and tell Fisk to clear a space at the end of the vegetable garden—also tell him to get hold of a big barrel and a bit of tar. And Polly—"

"Oh, honestly, Pa. The whole dastardly plot was foiled, after all, in 1605. And Fawkes was drawn and quartered in public, wasn't he? It does seem a bit silly to go to so much bother at this point, don't you think?"

He waved an impatient hand at me like someone bothered by flies. "—I want you to call the Vicarage," he went on, "and tell them to bring along all their Cubs and Brownies and so on. Children in their wisdom understand these matters. 'Confound their knavish tricks'—that's the spirit. Get 'em busy making an effigy. And tell Nan to lay on plenty of the junk they like to eat—wieners and all that. We'll collect a whole lot of dry rubbish this afternoon, and—"

"Is that 'we' plural or royal?" asked Hamish.

"Faugh," said Pa, nettled. "The pair of you might as well have been drawn and quartered years ago, for all the use you are. I'll gather up the fuel myself."

Hamish, presumably as a matter of principle, let him work alone for half an hour dragging dead branches onto a growing pyre, and raking up dead leaves to add to it; but then he donned gloves and pitched in to help. By sunset an impressive pile rose high and dark against the last smear of crimson in the sky. After dinner we all went out to inspect the final preparations. It was quite dark now, and a light mist had begun to rise. Fitful gusts of wind rustled the dead leaves underfoot, and there fell into the cold air that hush that comes with the onset of night. In spite of my thick sweater and wool trousers, I was not warm. The whole ridiculous affair bored me. I was glad when the Vicar arrived with his busload of squealing, squirming children so I could escort them to the scene of the action and get it all over with.

"Hermione has a cold," Richard told me as we cut a path of light across the garden with our torches.

"How intelligent of her."

"She asked me to remind you about the jumble sale on Wednesday. Can you come to church and help her sort the things at ten?"

"Oh. Yes, of course."

The beam of my torch caught Crackers, a pale feline shape that shone astonished, luminous eyes at us as if we were bizarre apparitions. He then leaped high in the air and vanished.

At the bottom of the kitchen-garden, Fisk stood guard over the tower of fuel. Dragging their Fawkes effigy, the children squealed and swooped around the pyre like a flock of starlings.

"Don't none of you young buggers touch nothing," he warned them, "or I'll ave your guts for garters."

With a dramatic flourish, Pa lit a knotted branch that had been dipped in tar, and with it ignited the pyre. A scream of glee rose from the children as smoke and crackling flame began to swirl up into the darkness.

"Remember, remember," Pa chanted, "the Fifth of November — Gunpowder, treason, and plot —"

With barbaric yells of joy, the rosy-faced Cubs and Brownies tossed their limp effigy in an old blanket before hurling it onto the fire, which was now blazing high and spitting hot sparks into the dark.

"We'll be lucky if the local fire marshal doesn't slap a fine on us for this," muttered Hamish. But he stared at the twisting yellow flames as if they fascinated him, and so, in spite of myself, did I. Nan's head was thrown back to watch the red sparks swarm and spin high in the air before disappearing in the mist. When the children, shoving, scuffling, and kicking each other, joined grubby hands and began to circle the blaze, we all found ourselves a willing part of the chain. Faster and faster we ran the circuit, the smoke catching at our lungs, the leaping fire scorching our cheeks. Breathless I staggered along with the rest, Pa's hand tugging me along. His white hair was wild in the rising wind. By now a spark of primitive madness seemed to have found its way into everyone's blood. The children leaped and shrieked like savages. I was hot and gasping.

Finally the circle broke into groups and pairs of dancers who stamped and whirled on the leaf-strewn ground. Fisk tore off and threw away his battered hat, and pulled Nan into a grotesque sort of polka, only to lose her to Richard, who caught her round the waist and, for all she was nearly twice his size, spun her away with him into the dark.

With a great crash the fire collapsed on itself, sank low, and subsided in clouds of smoke. We came to a standstill then, hot, laughing, and out of breath, and began to herd the children indoors for their hot chocolate and frankfurters. The Vicar mopped his face with one end of his long muffler. Nan's cheeks were blazing and her large, light eyes had an almost dazed look.

"There!" said Pa triumphantly. "Wasn't that grand? There's nothing like a bit of the old barbaric ritual to cleanse the blood."

"Is that what it does?" Hamish asked me as with our respective limps we brought up the rear of the procession.

"Not exactly," I had to admit.

Dutifully I presented myself at the church on Wednesday at ten, only to find myself alone there, the vestry with its store of jumble articles firmly locked, and no sign of Hermione anywhere. For a few minutes I strolled along the nave reading inscriptions on tombs and looking at the time-torn, dim old battle flags hanging overhead, wistful jumble themselves of forgotten conflicts. My breath made a pale little event in the cold air. Nothing about the place was calculated to make solitude welcome. If anything it was colder inside than outdoors in the hard frost. My cane made an assertive clatter on the stone floor, and when I sneezed the resulting echoes seemed to beat against the thick walls trying to find an exit. The whole scene brought rather drearily to mind various Poe-esque titles like "The Premature Burial" and "The Tell-Tale Heart".

A quarter past the hour, and still Hermione failed to appear. My wanderings took me to the lectern, where the spread wings of a brass eagle supported a massive Bible. It was open at a passage of advice that I thought could be applicable only to someone in my own peculiar circumstances: "I say then walk in the Spirit, and ye shall not fulfil the lust of the flesh. For the flesh lusteth against the Spirit and the Spirit against the flesh; and these are contrary, one to the other; so that ye cannot do the things that ye would."

Here at last the sputter and clank of the Vicarage car announced Hermione's arrival, and I thankfully left St. Paul and hurried out to meet her.

"Good morning, good morning!" she called, thrusting her dishevelled red head out of the window. "Just give me a hand with these few boxes, will you? They aren't heavy."

That, I soon found, was a matter of opinion, but Hermione, clad in jeans and an old many-pocketed hunting jacket, lugged more than her share on repeated trips to and from the vestry. "Blasted Boy Scouts were supposed to be here for this chore," she grumbled. "But never mind. Manage it ourselves." By the time we had wrestled all the cartons into the Parish Hall, her face was purple with exertion and I was nursing two broken fingernails. Four long trestle tables had been set up to serve as counters. There were fourteen cartons waiting to be unpacked. A large poster on the bulletin board exhorted us to lift up our hearts, but I for one found this easier said than done.

"Now, Mrs. Pryde's daughter will be along to look after the clothes stall," said Hermione, surveying the scene with an experienced eye. "And Gladys Barton — I don't know whether you know her — works at the Post Office — she's offered to do the odds-and-sods table." She began to extract various objects in that category from one of the boxes: faded books, odd pieces of china, toys, pictures, and an old-fashioned meat-grinder. "She and Crispin Bagshot are going to be married soon," she went on. "Richard's calling the first banns on Sunday."

I had, in fact, seen Gladys Barton selling stamps in the Post Office. She was a meagre, sallow girl with prominent hare's eyes and a retreating chin. The thought of my warm, rosy Nan made me swallow back something that might have been rage.

"Now all we need to do," Hermione was saying briskly, "is to spread all this tat out and slap a price on each item."

I became busy with another box, which seemed to contain mostly old shoes curling upward at the toes. At the very bottom, however, was a chamber-pot lavishly decorated with forget-me-nots.

"Crikey," I said. "What kind of price would be right for this?"

"You look a bit wan," remarked Hermione. "And I feel rather drained myself after all this effort. But here's something that will put us right." With a grin she drew a large thermos flask out of a flap pocket of her jacket, deftly unscrewed the top, and poured generously into two plastic cups. I expected tea, but a pungent smell of gin spoke for itself. She lifted hers to me with a wink.

"Cheers, dear."

"Cheers." I tipped mine down swiftly.

"No problem pricing things. Just put about half what you think it's worth on the ticket."

"Right. Nan will be along later with the stuff she's baked for the cake stall."

"Bless her. You know, she makes one think how right those kind old country words are—words, I mean, like 'simple' and 'natural'. There's nothing derogatory. On the contrary, in fact."

"That's true." I allowed a second generous slosh to be added to my mug. In comfortable silence we finished off the flask.

"Ah, that's better," she said, slapping back the stopper. "Shall we get started, then? Shoes and hats go with the clothes. Kids' things at this end. Everything else is oddments." She hauled out a glass case containing a large stuffed fish which looked disparagingly at us with its one glassy eye. After a moment's thought, she wrote "50p" on its gummed price-tag. Getting quickly into the spirit of the thing, I labelled a Donald Duck lampshade "10p" and a copy of *Sesame and Lilies* "4p".

"You've got it," said Hermione. "Now this, on the other hand, is a hard one to value. We might even have to pay somebody to take it away." It was a large framed print of a buxom woman kneeling in a ray of sunlight at a casement window, face uplifted to a bough outside where a bird perched, presumably singing. Her hands were clasped around a bunch of flowers, she looked pious or slightly sick, and for no discernible reason all her clothes were slipping off to reveal large expanses of pink, lustrous flesh.

"Well, what d'you think?" she demanded.

"No, that's a masterpiece. Art on its highest level. Combines vague spiritual uplift and sex. I'd say price it at two pounds, and if nobody buys it, I will. I know a couple of people who would really appreciate it. Both men, of course."

"Of course. This is actually just Richard's kind of thing, you know. He loves big women."

"Does he?" I said, interested.

"Well, you must have noticed."

"Noticed?" I paused with a straw hat in one hand and a toasting-fork in the other.

"Not that you can feel anything but sorry for people like Edward VII. No wonder he ate so much. Those great cows of women would have squashed him like a mosquito otherwise."

"Hermione—"

"Now here's a pair of corsets—just look at those bones. Aren't you glad it's now and not then? I don't even wear knickers any more, myself."

"When you say noticed—"

"My dear, will you look at this china thing for putting hair-combings into. Isn't it nauseating."

"About Richard—"

She blinked at me. "What about him?"

"—Well, you said—" and I indicated the pink expanses of the kneeling lady.

"Eh? Oh, that. Yes, well, but in the circumstances, of course . . . " Here her voice trailed off absently. Glasses on the end of her nose, she closely inspected the embroidery on a purple tea-cosy, and appeared to forget I was there.

"In *what* circumstances?"

But Mrs. Pryde's daughter now clattered in with her red-nosed toddler in a push-chair, and I could only speculate, somewhat uneasily, just what it was that Hermione had begun to tell me. And the worst of it was that I couldn't foresee any time, really, when the opportunity to ask her was likely to come again.

It was clear before long (though nobody actually said so) that the revision of Pa's novel was not going well. Every day he closeted himself in his study, but at frequent, unpredictable intervals he would emerge to prowl restlessly from room to room, or stand in moody silence glaring out of windows. Soon the whole house fell under the pall of one of his worst glooms, his dissatisfaction spreading like a disease from one person to the next. He stormed into the kitchen one morning and demanded that Radio One be silenced, and that made Mrs. Pryde sulk and take it out on the char. Hamish made a harmless remark about Anthony Powell which caused Pa to stalk away and slam doors. Hamish then shouted at Ivan (admittedly a neurotic dog), who after that took to slinking out of rooms with the whites of his eyes showing, on no provocation at all. And the ripple effect next spread to me the following day at lunch when Nan produced a dish Pa did not recognize.

"What's this, then?" he asked, tossing his portion about crossly between knife and fork.

"Pigs' trotters, Pa."

"Pigs' *what?*"

"Trotters," repeated Nan timidly.

He stared at her. "And you expect me to *eat* this?"

"Richard likes them," she said, only half audibly.

"And why, I'd like to know, should the bizarre gastronomic preferences of a stranger be foisted onto me at my own table? You'll be offering me dog's tonsils next, I suppose."

With that he dropped knife and fork across his plate, plucked free and tossed aside his table napkin, and strode out of the room. Ivan slunk under the table. Hamish gave a sardonic snort of amusement, but Nan's eyes were full of tears. The pigs' feet didn't appeal to me much either, but I felt indignantly that something really would have to be said to Pa. As I followed him out, Hamish muttered, "Lots of luck."

He had not gone back up to his den but stood round-shouldered at the sitting-room's bay window looking out at the dry yellow leaves that drifted down through the grey air.

"Pa—"

An irritable hunch of the shoulders was his only reply.

"Let Nan make you an omelette or something. You've made her cry. It really is a bit much."

Silence.

"Because you know perfectly well her cooking is a sort of love offering."

Still no answer.

"Pa, just because your book—"

With this he turned on me so fiercely I stepped back, startled not by his anger so much as by the naked misery of his eyes and mouth.

"Just because," he said quietly. "That's it exactly. Nobody knows or cares. Not even my own flesh and blood. All this torment, struggle, and frustration — and nobody has the faintest idea. It's like being the only speaker in a planet full of mutes. The isolation. The hopelessness. And why go on? Who gives a damn? It's all nothing but trumpery, that's what all of you think. And maybe you're right. Maybe it's all a sheer and utter waste of time."

He turned away again to look outside. A sleety rain had begun to fall, rustling and darkening the carpet of withered leaves.

"The fact is, I'm finished, Pol. It's all over."

Long experience told me that while some of this was sheer histrionics, the rest of it was quite genuine, and it touched me in spite of myself.

"Look, Pa, this is just a temporary down. Gifts like yours don't just go away like a head cold — you know that. Why don't you just shove that book away in a drawer for a while, and put it right out of your mind. Then when you least expect it, you'll be ready to go back to it — the problems will solve themselves when you're not looking at them. This has happened to you before. It's going to be all right."

He shrugged again, but I could tell he was listening to me.

"Now, Christmas is only a couple of weeks off. Why don't you put the thing aside till the holiday is over. You said a while ago you wanted a nice, old-fashioned Christmas, so let's do that. We'll have a big tree and all the family down; wouldn't that be nice? Blindman's buff — a Yule log — the whole bit. We'll have fun, and it will do you the world of good. You've just been poring over that book too much — you need to get away from it for a while. It's as simple as that."

I was by no means really sure of this, but Pa's back looked a little straighter. He jingled change thoughtfully in his trouser pocket.

"We could play charades," I added casually. "Christmas ones."

After a silence he muttered, "Well, if it would amuse you and Nan . . ."

"Oh, it would. And cheer you up too, Pa."

Another silence. Then he said, "We'll make it a saturn-alia, to tease Richard. Be sure you ask him to everything."

"Whatever you say. You plan the programme and I'll start phoning people this afternoon."

"Well, go along and ask Nan for that omelette first."

I hurried off, careful to repress a smile. On my way across the hall I met Hamish carrying a handful of letters.

"Would it be safe to approach the master now without serious risk of castration? There's a doctoral candidate doing a thesis who wants an interview. And an offer from Harvard for his papers."

"Both sound good. Go ahead."

He glanced at me doubtfully. "Really? What have you been up to, Pol?"

"Nothing at all. Just cheering him up."

"You do realize that may not be the best idea? It was Freud, you know, who said, 'I have to be somewhat miser-able in order to write well.' "

"Oh Hamish, don't be such a drear. Trust me."

But he went on his way frowning dubiously.

As we plunged into preparations for Christmas, it struck me for the first time how much the whole celebration—at least in our house—centred on performance, role-playing, and various kinds of games. When all the kitchen help had been mustered to chop suet and stone fruit, the pudding was ritually stirred by everyone upstairs and downstairs, each one making a wish. A ring, a thimble, and a coin were dropped into the batter, talismans for the children of all ages. The char, whistling through her National Health teeth, polished up a huge silver punch-bowl so that Pa, sleeves tucked back, could practise various Dickensian rec-ipes. Neither he nor anyone else was at all put off by the fact that none of us really liked punch. Nan seemed the least involved in all this game-playing as she braided bread and laced mince tarts with brandy. She even firmly managed to ignore all Pa's wistful references to bringing in a boar's head with an orange in its mouth. Just the same, one night when we were decorating the hall, she surprised me by holding up a bough of mistletoe with a roguish look and shaping her lips into a kiss, as if one game at least had some charm for her.

Costumes and disguises preoccupied the rest of us for days on end. A red velvet Santa Claus suit left over from Christmases past was unearthed from somewhere and tactfully enlarged here and there to accommodate Pa's current waistline. Brushed and hung outdoors to get rid of its mothball aroma, it swung in the pale December sun like the absurd pantomime rig that it was. A major part of the Christmas Eve doings was to be a mummer's play performed by Jill and her cousins, and I spent many hours contriving child-sized disguises and masks for it. The house itself was dressed for the occasion with greenery imported from the hedges and garden. Ropes of holly and ivy entwined the hall staircase. A great beribboned wreath of silk fruit and flowers decked the front door. Familiar pictures on the walls peered out with an air of faint surprise from under crowns of bay and spruce. Most exotic of all was a kissing-bough erected with muttered profanity by Fisk on the staircase landing. It looked charming with its seven bright apples hung on red ribbons from an ivy frame, all its little red candles flickering. The drips of wax got ground into the carpet, and one of the apples fell on my head; but these things did not seriously matter.

By Christmas Eve the house was lit from top to bottom and spicily scented by the tall tree that stood in its tub waiting to be dressed. Ralph and Lally in fur coats arrived with Darling decked out in a red-ribbon bow that made him scowl. Bill's and Alan's children spun around like dervishes and got under everyone's feet. Pa, resplendent in his red-velvet outfit, genially wielded a great silver ladle over the punch-bowl, which sent up a fragrant steam of lemon, spices, and rum. Unfortunately the punch itself tasted quite dreadful. Soon the small cups were hidden behind ornaments or on windowsills while Hamish in another room discreetly dispensed less romantic gin with lime and Scotch with water. Richard and Hermione arrived, beaming, their arms full of gaily wrapped presents, and announced with satisfaction that snow was forecast for later in the evening.

Before long, Pa forsook the punch-bowl to marshal three of his grandchildren for the mummer's play. We all sat in a row before the dining-room archway, and after considerable giggling and scuffling from the hall, Father Christmas led in his little procession of performers in fringed suits and paper-bag masks. Jill brought up the rear, tripping on the tail of Pa's long academic gown.

"Here comes I, old Father Christmas," announced Pa, pacing out a circle.

"Good master and mistress, I hope you are all within,
For I come this very Christmas to see you and your kin.
I hope you won't be fronted, nor still take any offence,
For if you do, pray tell to me,
And I'll begone before I commence."

Here I caught Ralph's eye, which looked so glum I thought he might actually accept Pa's offer. But Bill's middle son was now front and centre, proclaiming in a voice muffled by stage fright and the braces on his teeth:

"I'm King George, this notable knight,
I shed my blood for England's right."

His sibling then stepped forward to squeak as he lifted a paper sword in his pipe-cleaner arm:

"I'm the gallant soldier,
Bullslasher is my name,
Sword and buckler by my side,

I mean to draw the game."

"Don't thou be so hot, Bullslasher!" said Pa in a voice shaking with laughter. The brothers belted each other unconvincingly ("considering," their father said in my ear, "how much time they spend hitting each other every day"). Eventually one of them, after a sharp nudge from Pa, fell down. He scrambled up again to mumble:

"Mind the lists and guard the blows,
Mind thy head and thy poor old soul."

But in spite of this brave defiance, the King then dropped, killed for the second time.

Jill, who had been quietly sucking her thumb in the background while she waited for her cue, now came forward. She carried an outsize pair of pliers and a half-inflated balloon on a stick. Unlike her cousins she spoke up boldly, flashing her bright eyes at the audience through the holes in her mask.

"Here come I, the notable Doctor,
I have brought some pills to cure all ills,
Hipips, the phipps, and palsy—"

Here she broke off, half dissolved in giggles, but Pa's eye sternly quelled her.

"Then cure this man!" he commanded.

She whacked the prone King George smartly with her balloon, asking, "Do you feel any better?" His answer was a kick not to be found in the script provided by the Vicar's antiquarian library. She whacked him again. "I have the toothache," he mumbled. She then stood over him and mimed extraction of the tooth, the other two clasping her around the waist to help tug. When the tooth came out they all fell down. Jill shouted:

"Look at this elephant's tooth!
See what quick quack doctors can do!"

She pretended to dose him with the balloon, adding,

"Here, take a little of this flip-flop,
Pour it down thy tip-top."

King George then jumped up, and the whole troupe, flushed with triumph, marched once round in a ring and then out. Loud applause followed them.

"Isn't it a pity these cultural leftovers are so confusing as well as dull," said Lally, patting back a yawn. "I really think if it had lasted any longer I might have gone quite mad. The whole thing reminded me a bit of those folk-dances, you know the ones, where men clump about with bells on their ankles and funny hats, all of them waving handkerchiefs like lunatics. One's afraid to ask what it's all about because the answer would obviously be so indecent."

Ralph turned to give her a rather sour look of rebuke, so I did not agree with her out loud. Nan, sitting next to me, was gently rocking Jill's little sister, who had fallen asleep in her lap. I expected Richard, who stood behind us, to provide Lally with a detailed lecture on the Chudlington Mummer's Play (text transcribed in 1893), but he was looking down as if bemused by Nan's round arms folded around the child.

I slipped away to get myself a drink while the mothers rounded up their young and herded them upstairs to bed. They were all bribed with a sugar-dusted mince tart, and threatened with dire consequences if they didn't go instantly to sleep. Once they were gone, all the adults congregated around the tree to decorate it with candy canes, paper chains, tinsel, and spun-glass ornaments two generations old. All, that is, except Lally, who had drifted after me into Hamish's little study to help herself to a rather large drink. With a sigh she lowered herself into the room's only comfortable chair.

"Polly, have you got any money?" she said.

"Money! Well, hardly. All I've got in that line is nine

hundred pounds a year my old Aunt Marjorie left me. And she only did that because she was dotty. Why?"

"Oh, I thought you maybe had Bard's insurance or something."

I looked at her curiously. "No, that went to Doris. He meant to change it over, but never got round to it. There wasn't anything else. Even the car was a total write-off."

"Pity," she said, and with marvellous simplicity added, "Because I was going to ask for a loan. Rather a huge one, in fact."

"Oh, really. Well, I'm afraid you're out of luck there. Ralph's in difficulties again, is he?"

"That's it. Really, the poor dear does have the foulest luck. His stocks . . . something about oil . . . the price has gone up or down or something."

Lally's vagueness had for years been a family joke. Olivia swore she once referred to some grazing animals in a field as "those cows or sheep or whatever they are". But there was nothing very comic now about Lally's heavily veined hand plucking at the silk fringe of her skirt. She looked both tired and unwell, with her white fluff of hair laid back against a cushion, and it was easy to remember that she was well into her fifties.

"I'm sorry, Lall."

"Oh, not to worry. I suppose it will all sort itself out somehow. I've sold my jewellery. And Ralph will have to give up one of his clubs. But that isn't going to be nearly enough, I'm afraid. We may even have to sell the flat un-less—"

Sure enough, the handsome ruby and emerald dinner rings she always wore were missing from her hands. Poor Lally, I thought. It takes talent and hardihood to be deprived, and she had neither of these assets. It would be just as hard for her to give up her Dolphin Square address and her Harrods account as it would be to go on welfare.

The fact that this value system was ridiculous did not make it any less poignant.

"Well, I daresay Monty will help us out," she went on, closing her eyes. "He has before. But he seems so . . . so up and down lately, doesn't he, and that makes it awkward to ask him."

"Yes, it does. But it's Christmas, after all. And as you say, he's helped before."

"True. I suppose, Pol, you wouldn't ask him? — I mean, it's only five years ago, or three, or something like that since the last time, and—well—it's really a damn big sum . . ."

"I don't suppose you know exactly how much."

"Oh, Ralph can tell you all that."

"You know, Lall, I think it's better if we leave it between him and Pa."

"Well, perhaps you're right. But Ralph is so *low*, poor man. Business has been shocking, for one thing. None of his authors are making any money these days. No new book from Monty for ages, has there been, and he's always been the one big success in Ralph's stable."

"True. I'm not sure it would be a good idea to mention that to Pa, though. Shall I give you another drink?"

Hamish put his head in at the door and said, "Come on, you two. No loitering. You're wanted in the sitting-room for some Druidical nonsense or other."

"All right. We're coming."

Typically enough, Lally was soon playing snapdragon, snatching up blazing raisins with little shrieks of gaiety; but Ralph remained folded in gloom all the rest of the evening. Of the two of them, though, I felt sorrier for her.

"They wouldn't let me have a boar's head, you know, Richard," said Pa, moodily eyeing the plump and glossy goose Nan had just set before him on its huge platter.

"Never mind, my dear fellow. It's always sounded a

rather repulsive business to me. The procession bringing it in used to include 'a bloody sword drawn', you know, and pages, 'each with a messe of mustard'. Not really very tempting. As for brawn, it's nothing like as delicious as this noble bird will be, I'm sure of that."

"Why—are—we—waiting!" the children chanted; so Pa, with a resigned flourish of implements, set about his task. Nan's face had been clouded with anxiety, but it cleared as the first tender slice came off the knife. When he plunged in a big spoon and brought out the first dollop of oyster stuffing, its rich steam sent a cheer around the table.

Just enough of the predicted snow had fallen to powder the ground picturesquely between the house and the church where, to please Richard, we had all attended morning service. Now the day had turned frosty and foggy, and to promote indoor cosiness we had drawn the red curtains early, and lighted candles everywhere. There was even a log fire in the dining-room hearth, though we seldom lit it, because the person sitting nearest was so likely to feel like a bit of roast meat himself before long. Lally, however, took that place, sweetly proclaiming that she never felt too warm, especially in the country, where it was always draughty, owing to all those dreadful open spaces, fields and things. The sooner everything in this world was built up and decently paved over, she said, the better she'd be pleased.

The goose, now reduced to an ignominious rubble of bones, was taken away. Glasses of burgundy were refilled. Crackers were pulled, and ill-fitting tissue-paper hats were put on. Quarrels among the children, snatching each other's plastic prizes, were slapped down by parents. After a dramatic hush was imposed by Pa, the lights were put out and Nan made an effective entrance with a pudding the size of a cannon-ball, all ablaze with little blue flames. Shouts of greedy joy from the children greeted it, and Pa wielded his serving-spoons with a will. It was rich and moist with fruit and dark with stout, and those of us already satiated with goose looked at it rather dubiously and refused the hard sauce.

"Makes you want to fall on the bloody sword," muttered Hamish, but Pa relentlessly served everyone a large portion. We all probed our helping for the hidden prizes and cheered again when Nan held up the ring, Lally the thimble, and Ralph the big 10p coin.

"Possibly excepting the thimble," Pa said, patting Lally's hand, "a thoroughly suitable outcome. Nobody could say a life of pious toil is likely to be *your* fate, my love; but wealth for Ralph — marriage for Nan — splendid. Altogether appropriate." He sent the decanter of wine around again, and Ralph did not refuse it. I caught his eye and he shrugged. Evidently he had not yet told Pa about his predicament. By now, however, Pa's mood was so radiant I was sure Ralph would seize the first opportunity to do so.

Once the table was cleared, Pa decreed games to shake down the meal, so poor Ralph had to bide his time and help, with as much good humour as he could muster, to push all the sitting-room furniture into corners, to make room for blindman's buff. After all that food and wine, none of us had the strength to refuse to play, not even the teenager whose most frequent remark was, "Do I have to?" Soon the game was in full cry, with Pa, eyes bandaged, stalking and pouncing with fearsome, predatory clutches. We all shrieked and dodged around him as vigorously as the children did, though the three-year-old prudently kept her distance and her dignity. This game was followed by a rousing bout of hunt-the-slipper, after which all the young ones swooped off upstairs to settle around the television. The rest of us, rather breathless, sank into chairs. Pa stirred the fire to a blaze, and a blessed quiet fell.

"Dear, dear," said Richard, dusting down his dishevelled clerical blacks. "I haven't had such fun for years. My arteries will never be the same."

"The best part of exercise, just the same, is when it's over," Lally said, and no one contradicted her.

"Now is the time," said Pa, rubbing his hands together, "for reading aloud or telling stories, the more exotic and grotesque the better. Everyone must take a turn. But first the wassail-bowl. Ale, eggs, ginger, and roasted apples. Nan's set it up in the dining-room, all hot and spicy. Let's go and get some—I'm thirsty, for one."

We all trooped out after him, and in the hall where the big bough of mistletoe hung from the chandelier a certain amount of laughter, scuffling, and embracing broke out. Pa gave Hermione a hearty buss. Richard not only planted a smack on Nan's lips but accompanied it with a Rabelaisian slap on her haunches, which she seemed to enjoy. For myself I was careful to stay close to the wall and keep out of everyone's way.

The wassail-bowl smelled richly of sugar, cloves, and nutmeg and we helped ourselves to it with discretion. Nan topped up each cup with a little hissing crab-apple. We drifted back to the fireside rather lethargically, this time ignoring the mistletoe.

Pa drew Nan down to sit on a stool at his feet. She was still flushed and smiling from the horseplay in the hall. Her loosened hair caught the firelight and shone in the dim room like gold.

"Ah, the joys of domesticity," Pa said, stroking her cheek lovingly. "And it's women we have to thank for it—lovely, warm, giving women, smelling of bread and milk and babies."

"Yes, poor wretches," murmured Lally; but Pa ignored her.

"True," said Richard, gazing at Nan as if he could not look away from her. " 'A good woman is above rubies.' And yet—"

"Oh, come come. How can there possibly be any demur," Pa asked jovially.

"I say 'and yet' because—" began Richard.

"No, no; the wretched state of bachelors, relicts, single men of every persuasion—their abstinence becomes indecent in the presence of a ripe, beautiful woman. I confess it. Bachelorhood has been forced upon me, but I deplore it entirely. Don't you agree, Ralph? I don't ask that cynical misogynist Hamish, who is beyond redemption; I ask a happily married man."

"Well, when you say married . . . but oh yes: above rubies," Ralph agreed. His face was impassive, as if the subject did not really interest him, and he glanced neither at Lally nor at her ringless hands. Not for the first time I wondered how much he felt for her, or for anyone.

"And yet," Richard repeated, "the loving-kindness of women may after all be a destructive thing, because it's so sensual. It's entirely hedonistic, you see. They create fleshly comfort; they give pleasure—"

"And you call that destructive?" cried Pà.

"Yes, if it creates conflict between the flesh and the spirit. As, very often, it does."

"But why in the name of all that's sane should it do that? Even religion, which is so often crackpot, calls matrimony an honourable estate. Doesn't the C. of E. tell us it's a sacrament?"

"Quite so. But none of the founding fathers claim it's the ideal state, you know."

"The best Saint Paul could find to say for it was that it's better than burning," put in Hamish. "Though I must add that his views on women make mine come over as radically feminist."

"Between the flesh and the spirit there can be no real reconciliation," said Richard. There was such sadness in his voice and in his face, half turned away to stare into the fire, that we all stole a curious glance at him. All, that is, except Lally, who had sunk into one of her little dozes.

"Now, I fail to see how on earth you can possibly uphold

such a view," Pa said. "It's downright unhealthy. And irrational to boot. Why, Richard, you've married couples and called down the blessing of almighty God on them countless times."

"I bless everybody, Monty. And clergymen don't — I don't — marry anybody. They marry each other."

"That's a quibble, man. You've been married yourself."

"Quite right. I was much younger then."

Suddenly I remembered the Bible in church the day of the jumble sale, and knew who had left it open at that passage. I tried to catch Pa's eye, but it was too late to stop him.

"The service tells us that marriage is not only honourable, but holy — 'instituted of God' — even though my own fell damn well short of that. So how can you possibly —"

"Ah, marriage is well indeed for those who need it. But the life of the flesh is at war with the life of the spirit. And that is the better life, there is no question about it."

"But there certainly is —" began Pa. Richard, however, had turned his head to confront him with a troubled, honest, almost desperate look in his blue eyes.

"Five years ago, you know, I took a vow of celibacy," he said.

There was a brief silence. It was not the sort of remark easy to top in any gathering. We all tried without success to think of anything to say that would not be ridiculous, or embarrassing, or both. After a moment, Hermione asked Nan for the recipe for the wassail-cup, which was probably the best anyone could have done. With relief we turned to topics like the Thatcher government. Richard gave himself another cup of hot ale and began to discuss the prospects for Manchester United with Ralph. He looked quite serene now, as if relieved to have declared himself. As far as I could tell, Nan had not really understood his confession, and he did not look in her direction, there being, perhaps, no longer any compulsion to do so. Pa was chatting brightly now about his plans for Twelfth Night, but a baleful glint in his eye told me he understood the situation only too well. Poor Ralph, I thought, had better wait a little longer before approaching him.

At breakfast next morning, Alan said, "My business won't look after itself forever, Pa. We have to get back before New Year's Eve — that's one of my busiest times. If you really want us here for a Twelfth Night party, it will have to happen tomorrow."

Bill agreed that he too should get back to town, and Pa snorted with scorn that as usual their priorities were all wrong. Not until the daughters-in-law weighed in on their husbands' side did Pa yield with a good grace. Though both wives bored him considerably, it was his invariable policy to be charming to them, as if to compensate them publicly for having chosen such lacklustre mates. Now he sent us all scurrying to put preparations for a Twelfth Night celebration in hand for the next day.

"Get hold of the staff, Pol; they're all invited to lunch tomorrow. Hamish, will you and Lally lay on a present for each of them — Canterbury will be full of Boxing Day sales. And Nan, you whip us up a big Twelfth Night cake."

"What about asking the Vicar and —" I began.

"No need to bother them," he said impatiently. He then retired to his study, behind whose closed door later could be heard light, intermittent snoring.

I spent the afternoon chopping peel and pasting up gold-paper crowns for the rulers of the revels. Lally wrapped presents and lent a gold lamé stole to drape the Queen's throne—by prearrangement Jill's, Pa having no use for the vagaries of chance. Ralph, looking rather grim, went for a long, solitary walk with the dogs.

In due course, grinning and nudging each other, Mrs. Pryde with her daughter, the charwoman, and the scullery-maid filed in and took our places at the dining-room table.

Oldfisk brought up the rear. He was wearing a curious green tweed cap with ear-flaps, as if he feared the climate indoors might be hazardous to his health. The sight of Pa and me in aprons, waiting for them with respectfully folded hands, sobered them momentarily; but when the beer and wine began to flow they quickly got into the swing of the thing. While we scurried about serving the food, they began to call out orders and complaints. In no time cackles of laughter rose as our hirelings took their revenge, shouting for more drink, unbuttoning and belching freely, spilling and messing crumbs with abandon. Nan, though she looked rather sombre as she carried trays and changed plates, was more or less at ease in her usual role, but when Fisk actually patted her bottom as she passed by, Pa became noticeably flushed and cast a withering glare at his employee.

Mrs. Pryde had a streaming cold, but I have never seen a woman enjoy herself so recklessly. At the height of the revels she gave a Bacchanalian shriek and hurled her wineglass into the fireplace with a crash. It would hardly have surprised me if she had demanded Pa's head brought in on a platter for dessert.

Things quieted down a little only when the children came in after their meal in the kitchen. Nan cut the big cake, careful to see that Jill got the portion with the bean in it. At this point we all exclaimed with loud surprise. Ceremonially she was then robed in a sequined evening sweater of mine, throned on Lally's stole, and crowned by Pa. Her choice of King was Boris, who was persuaded with some difficulty to take a chair beside her. His crown embarrassed him greatly until it occurred to him to eat it.

"Now," said Jill with satisfaction, "you all have to do what I say, because I'm God. I can do anything I like."

"Well, almost anything," murmured Pa.

She flashed her eyes at him. "Give me a glass of wine, Polly Poodle," she commanded.

I provided a small one, generously watered. She swigged it down to admiring laughter from the staff. "Chip of the old block, eh?" they said to each other. "Cheeky little kiddy. Just our Arleen's age."

"I can say any bad words I know," announced Jill, "and nobody can smack me."

"What's the worst word you know, then?" Pa inquired.

"I wouldn't ask," warned Alan.

Jill took a moment to think. She squirmed on her throne. Her face turned a deep pink. We all waited expectantly. At last she whispered, "*Belly.*"

There was loud applause. More than a little drunk by now on wine and power, she shouted, "Knickers! Pee-pot!"

"Right, and I think we'll cut it off right there," said Pa. He slung the giggling Jill across his back and trotted her out of the room, thus marking the end of the party.

Not long after that, we saw off the two families in cars packed with Christmas loot. A post-children hush then settled over the house, in which could be heard the faint hiss of pine needles falling off the tree. The staff having gone cheerfully back to the village in a taxi, the rest of us set about a massive clean-up of the kitchen and dining-room. Exhausted after this unfamiliar labour, Ralph and Lally went early to bed.

At some point, however, before they drove away next day, Ralph must at last have put his question to Pa, because when a little later we sat down to an early supper, Pa looked not only tired like the rest of us, but greatly bothered.

"So," I said, "Lally told me. It's too bad."

Pa shoved back his chair irritably. "Ralph is fifty-four years old, and this is the *third* time he's landed himself in this kind of mess by gambling on the market. I just don't understand it. He seems to be incapable of learning from experience."

"Well, you could say that about the whole human race, maybe. But I do feel sorry for Lally."

Hamish excused himself and left for bed. We heard him yawning on the stairs. Now only Nan was left at the table with us. Her shoulders were round with fatigue and her nose was pink with the start of a cold, but she made no move to go.

"Yes, but Lally damn well ought to control him better," Pa went on restlessly. "She's quite shrewd, you know: women as silly as that generally are."

"Oh Pa, it's not fair to blame poor Lal. Nobody could control Ralph—a man who's always had his silk shirts made to measure, as if that were the only thinkable thing to do about shirts—it's bred into him, that kind of thing. He told me once that after he retired from the I.C.S. his grandfather used to send his laundry back to India to be done."

"Be that as it may, he's landed himself in it properly this time," said Pa grimly.

"What did you say to him, then?"

But Pa was stirring his coffee, his face gloomy and absent. "Money," he said heavily. "What a curse the stuff is. The misery it brings—whether it's having as much as I do now, so Ralph can put the bite on me, or not having enough, as in my young days."

"But Pa, your parents weren't poor."

"Poverty, my dear, is a relative term. They had enough to live on, yes—but nowhere near enough to match their pretensions. I was sent to the best private school in Ontario, but my father really couldn't afford it, so my fees were always late—sometimes months in arrears. There was always trouble getting the uniform and the books. Everyone in the school knew this, in the devilish way of such places. Can you imagine the humiliation of that for me? Our house was the sort of place where there might be a new oriental carpet on the floor, but the sheets were in rags. My mother would serve shrimp salad to impress her bridge friends, and then open a tin of beans for the family dinner. It made me a neurotic about money for the rest of my life."

I considered this more or less true. Pa was a curious blend of easy-spending, even grandiose, ways, and petty thrift that made him a saver of paper-clips, a bargain-hunter, and a fiery preacher against waste in the kitchen.

"But what did you say to Ralph, Pa? Are you going to bail him out?"

He turned a forbidding eye on me as if I were implicated somehow in Ralph's shortcomings.

"Why should I do anything of the sort?" he demanded.

"Well, only that he's been a friend for—"

"The man is simply irresponsible."

"That may be true. But he's made plenty of money for you in the past."

"That's no reason why I should make any sacrifice for him now. I'm not a millionaire, you know."

"I thought maybe you were, Pa," I said dryly. "Or close to it."

"Well, you're wrong. I'm nothing of the sort. And Ralph has no claim on my little nest-egg. It's little enough, God knows, with the family responsibilities I have, and you know well enough how true that is, Pol. Let him sell that flat of theirs and trade in his Rover. I don't think he even *knows* there are cars in a lower price bracket than that. As for shirts, let him go to Marks and Spencer's, like all the rest of us. Maybe then he'll think twice about speculating like a bloody fool. Well, I've told him I'll think about it for a week, and I might find him a little cash, but no way am I going to shell out the whole amount—not given his character, and my age, both of which strongly suggest I would never see it back. No, I'll see him starve first."

Nan suddenly got to her feet and turned to him, her mouth open to speak. There was only a shocked second for me to see how paper-white her face was before she crumpled at the knees and fell to the floor with a loud, alarming noise.

"Good God!" said Pa, leaping up.

We lifted her by the shoulders, called her name and tapped her cheeks, but it was a minute or two before she opened her eyes. She looked at us as if she could only with difficulty recognize us. I chafed her hand, which was deathly cold. She moved her lips uncertainly and said something that sounded like "alpha".

"What did you say, love?"

But she didn't answer. As far as I knew, Nan had never in her life fainted before. Come to that, I could never remember her ever being ill, even for a day. But she was so pale now that it frightened both of us.

Hamish, in a gown hurriedly slung on over his pyjamas, came bursting into the room. "What is it?" he said. "Are you all right? I thought maybe you—" His eyes went from me to Pa before he seemed in his agitation to notice poor Nan on the floor. Then he poured a glass of water untidily from the sideboard pitcher and squatted down to offer it to her.

"It's all right," I said. "There's a nasty kind of flu going around the village. Come on, Nan dear. Let us help you to bed. That's all this is, a touch of flu."

"Is it?" muttered Pa. "Is it?"

4
The Queen of Swords

Within forty-eight hours Nan's temperature was so high that it was clear she needed a doctor. Pa and I looked at each other helplessly. Bagshot, we silently agreed, would not be a good choice. Eventually we called a clinic in Canterbury and a brisk and tweedy little lady doctor of about seventy was soon at the door. She inspected Nan, who lay there flushed and restless. Then she said, "Don't like the sound of these lungs. She ought to go into hospital." "No," we both said together, and the doctor looked at us in turn sternly over the tops of her glasses.

"No offence meant," Pa added. "But hospitals, I can't help feeling, are terrible places, full of machines and death and germs. Last time I was there, I went in quite well and came out with hepatitis. I'm sure we can look after her better here. Besides, as you can perhaps see, this particular person is — well — if she found herself alone there among strangers, it would—"

"She's never been away from home before," I said.

The doctor looked again sharply at Nan, putting together psyche and soma with speed and deftness.

"Well, all right, then. It means close care and attention, you realize. If this bronchitis develops into pneumonia . . . well, it hasn't yet, and let's hope it won't. I'll start her off on tetracycline every four hours, and you'll call me at once if the breathing gets difficult. I'll pop in again tomorrow to check the lungs. Watch her carefully."

There was no need to tell us that. Pa and I had been alternating bedside shifts for the last twenty-four hours, not because we were afraid she might die, but because I for one was haunted by a gnawing sense of guilt. And he shared it, I was virtually certain of that. Twice now we had actively or passively manipulated events around her, no matter that our motives were good. A delicate system of checks and balances had been somehow molested, and Nan was now ill. At any rate, those were the connections as I saw them. And soon afterward we did become truly afraid, because she grew steadily worse. Her soft lips cracked with fever. She tossed and muttered a perpetual blurred gabble in which we could not distinguish a single word. Sometimes she did not seem to recognize us but called us by different names, or mumbled to us to go away.

The doctor pursed her lips between the branches of her stethoscope. She phoned and arranged for the import of a nurse and a tank of oxygen. For a day or two there seemed to be no sound in the house but Nan's tight, hard bark of a cough like that of a sick dog or fox. We tiptoed around, trying to hide our fear from each other and from Hamish.

At last, however, her temperature dropped. Her hair darkened with sweat and she drifted into a quiet, normal sleep. A day or two later the nurse clapped herself into her hard-worked little car and set out for another case. "Keep well," she advised us heartily. "This flu is a real brute. It's killing off old people like flies. Cheerio."

"Jolly soul," remarked Pa, scowling, as she disappeared down the drive.

"Yes, but she has a point there, Pa. You're looking really done up, you know. If you're not careful, we'll have you down next with something. I'll sit with Nan tonight, just to make sure she's all right, and you get a decent night's sleep for a change."

He was in fact so tired that he went straight off to bed without even a token argument. Hamish offered to take over for me, but I shook my head. "Why are you martyring yourself?" he asked angrily, and stumped away without waiting for an answer. I knew there was no real need to sit up with her now — not on her part. But there was on mine. I wanted to be near her, just to look at the calmly sleeping face and listen to her easy breathing.

A blue chiffon scarf had been swathed around the lampshade, so the only light in the quiet room was dim. The drawn curtains, woven on Nan's own loom, closed us into a reassuring domestic warmth. From time to time the downstairs clock chimed the hour. Nan occasionally woke, smiled at me vaguely, then slept again. It grew later, and then earlier. The old house in the small hours creaked and rustled, and these little sounds magnified themselves uncannily, making my nerves prickle. I could hear the sigh of a light wind in the bare tree outside, and the fret of its stiff twigs against one another. Somewhere far away a rabbit shrieked faintly and made me start. A searching kind of loneliness came over me so powerfully I once actually got up to go and waken Hamish; but it passed. Then, gradually, a sort of numbness crept through my flesh. I was neither asleep nor awake. I was afraid to look in the bureau mirror for fear there would be no reflected image there.

At last I dragged myself stiffly to my feet. Careful not to rouse Nan, I crept to the window and pushed aside the curtain to look out at the sphinx face of the night. All that could be seen was a faint glitter of hoar frost on the ground, like an echo of the dim dust of stars overhead. Nan slept deeply, quietly on, and I envied her. I put my forehead to the cold pane of glass and longed to feel something—anything—that could draw me into the world of the living, and away from the world of the dead.

"Yes, thanks; much better now. Still weak, of course. Quite content to spend most of the day in bed. Mm. It's slow. The doctor says it will take a while to get her strength back. But she's on the mend, that's the main thing. Nice of you to call, Richard. Ah, that's kind, but Pol and I stick close to home these days ... yes. Thanks anyway. Some other time, perhaps. Best regards to Hermione."

We heard the receiver of the hall telephone returned to base with a decisive click. Pa came back to the card-table where the three of us had been sitting by the fire, after first making a detour to the drinks table to refill his brandy balloon. Hamish had picked up *The Times* in the interval, and I had laid out a game of solitaire to pass the time. I scooped the cards together now, yawning.

"Another round, Pa? Or have you had enough?"

"Enough. It's too easy to beat you."

"That's because you have no principles at all. You're such a shameless bluffer—sometimes you even *pretend* to bluff."

Pa smiled as if this were a compliment, which in a way it was.

Hamish refolded his newspaper and took off his glasses to rub his eyes. "I am whacked," he said. "Going through all those cartons is the most incredible chore. I hope you make Harvard pay through the nose for it."

"That is my firm intention. But you're not the one who has to read through every word of it. You can't even begin to imagine how dreary that is. My whole life is in those bloody boxes—and all it amounts to is a monstrous heap of trivia—scrap paper that should be tossed on the fire."

"Oh, come on, Pa. Look at it this way — somebody is actually willing to pay for the contents of your waste-baskets since 1950."

"Will you call Ralph tomorrow, or shall I," asked Hamish, "about all the stuff in his files? There must be tons of it there to be sifted through. What a heartening thought."

Pa sighed. "No doubt there is. No doubt. This whole stupid business is going to take us weeks more, when I should be getting on with my book. But there it is. Has to be done, I suppose."

"But you know between us Ralph and I could do a lot of the basic eliminating and sorting, if you'd just let us get on with it."

"Well, we'll see. Perhaps he'd better bring it all down here some time—when Nan's better, that is. There's no big hurry, after all."

Hamish twitched his close-set lips as if to answer, but thought better of it, and got up to replenish his glass instead.

"The worst of it," Pa went on, moodily swirling the brandy around in his snifter, "is that the whole exercise illustrates so accurately what Johnson called The Vanity of Human Wishes. Those boxes are full of aborted plans. Disappointments. Lost opportunities. So much debris of defeat. Three sets of divorce papers, for instance. Reminders that in the end everything goes—and everyone."

"Small loss, in a couple of instances, from all I've heard," said Hamish briskly. "I understand the third Mrs. Weston was a devotee of budgie-birds and Christian Science. Havers, as my Highland cousins would stay."

"Furthermore, Pa," I put in, anxious to derail this gloomy train of thought, "she didn't so much leave you as get the push, you know. Be honest, you loathed those budgies. And you had a lot to thank us kids for. Did you know—I'm sure you must have seen it—we had a whole secret code of signals we used to hassle her with? All bland innocence one minute, and the next it was pulled ear-lobes, drooped eyelids, little finger touched to the end of the nose. And her own kid (remember fat Patty?) used to join in. Surely you knew what was going on. No wonder she felt like the victim of a conspiracy. That's exactly what she was."

"Brats," said Hamish admiringly. "You couldn't have been more than seven then, Polly. And you never got caught at it? Dumb insolence, they call it, in the army. Very effective. What else could she do but quit."

"Do you mean to tell me that you little fiends—" began Pa. "And butter wouldn't melt in your smug little mouths the day I told you she was going. So it's you I have to thank for—" He stared at me as if outraged. Then he put down his glass and covered his mouth with his hand to hide a smile.

I was coming out of a Canterbury shoe shop, picking my way with caution around a patch of ice on the pavement, when someone called my name. Across the street, waving a mittened arm, was the familiar, cubic shape of Hermione. She wore a long tartan cape and a broad-brimmed, wimpled hat worthy of the Wife of Bath.

"How nice to run into you!" she shouted, as dozens of French schoolchildren straggled between us on their way to the cathedral in a storm of discarded paper and shrill chatter. "Come and have coffee with me. There's a nice little hotel over there, just outside the precinct." I shifted parcels to look at my watch. "Well, I have to meet Hamish in half an hour—"

"That's right then. Come along," she said crisply. "Don't let's hang about in this wind." The sky was a bold, almost Canadian blue, and there was a sharp wind scouring the streets like a wire broom, driving a thin dust of snow in shifts and eddies over the cobbles. I was not sorry to find myself hustled into the panelled lounge of a dim little hotel that smelled of cats and pork pies. A small coal fire glowed in the grate like a sleepy eye.

"There, that's better," said Hermione, dragging two chairs close to the hearth. She unbuttoned her cape and several layers of cardigans, but left the wimpled hat in position. "Well, my dear, how are you? Ages since we saw you last. (Two coffees, please. And a few biscuits, if you have 'em.) Nan's quite all right now, I suppose?"

"Well, she's still not quite . . . gets tired easily . . . hasn't got her energy back yet, really. The doctor says that's to be expected, though."

"Really? But it must be over a month since—"

"Yes. It was a very mean virus. Left people really low. The rest of us were lucky to escape it. Mind you, we've had our share of suffering. Ever tasted Mrs. Pryde's cooking? It's people like that who keep alive the tradition of British cuisine — she's a master hand with the scorched potato — the soggy cabbage. And the things that woman can do to an innocent lamp chop you'd hardly believe."

"Then you must all of you come over to dinner," declared Hermione, stirring her coffee with a masterful hand. "Shall we say Tues—"

"It's nice of you, but I'm afraid Nan isn't really up to going out yet. Thanks anyway, but . . . as for Pa, he's working hard these days sorting his papers to go into a university archive collection. And his agent's coming down this weekend with crates more of the stuff, so—"

Hermione gave me a sharpish glance. Then from a pocket of her cape she produced a flat hip-flask, uncapped it, and poured a slosh into each of our cups.

"You are naughty," I said with approval. "And inventive. What a combination! — Actually, the gin does wonders for the coffee."

"You think I'm an alcoholic, don't you?" she remarked with a mischievous smile. "But you're wrong, Pol. I don't drink to drown my sorrows — that's what alcoholics do, poor miserable sods, trying to escape their misery. It's quite different in my case, you know. I am happy. I drink to celebrate."

I looked at her curiously. "To celebrate what?"

"Why, life, dear. Life. A tot now and again is not only

fun, it's a sort of act of worship. Not Richard's kind, of course, but worship just the same."

"It must be wonderful to believe in God. That would make everything so simple and easy."

"Oh, you're wrong there. It makes everything very, very hard. Ask Richard some time. No, what's easy is to be like Schiller. He's supposed to have said to God (though why in French I can *not* imagine), "Entre nous, je crois que vous n'existez pas." What superb cheek. Of course that simplifies everything. But life itself — that's what's so marvellous. All we're given. Forty years I was married, you know. (That is, after a youthful mistake with a weight-lifter. But that only lasted a year. I don't count that.) My Kenneth was such a dear man, and I had forty years with him. All that loving friendship. Richness."

"And then he died. How do you work that into the celebration?"

"Nobody ever said good things last forever, did they? The point is, we're given them. And that's not only enough, it's far more than we deserve, yes? Cheers." She emptied her cup and waggled it at the woman behind the bar-counter, who reluctantly left her study of an article on Sid Vicious to shuffle over with more coffee.

"Well, I suppose you'll be going back to your London life one of these days," she said, once more topping up our cups from the flask.

"Yes, in a week or two. Just waiting for Nan to get back properly on her feet. I'd have been off long ago except for that. It's been one thing after another, really . . . " here my voice trailed away rather feebly. "I mean, ever since I came to Seven Oaks, things seem to have detained me here . . . without intending to, I seem to have become involved . . . well, you know what families are."

"That I do. I came down for a week to tidy up after Richard's wife died, and that was twelve years ago. He needs me."

"Does he?" I asked, tempted onto risky ground.

"You must know that. He walks a tightrope in the dark, poor little man. Sooner or later everybody draws away from him. As your family has done."

"Hermione, it's not—"

"Don't say any more. I know how it is."

There was a brief silence. I stared into my coffee-cup. After a moment I cleared my throat to utter some platitude or other, but then I saw that she was smiling to herself, so lost in some thoughts or memories of her own that she was hardly aware I was there. All at once I felt a sort of relief that was almost as good as happiness.

"I do like you, Hermione," I told her warmly.

She looked at me with her keen, percipient old eyes. "That's what people say when what they'd really like to do is explain, or apologize. I know how it is, Pol."

After that, I began in something of a hurry to collect my parcels and hump my coat back on. It is not comfortable to talk for long with anyone as truthful as Hermione. I bundled together my shopping and hurried her out into the street.

"Hamish is waiting for me at the library—afraid I've kept him waiting ages—thanks so much for the coffee. Give my best to Richard, won't you." There are no accidents, we're told. It was undoubtedly my haste to get away (possibly combined with the gin) that made me fail to notice a streak of ice underfoot. I shot forward. My ankle twisted as I struggled to regain balance; then I fell clumsily to the pavement. With a derisive clatter, my cane bounced several feet in the opposite direction.

A passing teenager dressed in studded black plastic, her hair dyed pink and teased into a halo of spikes, bent and picked me up as easily as if I were a child. She and Hermione (who had retrieved the cane) steadied me between them. We all gazed at my ankle, which began to swell visibly even as we looked at it.

"Let's help her to this bench. You hang on here, dear, till I get back. Put your foot up—that's it. I'll run and fetch Hamish. Won't be a minute."

She set off at a rapid jog-trot toward the library. The pink-haired girl offered me a cigarette, and, when I shook my head, a stick of gum. Two boys in wing collars from the King's School, a street violinist, a passing dog, and a fat housewife lingered to watch me watch my ankle swell on the cold bench.

"Rotten luck, innit," the punk girl said kindly. "Them street people want their eads lookin into, not puttin down a bit of sand." "Ass right," agreed the fat woman. "My old Gran, she broke er elbow up the Buttermarket last week. Shockin. I dunno what they do with our rates, I'm sure." "Ah, right you are—ere's the boy friend," said the punk girl. "Ta-ra." She gave me a friendly slap on the shoulder before making off.

Hamish, his face ruddy, plunged out of the car and elbowed his way through my sympathizers. "What the hell have you been doing to yourself?" he demanded breathlessly. Somebody else had asked me the same philosophical question not too long ago, but I couldn't remember where or when. "You're just trying to attract my attention," he said. "Admit it."

The fat woman was smiling broadly. "You wish," I said, glaring at him.

"I'll be off then," Hermione said tactfully. "Give you a ring tonight. Take care."

"Thanks," I mumbled, trying not to sound bitter.

"Ups-a-daisy, then," Hamish said. "Let me have the pleasure of lugging you to the car. We'll stop in at the hospital and get you X-rayed."

Grimacing with the effort not to cry, I waved goodbye to what was left of my audience as the car pulled away. My ankle was now throbbing viciously. "Oh shit," I muttered. "*Shit.*"

"Cheer up," advised Hamish with his grim smile a centimetre wider than usual. "Look at the sunny side, love. Your pa won't be a bit sorry if this means we'll have you around a bit longer. As for me, it will be a treat. A bouquet of goldenrod for the old hay-fever, that's what you are to me, dear. Right? That's better. I hate tears."

When Ralph came down that weekend with Lally, there was a faint but perceptible coolness between him and Pa, and not even her inconsequential chat could cover it. We sat down to dinner and the conversation, punctuated occasionally by sticky little silences, centred on topics of stunning non-interest like Nan's recovery and my sprained ankle.

"Well, lucky it was nothing worse," said Ralph.

"Oh, absolutely," I said.

Pa cleared his throat. Hamish said, "The trouble with Pol is that she's never grateful for small mercies. Like the opportunity to suffer and grow spiritually."

A silence fell. Lally looked studiously at her finger-nails. Ralph cleared his throat.

But Nan had spent several hours in the kitchen that afternoon, and when she came in, smiling, with the big tureen of soup, it was touchingly clear how pleased she was to see Ralph. The soup was egg and lemon, his favourite. It was followed by another dish he liked, beef Stroganoff delicately flavoured with garlic, sour cream, and morels. The cleverness of this choice struck me only near the end of the meal, when I remembered it was also among Pa's favourite main courses. By the time dessert was cleared away—a feathery apricot soufflé (which Pa also liked), his rather remote politeness had warmed a little, and he confided to Ralph how much sorting his papers depressed him.

"Now, I would have thought it would have exactly the opposite effect," said Ralph, lifting his eyebrows. "There it all is—the accomplishment of a distinguished literary life. How many people are there, after all, who can catalogue and weigh up their success like that? What an ego trip you ought to find it."

"Don't bother being polite," grumbled Pa. "It's all just so much dross."

"Come on, Monty, it's not like you to downgrade yourself. Or your art."

"Pah. What does it all amount to, when you get right down to it? Words, words, words. All a lot of nonsense."

"You're not serious. You couldn't be."

Nan now came in with a richly crumbling Stilton. She had lost a little weight and still looked rather pale, but she gave Ralph a sidelong smile as she set down on its board near him his favourite cheese. He paused without self-consciousness to kiss her hand before going on. "I'm perfectly serious. If you had to say which people are most influential —that's to say, most powerful—on this earth, it would have to be writers. They may not sit in the seats of the mighty like politicians or generals, but they shape the perceptions we all live by. Take, for instance, the concept that the sun rises and sets. Every six-year-old today knows the sun does nothing of the kind, and yet we all go on talking about sunrise and sunset. And that's because writers centuries ago implanted that image, and now it's so entrenched it can't be destroyed. So much for science. That's why I say writers are supremely powerful people. Good writers, of course. This Stilton looks superb, Nan."

"I think," said Pa, suddenly casting down his napkin, "that we'll ignore this rather second-rate claret. Cheese like this—the noblest of them all—calls for some of my '67 Crozes. Fetch us up a bottle, would you, Hamish?"

When this was done, and fresh glasses were filled, he lifted his to Ralph and nodded at him quite cordially. Lally, who up to now had eaten very little, now helped herself liberally to cheese. "Yes," she said, "it's quite true, when you come to think of it, about writers. Just imagine how utterly boring life would be sometimes, without books and things to read. At the hairdresser's, for instance, or waiting for the dentist. As for airplanes — why without something to read on them, one could easily go mad worrying about how they stay up. Think of all the crimes that would be committed — all the suicides that would happen — out of sheer boredom—if there were no writers to take our minds off things."

Pa looked at her with delight and began to laugh. Ralph joined in, and Lally beamed all round the table with her delicious smile.

Mrs. Pryde went off that Monday with her daughter's family for a winter holiday in Benidorm, and our char, recently married for the third time, came down with cystitis and retired temporarily from public life. My ankle kept me more or less immobile, and Nan was still not entirely herself. In spite of all this, Pa urged Ralph and Lally to stay on a couple of days into the following week. To do him justice, though, he cheerfully pitched in to help with the domestic chores, though these were as unfamiliar to him as the rites of some remote, exotic tribe. To see him dusting ornaments, or in Laocoön entanglement with the vacuum cleaner, for instance, was an experience it would have been a pity to miss.

The night before they were due to leave, however, Nan looked so tired that Pa pulled off her apron and sent her to bed. She moved slowly out of the kitchen, pausing only long enough to pick up Crackers, her usual night partner, though how she could sleep with that hot, noisily purring bulk like a lead weight on top of her I never could fathom. Hamish collected the dogs and took them out for their last run, while I heaved myself up on a kitchen stool to scrape plates into a bin. Pa, with some perplexity and hesitation, began to stack the dishwasher.

"Where do the cups go?" he asked, peering at the rack

through his bifocals. "No wonder they give degrees these days in the administration of kitchens. Surely none of this sauce muck will come off the forks, will it? I think we'll just throw away our dirty dishes from now on, till Mrs. P. gets back. Ah, the cunning of that fox Lally, pretending to fall asleep over her Courvoisier. And good old Ralph, popping off to bed with a cheery goodnight-all. He seems to think the *elves* clear up after dinner."

"A lot of men have that theory."

Pa paused, a fistful of cutlery in one hand. He appeared to be thinking about something quite other than what we were talking about. His book, I thought tolerantly, or perhaps those eternal papers, now stacked in heaps and bulging out of files all over both studies, where the sorting process seemed to make little or no headway. But when he pulled himself out of this reverie and went back to stacking plates, it was to speak about Ralph.

"You know, Pol, about his problem, I've been—a touch intolerant, perhaps ... it *was*, after all, bad luck about those stocks."

"Was it?"

"Well, granted that the man is prone to plunge ... Just the same, I think now I might have been a bit more ... " Here he glanced at me as if curious to see how I might react to this admission. For my part, I was curious too, and stopped rinsing pots to look at him.

"Are you thinking of helping him out, then, after all?"

"Ah — well — just possibly I might be able to suggest some kind of—"

"Well, that will be a big relief to Lall. And to him too, of course."

"After all, they're old friends. And he's been a valuable agent. I trust him absolutely in my own affairs."

"Yes. He's good about anything that isn't *personal*. Maybe not a bad way to be. It certainly simplifies things. For him, anyway."

"The thing is, though, I think it would be easier all round if I were not the one to reopen the subject. After all, he has his pride. What I'd like you to do before they go tomorrow is just hint to him that if he could bring himself to ask my opinion, I might have one or two useful suggestions about the whole dilemma. Could you do that? I'll suggest they come down to us again in a couple of weeks, and then—"

"I suppose I could do that. But what did you have in mind to do for him, Pa? It seems to have been a lot of money down the drain this time."

"Oh, there may be ways and means . . . some arrangements could perhaps be made," said Pa vaguely. He turned the sauce-boat around in his hands as if interested in its pattern.

"What do you actually think of Ralph?" he asked.

"Think of him? Why, I don't often think of him at all. You know how it is with somebody you've known so long . . . they get sort of indistinguishable from the background. Camouflaged by the daily round, as it were. Not like somebody you meet for the first time—they come on loud and clear as space invaders." Even as I said this, though, Hamish intruded into my mind without knocking, and I remembered that these days he had a way of emerging out of my particular background from time to time in a quite inconvenient sort of way.

"Yes, but you must have some opinion, Pol. He's quite attached to us all, wouldn't you say? I mean genuinely attached. Especially to you girls."

I jerked my mind back to Ralph. "Oh, I suppose he is, in a way. But Ralph's basically a very self-centred man."

"No more than most childless people are. It's a pity he and Lally never—"

"It's not a pity at all, Pa. There was nothing accidental about it—surely you knew that. They're childless because Ralph insisted on it. Lally told me once she wouldn't have minded having one . . . and for her to say that . . . anyhow, she's had one abortion that I know about."

"I still say it's a pity. A man doesn't know what family means until he has one. Look at those brothers of yours. And their dull wives, such excruciating bores I can hardly remember their names. Their total accomplishments are nil, but they've produced a few nice brats, haven't they? Ralph would have been a different man if he—"

"Oh Pa, come on. Generating young doesn't build character. It just overpopulates the damn globe."

With a shrug Pa went back to racking plates. "Have it your way. But what I sometimes think is that Ralph and Lally haven't maybe been the best combination. They're too much alike, or something. Ralph would be quite different if he — I mean he needs — oh well, maybe you're right. I just wondered what your basic impression of him was. You're a pretty shrewd little judge of character. Sometimes, that is."

"Thanks," I said tartly. The temptation was strong to add, "Look, approach him yourself. Leave me out of this." But then I thought of Lally. And of Ralph, kissing Nan's hand for the Stilton. I had to admit that, whatever his faults, he was after all as fond of us as it was in his nature to be. So I said instead, "All right, Pa. I'll speak to him before they go tomorrow."

A couple of days later Pa went to Paris for the inside of a week, to attend a PEN conference, and Nan, Hamish, and I at once dropped into lazy, even supine, habits. We slept late. Meals dwindled to pick-up snacks in the kitchen, and the vacuum cleaner was left strictly to its own devices. A deep quiet settled over the half-empty house, broken only by the occasional drowsy whirr of Nan's spinning-wheel. The dogs snored by the fire. Hamish nodded over the newspaper. Dust settled on the papers in both studies. Except that the hall clock ticked on, the three of us might have been under a sleeping-spell like the characters in a fairy tale. When the phone rang late one evening it made me jump and startled Crackers, who had been asleep on my lap, into one of his flying leaps.

"Who the hell is that, at this hour?" grumbled Hamish. He tossed down his book and stumped off. The silence regrouped itself. I settled back comfortably in Pa's big armchair, pushing the hassock that supported my swollen ankle a little nearer to the fire. It had sunk to a red glow, but I was too lazy to drag a log out of the basket to revive it. The only sound in the room was Crackers' tongue busily grooming his white bosom by way of restoring dignity after his recent flight. Sleet began a delicate rapping on the window-pane. I glanced at my watch, wondering idly what could be keeping Hamish so long. It was more than half an hour before he came back into the room with a face so tightly locked I knew at once that something had happened.

"What is it, Hamish?"

"Call from Canada. My brother in Halifax."

"Oh? Not bad news, I hope."

"Not exactly. She was ninety. My mother, I mean. In a nursing-home for the last four years."

"She's gone, then? I'm sorry."

He stood looking blankly into the fire as if waiting for something to happen.

"I don't think I've ever heard you mention her," I said tentatively.

"No. We never were what you could call close. She was not the kind of person that . . . I mean, she was a woman completely without tenderness." Squatting, he pulled a log from the basket and tossed it on the fire, producing a red eruption of sparks. "Fiercely upright, tough, strong, she was all of that. Made men out of her sons by sheer iron will-power. That is, she did with three of them. My two older brothers are doctors. The youngest is a provincial cabinet minister. I was her one failure."

"Don't be silly, Hamish. After all, you have two degrees."

"Certificates of competence in nothing that matters, Pol."

Stiffly he lowered himself to sit on the hearth-rug and hunch over his own knees. His face was a little turned from me. What he said seemed quite random, even irrelevant, until I realized he was not speaking to me at all, but addressing himself, as people do in shock.

"Funny, all this news does is remind me how bleak and poor our house was, as if it expressed her whole personality. The darned socks. Margarine scraped thin on the bread. Porridge and salt fish—we lived on that all winter. My father was only just literate, you know. He worked in a cannery all his life. He was a gentle, defeated man, and she had nothing but contempt for him. She was like dry ice smouldering in the house. Learning, in her view, was the pathway to success—that was its only value to her, and she forced her obsession on us without mercy of any kind. My brothers sat up over their books till all hours. Fergus ruined his eyes — there was no money for glasses — and Sandy wrote his finals with pneumonia—nobody dared to fail. She caught me once trying to sneak out of the house instead of doing my homework. I was a big lad of thirteen, but she took a stick to me until it broke in her hand. Next morning it was off to school with my welts and a swollen eye. The Children's Aid would be after her today, but in that community she was much admired. What a woman. You couldn't like her, but by God you had to have a certain respect. I ran off to war like a kid playing hookey, but I came home in the end, and under that grim eye, off I went on my new plastic foot to library school. Yes, she was one tough woman; I'm surprised, really, she ever allowed herself to die. Not that, in a way, she ever will, as far as I'm concerned."

There was a silence. Sleet was now lashing the window in steely gusts.

"Most parents are like that, more or less, aren't they," I suggested. "Between the enormous influence they have when we're too young to resist, and the genes they've handed on to us willy-nilly, how can they ever die? They can be six feet under and we'll still be sweating away trying to please or satisfy them—and never, ever, really making it. It will be that way with us and Pa, for sure. Whatever we do—wherever we go. Most of all maybe when we rebel. And you can't even hate them for it, because how can they help being what they are?"

"Was it rebellion, then, for you with Bard?" he asked, looking intently into the fire.

I felt the reckless impulse to be honest both with him and with myself. "Of course a lot of it was obsession. Sexual. Your basic Jocasta complex. But of course even if I'd known this at the time I never would have admitted it."

"Family ties," he shrugged. "Like nooses, aren't they. Nobody can escape the damn things."

"Well, my mother tried. I think maybe she thought she could liberate us as well as herself—I mean by taking off the way she did. Specially from me, I think when I'm really down. Because I was a mistake. She was pretty detached from me right from the start. By the time I was two she'd been planning her getaway for a long time. But the crazy thing is, when she did finally quit, all it did was pull Olivia after her, and lock the boys into kind of Siamese twins. And it orphaned me. Nan became my mother. And of course that's why I've been—I mean it's made the usual bond of sisters—oh, the hell with it. Why am I drivelling on like this? Do you want a drink, Hamish?"

"No."

"Neither do I, really."

"It's late. I suppose we'd better go up."

There was another, easier silence. The fire sank into

itself with a soft, collapsing noise like the inarticulate sound made by a sleeper.

"But I wish I could have loved her," he said.

"Yes."

"She didn't really want that, of course. But it lays a lot of guilt on me, just the same, that I never could."

"Yes, it would, I suppose. Unfair, isn't it."

"Well, she would have thought it a sinful waste of money for me to fly back for the funeral. So I don't need to be racked with guilt about *that*."

"Better than nothing, isn't it."

He had turned his face away again, but one of his hands reached out to clasp my good foot near him on the hearth-rug. It was a grip so firm and so silently eloquent that for days afterward I seemed to feel it there, holding me fast.

Nan tried to help me pass the time while my ankle healed by teaching me to knit, but I was not a good student. The needles in my hands might as well have been chopsticks for all the help they were in my attempt to make a scarf. Time after time her patient fingers put the work right, but, left to get on with it by myself, I soon got into fearful complications, once even knitting the scarf to the sweater I was wearing. Crossly I cut myself free with wide snaps of the scissors.

"It's hopeless, Nan. The womanly crafts just aren't for me. You have to have more confidence either in craft or in womanhood than I've got. And I'm far too old now to change, even if I wanted to."

She was at the workroom window, which she had opened wide to admit the fresh air of a mild, spring-like day. As usual, she gave no sign of having heard me. The knitting in her own hand hung idle as she looked out at the leafless web of the trees shining against the clear, pale-blue sky. Her large, calm eyes were focussed on the air as if it were a tangible thing. She was smiling faintly, and her fine, fair hair stirred a little in the flutter of a light wind. She seemed as I looked at her to be listening with some inner ear to the whole pulsing, swinging rhythm of the earth spinning in its ozone globe. Her eyes were exactly the light blue of the sky.

The phone's double ring sounded faintly in the distance. The empty house seemed to trivialize the sound into all but total irrelevance. On the third ring I said vaguely, "Where's Hamish, then?"

There was a pause, as if it took time for her to hear the question. Then she said, "He took the dogs," and turned back to the window.

"Damn." Awkwardly I got up and mustered my cane. There was no use expecting any action from Nan. Telephones were of no interest or concern whatever to her: she simply ignored all calls, and of course never made any herself. This oddity was ridiculous, of course, and very inconvenient to the rest of us; but as I left her looking out at the luminous day I wondered whether Bell's invention wasn't after all a rather overrated affair. None the less, I dutifully picked up the hall phone and spoke our number into it.

"Polly?" said Pa's voice rather loudly.

"Hullo, Pa. Where are you—still in Paris?"

"No, I'm in London. At the club. I had dinner here with Ralph last night. We had a long, serious talk. And I think a constructive one." How confident and full of vitality he sounded. It was the warm, rich-timbred voice of a man half his age.

"That's good, Pa."

"We've—discussed a number of things. I've made a few suggestions . . . he'll need some time, of course, to consider all the angles, but on the whole he . . . seems receptive. Anyhow, among the things we discussed was their flat. I'm proposing that he sell the leasehold, which is worth quite a bit, and use the money to pay off most of his debts. There should be enough left to put a down payment on some little place for them in Canterbury or somewhere near by. Of course, that's no long-term solution, but it's a start. I've suggested he put an estate agent onto it right away, and while he's attending to all that, I'll bring Lally down with me. I've invited the two of them to stay with us while they hunt for a place of their own. The whole thing will be easier on Lally that way."

"Yes, I suppose it will. She's such a complete Londoner, though. I mean small-town life—I can't see her doing Meals on Wheels, can you, or making jam for the W.I.?"

"Oh, don't start raising frivolous objections at this stage, Polly. The point is, their lives have got to change radically, and I am trying to help them make the adjustments. Thinking what's best in the end for all concerned."

"Yes, but Pa—"

"Now, I'll be there with Lall, probably on Wednesday. Say Wednesday, if you don't hear from me before then. She'll have all her clothes with her, so make sure the wardrobe in the big guest room is cleared right out. Put flowers on the dresser. And tell Nan to make something nice for dinner. Lally likes chicken. Ralph will be able to join us by the weekend, I should think. And it would be best, Pol, if you didn't discuss any of this with Lally just yet. She isn't capable of understanding all the ins and outs of the situation—it would just upset her. All right?"

"You mean she doesn't know yet the flat is being sold? Well, you must know what you're doing, Pa, but I—"

"Good girl. See you Wednesday, then."

He hung up briskly. I put down the phone. As soon as his voice was gone, I was left with a vague sense that more was going on than his words actually conveyed, and I wondered rather uneasily what it might be. However, living with Pa never left one with much time for idle speculation.

I went off to give Nan the news she was to get ready for long-term house guests. That would bring her down to earth for a while.

When I hobbled downstairs to greet Lally, it struck me that she had grown smaller. She stood in the hall looking rather forlorn amid a sea of luggage, with sequins of melted snow winking on her fur coat, and Darling tucked under one arm like a velvet muff. Her newly set and sprayed hair looked like a silver wig in the overhead light. She turned a cool, scented cheek to me and I put a kiss on it. Her gloved hand felt light and thin in mine.

"Well, Polly," she said. "You must think we're like some bothersome disease, we recur so often."

"Nonsense!" cried Pa from the door, where he was stamping snow vigorously off his shoes. His face, with cheeks red from the cold, radiated energy and confidence. "We need you to liven up this mausoleum." He deftly removed her coat and gave it to Hamish to hang in the cloakroom. She was wearing a beautifully fitted dark-blue dress that gave her fine skin a pearly pallor. This new look of delicacy and woe, I had to admit, was highly becoming, and it was evident that Pa thought so too. He pushed her favourite chair close to the fire and pulled the heavy curtains close to exclude any possible draught.

"Now, Lally dear," he said, rubbing his hands. "A nice dry martini is what you need, right? Hamish knows just how you like it. A twist of lemon, isn't it? That's the girl. You tuck into that."

When the drink was placed on a little table at her elbow she did manage at last to muster a wan smile. Darling underwent his usual inspection from our dogs (who always affected surprise — even disbelief — at his size, shape, and very existence), and then hopped into her lap, where he settled with a sniffling sigh. Nan brought in a dish of hot canapés and offered it to Lally with her slow smile.

"No thanks, dear, I'm eating less these days. Training for poverty. Not that I intend to give up drink, you understand—just that if it comes to a choice, I prefer it to food."

"Come on, Lally, enough of this Little Match Girl act," protested Pa. "Things aren't that bad, and you know it."

"I know absolutely nothing about it, Monty. Ralph has gone all silent and tight around the jaws. He may have plans, but I have no idea what they are, I can assure you. As far as I know, once the flat's sold, we'll have to live on thin air."

"My dear woman—" began Pa, but she went on, fixing a plaintive gaze on me from under her blue eyelids. "We're apparently meant to live in some appalling two-up-and-two-down near the tannery, Pol, in rooms so small they make you want to scream, and eat fish-fingers for the rest of our lives."

"Lalage," said Pa sternly.

"Well?"

"Stop this at once. You should know Ralph—and come to that, me—better than that."

"I know him better than anyone should know anybody, Monty." There was something genuinely and sharply bitter in her usually soft voice. Her hand trembled a little as she set down her drink.

"Just believe me, we're doing our level best to make sure of your comfort," went on Pa more gently. "It's going to be all right, my dear. Trust me. Relax. Your worries are over, Lally. It's a sign of old age, you know, to assume that when things change, it's always for the worse. No, don't you believe it. These changes are going to be creative. Exciting."

"Also good for rheumatism and falling hair," added Hamish, setting down her refilled glass. Pa darted him an irritable glance, which he ignored. Nan picked up her tray, but as she made for the door, Pa stopped her with a gesture.

"Hold on just a second," he said. "Lally, I have a little

something here for you. Not exactly a present, because they were yours to begin with. But a little offering, just the same, to someone who's been dear to me for many years."

And from his pocket he produced three faded little jewellers' boxes, each holding in its velvet slit one of Lally's old-fashioned dinner rings. She looked at them dumbfounded, and I shared some of her astonishment. The gift and the tribute together had a certain drama it was impossible to miss, and I glanced at Pa in open curiosity. Among other things, I wondered why he had made a point of Nan's presence. But no answers were apparent anywhere in Pa's smiling face. I could only ask myself, baffled, "Well, what have we here?"

As we went into the dining-room, he threw an arm across my shoulders in an exuberant hug. "Ah, it's lovely to be home," he said. "Home with my girls, while I still have them, eh Pol?" He nipped ahead then to pull out Lally's chair, but she paused at the door to say to me in a low voice, "How lovely of Monty, about these rings. Nobody's ever in my whole life done anything so sweet for me." And I saw that her eyes were full of tears.

Ralph was expected by tea-time on Monday, but the dinner hour came and went with no word from him. Lally sipped her demitasse by the fire with no sign of concern, but Pa kept going to the window to peer out at the thick, yellowish fog that had rolled in from the Channel hours before. Time and again he prowled out to the hall to listen for the Rover's arrival. Each time he did so, Nan looked up from her knitting, her wide forehead creasing in a frown.

"They say the roads are dreadful," he fretted. "Ralph's a good driver, but the A.A. calls this the worst situation for years. Still, if he had the good sense not to start out at all, why hasn't he called us?"

"He's probably caught in some miles-long balls-up," said

Hamish, catching my eye. "At the Dartford Tunnel, perhaps. You know what *that* can be like, even on a perfectly clear day."

"More likely he's cosily tucking into a good dinner at some roadside hotel," remarked Lally calmly. "He'll call later, after his brandy."

"Speaking of which—" said Pa, going to the decanter.

"Yes, please," said Lally.

"No, thanks," Hamish and I said together.

"How can we pass the time while we wait?" Pa asked us fretfully. "I hate these gaps." He rummaged with a restless hand through the drawer where we kept various parlour games and packs of cards. "Not bridge—we want something silly."

"All the games I know are silly, specially bridge," said Lally. "But I have a tarot pack upstairs. If someone will run up and get it, I'll tell everybody's fortune, if you like."

"Well," said Pa, gazing at her appreciatively, "you yourself are a perfect Belladonna—the Lady of Situations, eh? But fortune-telling—no. Too absurd altogether."

"Absurd?" said Hamish. "It makes my Celtic blood creep. I believe in it absolutely when it's done by someone with the sight."

"What, you actually go for divination? Palmistry, tea-leaves, and all that? Shame on you," said Pa roundly.

"It makes as much sense as anything else, doesn't it? The theory that everything is fore-ordained, that is."

"Poppycock. There's no divinity that shapes our ends. We do that ourselves, for better or worse, as soon as we're out of our cradles."

"You like to think so. But what do we know about it, after all?"

"As a student of human nature, I know enough."

"Well, of course, you couldn't write novels if you didn't believe it's ego, not Fate, that makes the world go round. Your whole premise is that there's a connection between cause and effect. But as far as I can tell there's no link at all. That's why people read fiction—for comfort."

"Will-power," began Pa, "the power of personality — Wait. Was that—?"

He darted out to the hall, listened for a second, then came back to wander once more to the window and stare out at the blind presence of the fog. "Do sit down, Pa," I complained. "You're making us all nervous."

"If he doesn't believe in the unforeseeable, why is he so much like a cat on hot bricks?" Hamish asked me under his breath.

"Don't ask me," I muttered, because it was one of the questions that had been on my mind all evening, even though I agreed with Pa entirely about cause and effect, and had no time at all for fortune-tellers.

The hall clock struck the quarter after eleven, and Lally, yawning, announced she was going to bed. A moment later we all heard the crunch of tires on gravel and the muffled slam of a car door.

"Ah!" cried Pa triumphantly. He hurried to fling open the front door. Ralph came in, accompanied like a stage devil by a curling wisp or two of fog. He dropped his two leather cases on the hall carpet and rubbed both lean hands over his face with a groan of fatigue.

"Sorry to be so late. But it's been six bloody *hours* from the South Circular. The fog's lifting now, but from Rochester on, the visibility's been practically nil. Of course, once I got that far, there was no point in turning back."

"Come on in, my dear chap," urged Pa. "A stiff drink is what you need. Fly to the kitchen and get Ralph a bite of supper, Nan. Well, we've all been rather worried. Thank God you're here in one piece."

Ralph detained Nan briefly with a kiss, and then saluted Lally and me, but in a much more perfunctory style than usual. He looked very tired, and even when stretched out on the sofa with a drink he seemed, I thought, oddly unrelaxed. If he noticed the rings restored to Lally's hands, he made no sign; indeed, he seemed to avoid looking at her altogether.

"Yes, it's good to have you home safe," said Pa, giving himself another brandy. "Where the heart is, eh? Cosy to be all of us here together."

"Very cosy," said Ralph.

"How's your drink—all right like that?"

"Very nice, thanks."

There was an awkward little pause. 'Well, after all,' I thought, 'it can't be easy for Ralph to have his money problems taken in hand by one of his own clients, and everybody in the house aware of it. Sticky for anyone. And men aren't good at being grateful for that kind of help. I just hope it doesn't mess things up between him and Pa over the long haul.'

When Nan carried in a steaming tray with rolls, soup, and a dish of scrambled eggs tossed with bits of smoked salmon, he thanked her absently but put it aside while he finished the second whisky Pa had pressed on him.

"Now, you must be hungry, Ralph," he said robustly. "Let's see you destroy that food. It looks very nice, I must say. Wasn't aware we had any smoked salmon. *We* weren't offered any at dinner, I can tell you."

"I'm not very hungry, unfortunately," said Ralph. "Maybe I'll have just a bit of the soup. It's lovely, Nan, but I'm a bit done up."

"Well, in that case—" said Pa jovially. He took possession of the scrambled eggs and gobbled them down with zest. Nan waited patiently at the door for the tray, silent as usual, with Crackers wreathing himself in purring circles around her legs. From time to time Ralph stole a quick glance at her as if his attention had been drawn to something new about her; but she looked just as always, calm, detached, hair fly-away, apron crumpled.

"Let's see what's going on out there," said Pa, and drew

the window-curtains open. The fog had completely and arbitrarily vanished. A black and gold midnight stood there, framed in dramatic clarity. The sky was embossed with large, bright stars, and a brilliant moon flooded the bare garden with its disembodied light. We all stared at it, enchanted by the transformation. But when we turned away from the window at last, I saw that once more Ralph was looking at Nan.

" 'My high charms work ... ' " said Pa, slowly drawing the curtains shut again. "Ah, what an old necromancer God is."

"It was Prospero who bragged like that, not God," I said.

But Pa was drawing Lally to her feet. "Off to bed with you, my love," he said benignly. "And a good night to all, especially the traveller."

Floods of rain descended over the southeast counties in the first week of February, all but obliterating the countryside. The windows of Seven Oaks streamed so heavily that the familiar shapes of trees and paths in the garden trembled and blurred into ambiguity. Even the boundary between indoors and outdoors became indefinite when a loose roof-tile admitted rain extensively into my attic bedroom.

The dogs came in drenched and left muddy paw-prints all over the kitchen floor, but Mrs. Pryde and her daughter, their noses peeling with sunburn, took all this in their stride. They reported that it was good to be back—all that sun, enough to kipper you alive, they said, and nothing but that oily foreign muck to eat. Over their mugs of strong tea they looked out with something close to satisfaction at the leaden curtain of rain outside the kitchen window.

For the first time in months I began to sleep badly, sometimes waking in the small hours to sit bolt upright, my heart racing in causeless excitement or alarm. Then I would find myself unable to get back to sleep, but would lie there entangled in ridiculous, irrelevant memories that proposed themselves like riddles. One of these, for example, centred about a fight I had twenty years ago with Olivia, which made as little sense now as it had then. Her part (Helena) in *A Midsummer Night's Dream* seemed to me at the time a better one than mine (Hermia), for which Pa had cast me. This irritant was no doubt compounded by her costume, which was prettier than mine, and the fact that at fifteen she had a figure, while I was still flat as a paper doll. In any case, when at rehearsal she put just a shade too much emphasis into calling me "you counterfeit, you puppet", I flew at her in a rage, clawing and kicking, and Pa had to pull me off her like a furiously hissing little cat. "You are much too *passionate*, child," he cried, giving me a shake. This only enraged me further, and I bit him. In the end he recast me as Puck, whose costume was a boring tunic, and I had a whole new part to learn, so the contest was a draw. But what could possibly be the point of this random recollection, I wondered, watching the window whiten with morning. Pa could certainly not reproach me now for passion in any form. But for the rest of the day I couldn't help feeling a certain nostalgia for that fiery little rebel that used to be me.

Day after day the downpour drummed steadily on the roof and hissed down the chimneys. It streamed in a wet deluge from the guttering and pattered all night from the eaves. In these drenched conditions, it was not surprising that Ralph and Lally only once went to Canterbury to look at houses, or that they came home from that excursion silent and exceedingly glum. We all sat about apathetically by the hour flicking through magazines or watching television, like passengers stranded in mid-life at some boring existential air terminal. After a week of this, I was driven to knock on the door of Pa's study with a reckless disregard of the consequences.

He looked up frowning from the pile of old letters he was

sorting through, but at once pulled off his glasses, saying, "Come in, my dear. Give me an excuse — any excuse — to stop doing this."

"I thought we might go into Canterbury, just the two of us. I've got a bad case of cabin fever. There's a concert at four at the cathedral . . . it's something to do. I've told the others it's madrigals, so no one else wants to come."

"Yes, let's. As you say, the house seems to have shrunk a bit lately. Come on then—where's your diving-suit?" We muffled up in macs and boots and slipped out. The others barely glanced up to notice our departure.

Soon we were out in a sodden landscape where fields, trees, and sky had all been leached of color and reduced to various shades of grey. The wheels of cars ahead of us on the road cast up great, smoking fans of water from deep puddles. Trucks coming in the opposite direction periodically deluged our windscreen with a blinding cascade. Pa drove with circumspection, peering through the wipers' two clear segments and occasionally muttering to himself.

"Pa, there's something I want to say."

"Is there, my dear?"

"Yes. I've been . . . I mean, I haven't had a chance to talk to you privately lately, and—"

"Well?"

"Well, it's about Ralph."

"What about him?"

I shifted in the tight embrace of my seat-belt. "Well, this may sound a bit—I feel a bit of a peeping Tom, but—"

"Oh, do get on with it, child."

I took a breath and plunged in. "Well, Nan's making him a Fair Isle sweater. You remember he asked her to, though I've never seen him wear anything as folksy as that."

"Is this about Ralph's taste in clothes, then?"

"Hold on. Yesterday morning I passed her door and she was measuring it on him — holding it up to his chest, you know—and he put his arms around her and gave her a kiss."

Pa darted me a sharp look. "Did he now? And is that such big news?"

"Yes, but Pa, it was not just—it was—what I mean is, it was *sexual*."

How ridiculous my piping voice sounded, like some priggish child tattling to a teacher, and all about an incident as trivial as a kiss. But the little scene had stamped itself into my mind with morbid vividness: his mouth holding hers, his thin hand moving slowly down her back till it reached her buttock, which he gripped firmly to him. And she was perfectly still, not simply passive or unresisting, but immobile, like someone entranced. It was not, I was sure, something that had ever happened between them before.

"It bothers me, Pa," I said bluntly, "because it's tampering with her. It's wrong, like meddling with a child. She hasn't got much grasp of things, maybe, but to her Ralph is a kind of uncle, and furthermore, he's married to Lally. This new ploy is bound to upset her."

"My dear girl, do I have to remind you that Nan is thirty-seven? As for the rest of it, I trust old Mother Nature. The good old libido can settle any problems of that kind."

"Look, you are actually shocking me. You know as well as I do that Nan isn't up to dealing with a casual pass—or, worse, a serious one."

"Now what makes you so sure of that? Something instinctive—something perfectly natural like that—"

He broke off here to hunch forward attentively over the wheel as we crossed a small bridge over the Stour. It was normally a domestic, weedy little river of very modest dimensions and habits, but today it was swollen high, its brown waters roped with a powerful, thickly twisting current. The rush of it could be heard even through our closed windows. Pa waited until we were safely across before he went on, "My dear, you're fussing about nothing."

"Pa, I am trying to tell you that kiss was not nothing."

"Well, what of it?"

I stared at him. "You mean it's all right with you if Ralph—if he takes Nan to bed under the same roof as his wife—are you just going to smile blandly and say, well, Nan is thirty-seven, it's all perfectly natural?"

"Both of those things are true, you know."

"I don't understand you at all, Pa. All this laissez-faire isn't like you."

"Look, Polly, why do you have to assume we're talking about a cold-blooded seduction here? Why shouldn't his intentions be perfectly honourable? He's always been fond of her. It's time for her now—she likes Ralph—and why on earth shouldn't they marry, if they want to?"

"Marry! Why Pa, are you out of your head? What about Lally?"

"What about her?" he asked imperturbably.

"Oh, how can you say that! She would be *devastated*. They've been together—what is it—thirty-odd years!"

"Well, perhaps it's time for a change."

"Oh, come on, Pa. Lally's attached to him. She cares a lot. Surely you know that."

"They aren't married," he reminded me.

"Oh, of course they are, after all this time."

"She's used to his little flings, you know. That may be all this is, I suppose. And even if it's something more, I wouldn't call theirs a really deep bond, would you? Now be honest."

"Well," I said reluctantly, "it's not Tristan and Isolde, but all the same, they *are* attached."

"What a romantic you are, Pol, and after all that's happened to you, too—it's quite incredible. Now to me it's nothing but claptrap to say that Lally would be 'devastated'. She would be nothing of the kind. You know her better than that. As long as she's comfortable, the world could end and she'd hardly notice. As for feelings, she has about the same emotional range as that pug of hers. In the event of Ralph's marriage, he'd no doubt make some kind of modest provision for her, and that would be that."

"You talk about 'Ralph's marriage' as if . . . " Even as I said this, my heart began to knock about in a sharp, irregular sort of way. "You've discussed this with him," I said stupidly. "You've *arranged* it, haven't you? You've bought him. That's the truth, isn't it?"

"Now see here, Polly. All I've done is make Ralph aware that Nan will be provided for very comfortably after my death or when she marries. As you well know, I've been concerned for a long time about her future. It will be easy enough to protect her money from any possible—er—indiscretion on his part. And what on earth is wrong with a husband like Ralph—a kind old friend who will look after her, and whom she's fond of?"

"A selfish philanderer who'll almost certainly make her miserable. Somebody who'll take her as part of a package deal. Isn't that more like it?"

"My dear, nine marriages out of ten are compromises approximately like that."

I shook my head. "Pa, this isn't a compromise. It's an arrangement. And it's monstrous."

"Monstrous? It's nothing of the kind. Don't you know that most arranged marriages are highly successful?"

"But to manipulate them like that—no, it is monstrous. You're playing God again, and—"

"Polly, will you kindly use your wits. I am manipulating nothing and nobody here. They are both adults. What they do is entirely up to them. Who's forcing anything on anybody? They are perfectly free agents. And there are no serious obstacles at all. The age difference is neither here nor there — in fact, in view of her attachment to me, it seems quite suitable. There's a lot of genuine affection on both sides, as you know. More than that, perhaps. Have you forgotten how she reacted when I said I'd see him starve?—No, my dear. Far from being miserable, I can see her as entirely happy, living a quiet married life in the country somewhere and—"

"Look, Pa. The point is, would he take Nan with no money at all? You know he wouldn't."

"A rhetorical question like that simply has no validity at all. It's like those theoretical situations in that silly game Ethics, or whatever it's called. Doesn't apply here at all."

"But this isn't a game, Pa: it's somebody's life."

"I'm well aware of that."

I could find no answer to this but a baffled silence. He pulled up the car's hand-brake and I saw that we had arrived in a city car-park near the cathedral without my noticing it.

"Well, I give you fair warning, Pa, I don't like this, and I'll have nothing to do with it. Absolutely nothing."

"How very scrupulous of you. A little late in the day, though, isn't it, for all this moral integrity? If you were the parent of a person like Nan . . . well, of course you've never had a child, so—But I hope I can at least trust you not to interfere here, Pol. Believe me, if I thought Nan would be unhappy, I'd put a stop to it immediately. But I don't think so at all. On the contrary, in fact. So I intend to let things take their course, whatever that might be. You know I love her. Let her have this chance. You must see that it's a better future for her than . . . I mean, after I'm gone she'll have no one. I promise you that if the time should come when I see any threat to her peace of mind— well, that would be entirely different."

"You do promise," I said, catching at his arm as he opened the car door.

"I give you my solemn word. And you will promise me not to interfere, Polly. After all, you haven't made such a brilliant success of your own life. I think you can safely leave this to me."

We looked at each other.

"As long as Nan's happy. But I warn you, Pa, if—"

"That's agreed, then."

He stepped out of the car and deftly unfurled an umbrella for himself before opening one for me. I ducked under its shelter clumsily. The rain drummed down so powerfully it tilted the dome to one side. I had to cling hard to bring the curved grip upright with both my hands, and for a moment the downpour beat into my eyes so I could hardly see.

The rain persisted in its dreary, drumming fashion day after day. I did my best to put that conversation with Pa out of my mind entirely, on the grounds that in weather like this no one could possibly keep a sense of proportion about anything. Aware that I was more than ordinarily irritable, I tried to avoid communication with anyone, even the cat. When a bridge game was organized one afternoon, by tacit agreement nobody asked me to join it, and I retreated to the furthermost limits of the sitting-room as soon as conversation and laughter began to rise noisily around the card-table. Pa was making Lally scream with laughter over a tale of the sexual misfortunes of a friend of theirs. Even from the other end of the room I could not escape it entirely.

"And then he said, 'Well, honestly, I think the least you two could do is *stop* while I'm talking to you—'" Here he had to stop himself, hugging his own ribs and rocking to and fro in ecstasy.

"Come on," said Ralph impatiently. "Are we playing this rubber or not?"

"Not," said Hamish.

"Darling, you're terribly wicked about poor Rupert," gasped Lally, reaching over to squeeze Pa's hand.

"You stimulate me, that's why," said Pa, wiping his eyes. "You're the only woman I know who understands how divinely funny sex is."

As they so often seemed to be these days, Hamish's hard

blue eyes were on me with a sort of dogged patience I found oppressive. He tossed down his cards now and came over to the corner where I was trying to read.

"Why don't we go into town and see a movie," he suggested. "We wouldn't have to neck, but it might give us a laugh anyway."

"Oh, the flicks in that Canterbury place are always at least three years old."

"But there's my manly charm to make up for that."

"Hamish, you're altogether resistible."

Ralph had got up from the table to wander over to the drinks tray, and then away from it. Hamish stood looking at me with his head a little on one side like a bird considering a not very attractive worm. "You're ruder than usual," he said. "What's making you so scratchy?" Without waiting for an answer he turned away and asked whether anybody else would like to see a film. Lally accepted at once and drifted off to get ready — a process we all knew could take half an hour. Hamish stood at the window waiting for her patiently, chin lifted, whistling tranquilly. He did not glance at me.

I struggled out of my chair, tossed down my book, and wandered off to find Nan, whom I hadn't seen all day. To my surprise I found the door of her workroom not only closed but locked. There was a long pause before she answered my knock. Then she widened the door to admit me with some reluctance. Her face looked heavy and small-eyed with a sort of mute misery that made me suddenly fiercely angry.

"What's the trouble, love?" I asked, closing the door with care behind me.

She turned away without answering.

"Tell me," I persisted gently. She still said nothing, only fumbled the shuttle of her loom in slow hands.

"Is it Ralph?"

"Yes," she said, only half audibly.

"Ah. Well, what about him? Come on, tell me."

"Is it bad—" she began, and then stopped.

"He's been after you. And you want to know is that bad?"

She nodded.

"Well, I'm hardly the person to ask, am I, not with my—" From the hall Lally called musical goodbyes, and the front door banged behind her and Hamish. As I looked at Nan's lowered head, another flash of acute exasperation swept over me and I burst out, "Look, it's not a question of bad or good. Ralph and Lally are both free, aren't they? I mean, that's clear enough these days. All that matters is, do you really want him?"

"Oh yes," she said. "Oh yes."

"Well, if you feel like that, go ahead. Take what you want. Everybody else does. You can have him if you like. As long as you don't trust him you'll be all right."

Well before this was properly out, I wished it unsaid. Biting my tongue I stood there a moment trying to shake off a quite dire sense of the danger in words that should never have been spoken. But how much of my advice she had taken in or understood it was impossible to tell. In any case, I didn't linger to try. Driven by a frantic kind of bored impatience I was already halfway down the hall in search of boots and a mac. A long, wet, purgatorial walk in the rain felt like a necessity.

"Come on, Pa, just what the hell are you up to with Lally? Are you actually thinking of—why did you give her those rings?"

I woke next morning to find myself involved in this monologue which had jumped into my mind the instant after a dream vacated it: a ridiculous scenario in which my surgeon, dressed as Father Christmas, threw my cane away saying, "You're not allowed to have this any more."

A bright yellow light shone behind my print curtains. I

lay there for a moment looking at it in some disbelief. There
was no sound of rain, though I could hear a gusty wind
blowing. Someone was whistling gaily in the distance. Tossing back the blankets I padded to the window and opened
the curtains. Sunlight, warm and lavish, instantly fell over
me like a warm garment. The sky, on which a few little
puffs of white cloud floated innocently, was a bland and
radiant blue. Below me in the garden Nan, bare-headed in
her old sweater and cords, stood hands in pockets, serenely
contemplating the day. All that was left of the deluge was
a residual glitter on bushes, boughs, and grass. Green
shoots were spearing up out of the wet black earth. A skein
of small birds flew by on the wind. Our two dogs plunged
hilariously in and out of the shrubbery, their coats shining
like jet in the clear light.

I tapped on the window and waved to Nan, who lifted a
cheerful face and waved both hands in return. The red head
and stocky form of Hamish carrying two large baskets
appeared beside her, and he looked up to shout, "Get up,
lazy-bones. We're going into the village to shop. You've got
five minutes."

Five minutes later I was bundling myself into the car
after them, buttoning my jacket with one hand and grasp-
ing in the other a new-baked brioche to eat on the way.

"What's the big rush?" I wanted to know.

"Ducks," said Hamish. "A desire has been expressed for
canard à l'orange, and our mission is to grab three of the
brutes from the butcher for tonight, before he sells them
to anyone else."

The bright day with its gusts of fresh wind seemed to
give all three of us an almost heady feeling of well-being
as we bowled along. I munched my brioche greedily. Hamish whistled like a blackbird. In the back seat Nan hugged
Boris and Ivan, one in each arm. Once in the village, we
captured our birds without difficulty, to Nan's great satisfaction. "Nice duck for Ralph," she said, swinging the

heavy basket gaily. We separated then while Hamish made for the shoemaker with a brogue's worndown heel to be replaced. "I won't be long," he said, "and then I'll buy you two a coffee at the Swan. See you there in half an hour."

Nan and I idled along the High Street to amuse ourselves by looking into shop windows. They offered the usual village jumble: plastic toys and buns of the same consistency in the post office, and a Gifte Shoppe full of tea-towels, salad bowls, and pottery objects with mottos like "Silence is golden" on them. Rather to my surprise, Nan wanted to linger outside a dress shop in whose window a model wearing an electric-blue rayon evening gown stood in an attitude of scornful disdain. She looked so earnestly at this figure draped in its awful fabric that I began to laugh.

"You can't seriously fancy yourself in that! Come on, this wind is nippy." Suddenly a tremendous clamour of bells cast itself into the air over our heads and we both turned to glance over at the square grey church-tower only a few yards away. Nan said, "Look," and began to tug me and the dogs across the road where a little knot of spectators had gathered at the lych-gate to watch a bridal party emerge from the church door.

First to step out was the Vicar in his stole and surplice, blinking in the bright sunlight. A stout mother in yellow nylon came after him, blowing her nose, followed by a small bridesmaid picking hers. Too late to draw Nan away, I saw that the groom was Crispin Bagshot in a new navy-blue suit, his hair slicked powerfully back and his face wreathed in one great smile. The bride hanging to his arm also had a dazed look of joy about her, brighter even than her disastrous pink tulle dress.

In some perturbation I glanced at Nan, but she was smiling with a wide and generous delight at the whole group, even going so far as to wave at Richard in a matey sort of way. His blue eyes beamed at us kindly and he tucked his hands inside his wide sleeves to warm them. A photographer now began to circle the party, darting and pouncing here and there like a sheepdog assembling its flock. But it was Nan's face that held my attention. Her cheeks were flushed; her whole round, fresh countenance was radiant. As the wedding group disappeared into beribboned cars, she took my arm and hugged it to her. "What a pretty bride," she said, as if for once — maybe for the first time — she saw herself in a role, like everyone else.

Recent events on all sides had left me full of doubts and anxieties, but now with relief I felt some of these beginning to melt away. By accident or design, perhaps it didn't matter after all, if only things could turn out well for Nan.

"The Queen of Swords is your card, Polly. A dark woman, sharp and witty. Also someone who knows about grief. Are you going to tell me what your question is, or keep it to yourself? We can do it either way — whichever you like."

The firelight flickered on the picture card that Lally had laid down between us on the green baize of the card-table. She had turned off the lamp in our corner of the room, murmuring that concentration and a soft light were important. "You have to shuffle the pack with your own hands," she told me, "and put everything out of your mind except the question you want answered."

On the other side of the hearth, his legs stretched toward the fire, Pa was browsing through a large picture-book on France. Opposite him, in a matching pose, Hamish too held a book, but at intervals I felt his attention flick toward us. Ralph had drifted off to watch Nan work at her loom. The room was so quiet one could hear the hiss of burning wood on the hearth and an occasional whimper from Ivan, whose sleep was troubled by dreams.

"I'm not sure I really want to do this, Lall. Remind me it's all a lot of rubbish; then maybe I'll play."

"It's all a lot of rubbish," she said equably. "What's your

question, then?" Her small white hands, light winking on the rings, hovered lazily over the pack of cards.

"Oh, I don't know. The surgeon's checking me over on Friday. I wouldn't mind knowing the verdict, I guess." Half sheepishly I took up the pack and shuffled it.

"Sometimes the question asked isn't the one really in the seeker's mind," remarked Lally, half closing her eyes as if sleepy, "but that's all right. The cards can suggest answers to the real question just the same."

"In other words, it's all a load of rubbish."

"If you like."

"Right. What do we do next, then?"

She took the pack from me and began to set out cards on and around the first one, the Queen of Swords. This was a glum and broody lady holding an upright sword against a background of storm clouds. She looked reassuringly quite unlike me.

"These centre cards are to do with the present position," murmured Lally. "This covers her." She laid a card over the Queen. "And this crosses her," placing one crosswise over it. She then set out four cards clockwise around the first one. "These stand for the Goal, the Past, the recent Past, and the Future." Finally she placed a row of four more in a column on the right. "And these represent the fears you have, the influence of family, the hopes you have—and last of all, here on top, the outcome. Now let's see."

She gazed in a leisurely yet intent way at the spread of cards. "In the centre here we have crossing you the Hierophant. He represents a leader, somebody attached to orthodox tradition. The sceptre in his hand stands for creative power, both the physical and the spiritual kind. Somebody madly energetic, dear, not like you or me."

"My surgeon."

"Could be."

"Press on, then."

"And up top here is the Goal — the ten of Cups — ah. Attainment of the heart's desire."

"Great. A happy ending, then."

"Well, it's not quite that simple. You see, this card's the long-ago past — the Magician — powerful male dominance. And here's the Tower struck by lightning — that's recent. A disastrous change of situation."

I rubbed my knees, which were giving off twinges. "What's this future card say, that's more to the point — if there is a point. This beast with the horns on it, is that supposed to be the devil? And what's he got to do with these naked people in the chains?"

"That card represents bondage to the material world. Black magic. Destruction. But the bonds on the man and woman here, you see, are loose enough to be slipped off — in other words, they're more imaginary than real."

"It's all pretty ridiculous, you must admit. Let's get to the outcome. What's this last card with the wheel on it?"

"That's the wheel of fortune. It suggests things could go either way for you."

"So we've got no answer at all. That figures."

"Oh, I wouldn't say that. You see, this card nearest the last one influences it."

"This dude here in the robes?" I drawled, to tease her.

"He's the King of Cups, dear. A level-headed, responsible man. He's interested in the arts — a professional of some kind. Very well disposed to the questioner. A bachelor."

I burst out laughing. "The tall, dark stranger? Lally, honestly!"

The readers across the room glanced up and Hamish, closing his book, got to his feet and stumped over to us. He peered curiously at the little coloured squares of pasteboard with their arcane symbols, looking with particular attention at the King of Cups.

"You say every person here can be represented by one of these cards?" he asked her.

"That's right."

"Pull the other one, Lally," I said.

"No, really, you'd be surprised. What about the Magician here, for instance. He represents knowledge and the power to make things happen. He establishes his identity through his creativity. He succeeds on every level—thought, word, and deed. If that isn't our Monty—"

"To the life," agreed Pa, lifting his bearded chin at us with a grin.

Ralph now came lounging into the room, flicking bits of wool off the sleeves of his dark-grey suit. He looked as imperturbable and elegant as ever, but I wondered what kissings and touchings might not have been exchanged this last hour in Nan's workroom. The thought gave me a queasy sort of pang. Hamish gave his shoulders a jerk and drew a little away, as if he caught some contagion of uneasiness from me. Crackers came into the room on noiseless pads and took up a statuesque seated pose to gaze through half-closed eyes at the fire.

"And what would Nan's card be?" I asked, more for something to say than because I really wanted to know.

"Oh, she'd be the Queen of Wands," said Lally, laying a court-card in front of me. "Loving. Chaste. Practical. A fair, blue-eyed woman, a home and nature lover. And see the cat at her feet?"

"Yes, and see that great club she's clutching, and the grim expression on her face," remarked Pa, who had abandoned his book and strolled over to join our group around the table. "I'd say the lady's less like Nan than Oldfisk is."

"But after all," said Hamish with a shrug, "life's a kind of card game, so why shouldn't these cards make sense? We're all dealt a hand at the start. You will be black, female, beautiful, brilliant. You will be male, deformed, retarded—"

"Don't be so hard on yourself, Hamish," cried Pa. He casually fanned out some of the cards, though Lally did not

seem to like his touching them. "Pity the image of life as
a card-game has become such a cliché," he said, "because
it's a damn good one. Of course it's a game — partners or
solitaire — but obviously it's the wild cards, and how you
play your hand, that make all the difference."

"And can anyone win without cheating?" I asked, looking
at him directly.

"Probably not," he said. "But that's part of the fun."

As soon as she tactfully could, Lally scooped her cards
together. She wrapped the pack in a silk handkerchief
before returning it to a little wooden box, as if she actually
believed the whole thing was endowed with a kind of magic.

"No, divination is a lot of bunk," said Pa, giving a lock
of my hair a tweak, "but some Jungists actually do relate
the tarot symbols to archetypes of the collective uncon-
scious. And who knows, after all, whether Lally's subcon-
scious isn't as deep a well of truth as any other? Eh, my
dear?" He touched her cheek affectionately and added,
"I've been reading about Provence. Who needs any cards
to tell what a lovely life that would be, down there in the
white sun, with the olive trees. Heigh, it makes you long
to be out of grey old England, doesn't it? Would you like
a nightcap before bed, Lall? Anybody? It's nearly twelve."

No one accepted his offer and soon we drifted off to climb
the stairs to bed. Lally, however, stayed at the card-table,
chin propped dreamily on her hands. As I left the room I
glanced back and saw her take the cards once more out of
their box. Whose future was she trying to divine now, I
wondered. Well, heaven knew there were enough question-
marks in her own.

For several days after my appointments with doctor and
dentist, I stayed up in London in order to see Walt and a
few other friends, and pick up as much theatre gossip as
I could. Unfortunately there was not much satisfaction in

any of these exercises. A surprising number of the people in my address-book had divorced each other, lapsed into alcohol or paranoia, or simply disappeared. Some of the old cronies I did manage to locate looked at me as if vaguely surprised—and not greatly interested—to discover I was still alive. Even Walt could talk about nothing but his role as a bumbling cat burglar in a new TV series. It was for some reason annoying to feel myself an outsider in my old world, even though I had no very powerful urge to rejoin it.

The whole interlude, in other words, left me feeling restless and more than usually perverse, so I caught an evening train down to Canterbury without letting the family know I was coming. I was particularly unwilling to be picked up like a parcel at the station by Hamish or anyone else. Instead, I hired a taxi driven by an evil old man with brown teeth and a loose, rattling cough of grisly frequency. To make matters worse, he kept slewing around in his seat to eye me with senile lechery. The drive seemed to last about a week, but it ultimately had the effect of making me better pleased to get home than I'd expected to be.

When I let myself in, Boris immediately rushed into the hall, skidding on the rug and barking hysterically. It was his dim-witted conviction that every newcomer, no matter how familiar, was an armed robber. I tapped him over the nose with my gloves and told him to shut up. Such as it was, though, his was the only welcome I got. No one at all was about, though a considerable noise could be heard behind the closed dining-room doors. Then one leaf of the doors popped open and Hamish looked out.

"Why the devil didn't you call me?" he said, closing the door behind him to cut off the babble of voices.

"Well, actually, I rather wish I had."

He took my hand in his hard, square one and looked at me sharply.

"What did the quack say about your leg?"

"Oh, he seemed reasonably satisfied. Says I probably won't get arthritis much before I'm forty."

"That's great news."

"He's a glum sort of man."

"You look a touch glum yourself. Are you?"

"No."

"That's a lie."

"It isn't."

"I always know when you're down, Polly. Your lower lip sticks out in two halves." He looked hard at my mouth. "And one of these days, I am going to alter the shape of that mouth of yours once and for all."

Sharply I twisted my hand free of his. With a faint, grim smile he turned to fling open the dining-room doors for me with a flunkey's ceremonial flourish. With as much dignity as I could muster, I walked in ahead of him.

Everyone around the table was laughing and exclaiming or calling out encouragement to Pa, who was easing the cork expertly out of a champagne bottle. The Vicar was there, his blue eyes bright with expectation, and Hermione across from him chimed two wineglasses lightly together with the triumphant smile of a small child playing a triangle. She was wearing a sort of Spanish mantilla over her red hair, and one end of it had caught in the large brooch skewered to her bosom, pulling the lace askew in a devil-may-care sort of way. She looked very jolly and rather tipsy, as did most of the others. At the sight of me, Richard jumped up from his place beside Lally so impetuously he almost knocked over his chair. She watched it topple, then right itself, with vague interest, as if it were part of a movie about someone else's life.

"Welcome, welcome," said Richard warmly, dragging up a chair for me. "Sit here beside Hamish, my dear."

"Yes, do that, my dear," agreed Hamish, grinning.

"You've missed the announcement, but you're just in

time for the celebration," the Vicar went on, rubbing his small hands together.

Of course there was no need to ask what announcement. Ralph had his arm around Nan's shoulders. She was wearing her blue suit with its white blouse, and her hair had been cut very short and curled close. These things made her look unfamiliar and also quite strikingly attractive, though not with the innocent, unkempt sort of beauty she had before. In fact, the unfamiliar thing about her was that now she looked almost exactly like anyone else. And yet her fresh, natural self could still be found in her rosy face and shyly lowered head. She leaned against Ralph as trustingly as a child. I found I could not see her through a dazzle of tears.

"Now we'll drink long life and happiness to this dear couple," said Pa, filling glasses swifly, and pausing to drop a kiss on my head as he went around the table.

"Long life and happiness," everyone chorused. I stole an apprehensive glance at Lally, but she was raising her glass with the rest and smiling her delicious, drowsy smile. She looked more than usually alluring in her midnight-blue dress with a jewelled clasp on the shoulder which I couldn't remember having seen before. Hamish followed my gaze to this ornament. I carefully avoided his eye, which had a sardonic glint of amusement in it, though whether at Lally's expense or mine it was impossible to tell.

"Now we must settle on the day," Pa was saying as he topped up glasses. "What do you think, Nan? Some time early in May, perhaps? That's a lovely time of year, and why wait any longer?"

"Yes, make it early," said Nan.

"Have you no shame," said Ralph fondly.

"None at all." Her face shone with such frank joy that everyone laughed. Richard whipped out a small diary to examine its entries for May. "The tenth is free," he said. "Shall we say the tenth?"

Ralph spoke into her ear and she nodded. His usually pale, lean cheeks were a little flushed, but he was perfectly composed. It was a face that revealed no more of the inner self than his elegant clothes did: a perfectly conventional façade he had long ago constructed, behind which he was free to be his own man, whatever that might be. It was impossible to tell now from his pleasant smile what he might actually be thinking or feeling, and I looked away from him with a sort of distaste, only to find Hamish looking intently at me.

"Yes," he said quietly. "One wonders."

"Where are they going to live?" I couldn't resist asking him, because to this practical question at least there had to be an answer.

But before Hamish could speak, Pa tossed off the last of his champagne and said, "As for residence, I don't think the newly-weds could do better than someplace in a nice, unspoiled village like ours. I hear there's a cottage coming up for sale near the Vicarage, for instance . . . as for this place, it will be far too big for me now, of course. The fact is, I have immortal longings in me, these days, for the sun . . . maybe a nice little stone *mas* somewhere near Arles or Orange, eh Lally? Ah well, there's plenty of time for all that. Our job now is to organize this wedding, and I mean to make it a bash nobody will ever forget. Everything will drip, I give you my word, with Bach and Purcell, with orange-blossom and confetti and Mumm's. The wedding-gown will be a fairy-tale creation, and we'll set Alan to work at once on a mountainous cake. Everyone must come, of course—Olivia will stay away at her peril, so warn her, Polly—and as for you, my dear girl, of course you'll stay on here with us until the knot is tied. Jill and Liza will make charming flower-girls—we'll sleek their hair back and have Victorian frocks made for them—oh, it will be a sight to behold, I promise you, and a happy, happy day."

Pa's voice, which had been rich and strong, here faltered,

as if he were all at once touched by a pang of fatigue or doubt. The hand raising his glass trembled and he seemed to sway slightly on his feet. Hamish made an alarmed little movement toward him, but an instant later Pa was laughing and turning to the buffet for another bottle. He twisted off the wire deftly and then eased out the cork in a smooth, casual extraction that let nothing escape but a faint curl of vapour. "Yes," he said robustly, "I think it will be the happiest day of our lives."

5

"Into Air, into Thin Air"

Soon after the announcement appeared in *The Times* under "Forthcoming Marriages", Pa began to plan a big engagement party at Seven Oaks. He paced in and out of the sitting-room, gauging its potential for dancing, and tweaking critically at the curtains. "Palms and a little orchestra are really what this space calls for," he muttered, "but I suppose the mere suggestion will be howled down in favour of filthy hi-fi speakers in all the corners. Civilization is dying out everywhere."

"And a good thing too, if you mean tasselled programmes tied to girls' wrists," I said. "You'll be on about white soup next, I suppose—all that botheration mashing almonds into paste. Jane Austen is *dead*, Pa."

"But I am not!" declared Pa with triumph. "Now let's see—a white ball, maybe?—that would look nice. Or no— I have it—what about masks—a costume party. It will be great fun if we make it a masquerade."

"Will it?" I said.

"No," said Hamish.

"Come on, Pa. People look so silly, once you get over the joke of seeing the bizarre get-ups they choose. After that there's nothing left but the problem of dancing with Napoleon without losing an eye to his cocked hat, or if you're male, coping with a partner in a tutu and blocked shoes. Can't we just be ourselves and comfortable?"

"What did I ever do to deserve children who were born middle-aged," said Pa. "Put 'masquerade ball' on the invitations, Hamish. It will be enormous fun, you'll see."

Deplorably enough, he proved to be right. In no time we were all to some extent caught up in the childish but irresistible game of dressing-up. Not even Nan could entirely resist the fascination of a disguise. Pa had a stylized gold mask made for her, to complement her golden birthday-dress, and she wore it on and off for hours before the party, allured to find it hid her individuality completely and made her look rather eerily like an idol or a statue. Although we were supposed to keep our costumes a secret, before the first guests arrived there was considerable last-minute scurrying in and out of each other's rooms to beg, borrow, or steal various articles. But Nan reversed the process by coming to lay her mask down on my bureau with a smile, saying, "You wear it, Pol. I'll keep my own face."

I held the thing up and the mirror showed a metallized, rather sinister vizor through which my eyes glimmered with a submerged, almost apprehensive look.

"No, you're right," I told her, and tossed it onto my bed. My costume, a scanty affair of flimsy drapes, was meant to represent Titania in the form of a gaudy winged insect. I had once seen a ballet production in which Oberon was danced in a glittering outfit that made him look like a rather elegant stag-beetle, and with the help of my professional kit I now plagiarized his make-up idea. A fern-like pattern in blue-green paint decorated each cheek, to complement a pair of curly antennae springing from the head-dress. I drew a blue perpendicular line from eyebrow to eyelid, and carefully stuck several green sequins on my upper eyelashes. This made it difficult to see anything very clearly, but it did lend me a very exotic look.

"What's Ralph wearing?" I asked Nan. She was standing

behind me, absorbed in curling her new short locks of hair over her fingers. Her eyes were fixed, as if fascinated, on her own image in the mirror.

"He won't tell," she said. "But I'll know him."

"Hamish says his disguise is going to be a sandwich-board that says 'My Name is Hamish Grant'. I wouldn't put it past him."

"What about Pa? He won't tell either."

"We're not supposed to know, but I caught him borrowing Lally's fur-lined jacket. I'm pretty sure he's going to be a Renaissance man, like that Titian fellow in the velvet cap—there used to be a print of it in the nursery, remember?" The subject was a young man (which would not faze Pa a bit) — a muscular youth clutching the pommel of a sword, and at the same time gazing into space with the tilted head and absent eyes of a dreamer. It was obvious why Pa liked that combination of the active and the passive and hoped it would inspire his sons. But Nan appeared to have lost all interest in Pa's costume. With a glance at me she took up a bottle of my perfume and timidly dabbed a little on her palms and the base of her throat as she had seen me do. She tipped her left hand childishly to and fro to catch the light with her little engagement ring, as if bewitched by the new identity it gave her.

We heard the doorbell then, and Boris barking from his kitchen exile. Pa shouted up the stairs, "Come along—get down here, girls. James and John have arrived."

Once downstairs we found that prolonged earlier scuf-flings and thumpings from the staff had transformed all the main ground-floor rooms into a romantic setting for the ball. The carpets had been rolled away and the floors polished. In a corner of the hall, perched on the umbrella-stand, the life-sized doll, dressed in Pa's white tie and tails, had been set up like some benevolent household god to greet and bless the company. Yards of sheer dark-blue material pierced all over with little star-shaped apertures had been draped to cover the chandeliers. All the table lamps and wall sconces were swathed in the same dark perforated fabric. The effect was quite magical. It created a sort of indoor *heure-bleue* mystery which not only had charm but would make it quite difficult for the guests to recognize each other. Or so I imagined.

Shaking out my gauzy wings I went forward to greet James and his wife Marguerite. They had blackened their faces and put on hobo rags — to give publishers a truer image, he explained. She doffed a broken topper to me jauntily and said, "Hello, Polly."

"Damn. You're not supposed to know me from Titania, Marguerite."

After Pa had removed their tattered overcoats, he had to hurry to the door again, leaving me to usher them toward the bar set up in the dining-room. There James and John fell into chat with Alan in a clown suit, who was presiding over the drinks with professional aplomb. Marguerite, glancing cautiously around to make sure no one could overhear, put her head close to mine and said, "Polly dear, this engagement. Such a *surprise*. I mean, what about Lally? After all these years, it does seem—you won't mind my saying this, dear—just a bit bizarre for Ralph to . . . "

"Yes, I know it seems a bit—but after all, these things happen."

"Well, but she must feel—"

Just then, however, Lally herself appeared. She minced up to us in a beaded flapper's dress, the short skirt revealing a generous length of shapely leg. Her hair was bound close under a glittering silver cloche. In one languid hand she held a long ivory cigarette-holder. There was nothing actually in it, because Lally had strong anti-smoking views, but it gave her an effective final touch of jazz-age sophistication. Raising plucked eyebrows she smiled at us with her painted-on cupid's-bow mouth and went on to the bar, pausing on the way to dance a few slow steps of the Charleston.

"Well," murmured Marguerite, eyeing this performance, "she does seem to be taking it very well, I must say. Just the same, my dear, the whole thing—I mean, I find it very hard to get used to the idea. Where is Ralph actually *living* now? Not here, surely."

"No, he's staying at his club till the wedding. He comes down weekends, of course."

"But *Lally* is living here?"

"Yes. She's in a bedroom next to mine now. You and James will have their old room tonight, and Ralph will stay at the Vicarage."

"How very peculiar."

I had to admit to myself that it was, and that I was not finding it easy to get used to these changes either, but I had no urge to confide these thoughts to Marguerite. With relief I spotted Walt's freckled face in a suit of cardboard armour at the door, which gave me the excuse to hurry away from her.

People were now arriving thick and fast. The rooms filled with chatter rising in competition with the dance music which had begun to pump out of the various despised speakers. Pa had ordered all the windows open wide ("Costumes are always horribly hot," he said. "It's their only disadvantage"), but the air, spiked with perfume, spirits, and the occasional cigar or cigarette, soon grew very warm and heavy. I danced with Walt—a cumbersome and angular partner in his rigid encasement — but this made me so thirsty I soon passed him on to Hermione. She made a most improbable nun in draperies which she had tucked well up to free her legs. With a cry of "Cha-cha-cha!" she swung Walt off while I went to the bar in search of a drink.

"Here you are, little sister," Alan said, handing me a well-iced gin and tonic. I hoisted myself onto a bar-stool to rest my feet. The dancers turned and glided in the dim blue light. Richard, in a child's sailor-suit, twirled my tall sister-in-law around the floor. A straw hat hung jauntily down his back on its sling of ribbon. My brother Bill, his mild, mouse-coloured hair spiked up with gel, wore the boots, chains, and studs of a motorcycle thug. A tall guest appearing at my elbow wore black from head to toe, with a close-fitting silk mask on which a cat's whiskered face had been painted.

"Makes you wonder, doesn't it, all this dressing-up," I said to him, rattling the icy dregs of my drink. "Is all this projection or transference of identity sinister, or is it just good clean fun?"

"I wouldn't know, Pol," he said, with a burlesque twitch of his whiskers, and with a little jolt of surprise I recognized Ralph's voice. Nan came up and took his arm, smiling. He embraced her and moved off with her to join the dancers. I held out my glass to Alan for a refill. The two of them danced beautifully together, as if all his skill had been absorbed without effort into her clumsy body. Though Nan wore no mask, her flushed face was so open, so fully awakened, that she looked transformed. Ralph's black arm held her close; her golden skirts curled around his black legs. Her eyes were fastened to the cat mask of his face.

"You can build me another one of those," I told Alan.

"Again? Steady on," he said, surprised.

"Oh, don't be silly. It's just so hot in here."

I took my drink and wandered with it across the hall, picking my way among the dancers in search of Lally. I wanted very much to talk to her, without having any clear notion at all what I wanted to say. At last I caught a glimpse of her short skirt disappearing into the little office Hamish used, and followed her there. She had dropped into a chair and kicked off her silver shoes. Like me, she had a drink in her hand.

"Exhausting, isn't it," she said. "Close the door, Pol. Then nobody will make us dance."

"Lally," I said abruptly. "What's going to happen to you now?"

"Me? Why nothing very much. Monty tells me I'm welcome to stay on here as long as I like. That is, until and unless he packs it all in and goes off to France. Meantime, I can act as his hostess—housekeeper—social secretary, or whatever."

"Whatever?" I said.

She batted her mascaraed eyelashes at me mockingly. "Curiosity killed the cat, Polly. The idea is I'm to take some of the load off Hamish once Nan's gone. It's clearly understood, though, that I will cook absolutely nothing."

"I see." This by no means really answered my question, but it was evidently all she intended to say for the moment. After a pause I tried another approach.

"But I wish you'd tell me what you really think—I mean, feel—about Nan and Ralph. For one reason and another, I'm not—I'm not quite easy in my mind."

She looked at me. The thick make-up base on her face with its doll's circles of rouge might as well have been a mask.

"I don't think about it at all, Polly. What would be the point? It's done now. As for feelings, it's a long time since I had any worth mentioning. It's much the best thing about getting older. You care less and less about more and more."

"Really?" I blinked my sequined eyelids in an effort to focus her more clearly, but her face had no expression on it at all, or none that I could read.

"Really," she said firmly.

We sipped our drinks in companionable silence. Then I said, "Well, I'm glad if it's like that for you. Makes everything easier all round. But Ralph . . . will he be good for her, do you think?"

"That depends on what you mean by 'good'."

"Well, there's been such a change in her, hasn't there? I mean it has to be good that she's more—more *ordinary* now."

"Does it? Well, maybe."

"The thing is, will he be a good husband to her? It worries me, that."

Frowning, Lally rattled the ice in the bottom of her glass. "There's a bottle of gin in that little cupboard behind you, isn't there, Pol? Hoick it out and give us both a dash more."

I did this, prudently adding a generous splash of tonic to each glass.

"Well, will he? Be a good husband, that is."

"Who can tell? After all, years ago I *left* the kind of man people call a good husband, and what a blissful escape it was. So maybe I'm not the right one to ask. Now, if you mean is he a good lover, why the answer is oh yes, indeed. In his younger days he was very very keen . . . used to grumble because women only have five body orifices, and two of those, even with the best will in the world, aren't madly useful for intercourse. Even now, he . . . well, anyhow he's still virile, if that's what's worrying you. Almost excessively so. Very tiring, the whole business, I've found in the last few years. Almost more trouble than it's worth, in fact, is my view. But not in his. Nor ever will be, I imagine."

I thought about this for a moment. My head had begun to feel rather large, full and heavy. In case the gin and tonic might have something to do with this, I put my glass down with care on the floor, where it could not fall off anything.

"What I actually mean, Lally, is will he be good to her. How's he going to like living in the village, if they do that? Or if they live in some little flat in London and she has to entertain his sophisticated friends—how's that going to be? Eh? That's what I wonder."

"Fortunately," said Lally, calmly topping up her glass again, "that won't be any of my business, will it."

"Well, it bothers me. And I feel it ought to bother Pa. But it doesn't seem to, does it. Nothing seems to bother him."

"No, it doesn't."

"Why is that, do you think, Lall? She's his daughter."

"That's because he's a *man*, dear."

"A man? You mean he fathered her. I know that."

"No, no. Because he's a *man*."

"Of course he is. You're not making sense, Lall."

"Men," began Lally, and then stopped. She looked intently into her drink as if the rest of her sentence might have fallen into it. After a long pause I reached down, retrieved my own glass, and tilted it up.

"Men—" I prompted her.

"That's it. Men are all like that. It's a fact of life. Nan, like all the rest of us, will get used to it in time, I guess."

"But you were saying men—"

"Right. They're like egos on legs. Monsters. It's almost pathetic. They just honestly don't know other people exist. Specially if those people are women. You have to keep on reminding them. Then the nicer ones snap their fingers and say, 'By golly, yes! — sorry — you're quite right. My, my. Those things out there are *people*.' But then they always forget again. Every time."

This struck me as possibly the most profound truth ever uttered. It moved me. I looked with some intensity at Lally.

"You're a wise old owl, Lall."

"Damn right I am. Too bad it pays so badly."

Tears of pity and sorrow for all women had begun to entangle themselves in my sequins, and in my haste to prevent my make-up from streaking, I reached toward the desk to put down my glass. It promptly fell off the edge, splashing the carpet and my shoes with gin. Without another word, Lally and I rose and walked out in majestic silence to rejoin the party.

Pa had shed his furred jacket and pushed back his velvet headgear (a hat of Hermione's I now recognized). He seized

Lally the moment he spotted her and danced her out into the hall. I walked rather carefully to the foot of the stairs and after a pause began very, very slowly to climb them. There was no doubt about it now, something in those gin-and-tonics was affecting me oddly. So oddly that on the top landing I thought it best to sit down for a little rest.

After a while I noticed a large pair of reddish-haired bare legs in front of me. Above them was a tartan kilt, and above that again, a lace-frilled shirt with Hamish in it.

"My name is Hamish Grant," I said.

"What the devil are you doing up here?" he demanded.

"I am sitting here."

"Yes, but what the hell for?"

"Well, mostly because I can't get up."

He bent over me and sniffed. Then he gripped the banister rail, his back heaving in a soundless wheeze of a laugh. This seemed to occupy him for quite a while. Below in the hall I caught a glimpse of Walt peering about wistfully for me in the crowd. He lifted a drink to his mouth only to have his vizor clap shut at the crucial moment. Faintly, in a lull in the music, I heard a muffled "God-damn" from inside the armour. Spinning and dancing in the background were cats and nuns, kings and clowns and hoboes. I closed my eyes.

"Right," said Hamish. "Up we go, then. This is giving me a strong sense of *déjà-vu*." Clumsily he thrust one arm under my knees and lurched with me up the last flight of stairs. "My God, for a bug you weigh enough," he said, and dropped me on my bed with a gasp of relief. His red, squarish, smiling face looked down into mine. Very gently he drew off the green sequins from my eyelashes.

"Don't go," I said, holding him by his lace jabot. "Why don't you kiss me?"

"Because you're drunk," he said, jerking himself free. I saw with mild surprise that he was extremely angry.

"Sleep it off, Polly," he said roughly. "Ask me again, when you're sober, if you have the guts. But don't ever make a pass at me like that again."

He threw a quilt over me and the last thing I saw was his hard, straight back moving quickly away.

March opened with an early spell of warm, sunny weather that greened the fields and brought up a rush of yellow-eyed narcissus and tall daffodils in the grass. A cuckoo called from the woods, and a perfect din of courting birds broke out at dawn every morning. "Silly buggers, aren't they," remarked Hamish. "You'd think they'd remember that all *that* leads to is a nestful of brats. As for flying all the way back from Africa every year—they only do it to impress poets and other crazies." He drooped the eyelid nearest me in a wink. I pretended not to see it. My recollections of the masked ball were dimmish but uncomfortable, and I was no longer able to talk or laugh at all easily with him. Perhaps it was this shift in our relationship (if that was the right word for it) that made me irritable, even morose, in spite of the mild gaiety of springtime. But in all the flutter of bridal plans and preparations in the house no one noticed my mood. Hamish in particular seemed entirely unaware of it, which for some reason I found no help at all.

One bright morning Pa strode into the kitchen where Nan and I were making soup, and clapped his hands so briskly together for attention that I dropped my vegetable-peeler to the floor.

"Oh Pa, must you be so dramatic?" I grumbled.

"Come along now, both of you," he said. "Leave all that. We're going out. Dawson, the estate agent, has just called. That cottage near the rectory—it's come on the market at last. We can pick up the key this morning and have a look around before it goes on their list. Decent of Dawson to let us have first chance, because with housing the way it is, the place is sure to be snapped up in no time. Come on, girls — I'll shake Ralph up and we'll go along right away."

Nan was already untying her apron, but I went on cutting up carrots. "You don't need me," I told Pa, but he said, "Yes we do. *Come* on, girl," and pulled me to my feet. Shortly Ralph, in cords and his new Fair Isle sweater, joined us in the Daimler. Boris crammed himself in at the last minute after Nan. In the distance Hamish could be seen on the terrace stretched full length in a long chair. He was chatting over coffee with Lally, and Darling was curled domestically between them. Something that might have been a smile widened his lips as he waved us goodbye.

We shot off toward Canterbury past trees and hedges in new leaf that twinkled and glittered in the bright air. The first lambs jumped on the downs under a blue sky as glossy as silk. The cottage, when we pulled up at its gate, looked charming with its stone walls cloaked in ivy and a wisteria vine budding over the front door.

"Oh look!" cried Nan in delight.

"Easy does it, love," advised Ralph, taking her hand. "We haven't seen the inside yet."

Pa managed after some difficulty to unlock the door, and we stepped into an entrance hall carpeted with dirty newspaper and a litter of handbills that for months past had been thrust through the letter-box. The peculiarly sad, dusty chill of an empty house touched our faces.

"The old boy who owned the place was in hospital for a long time before he finally popped off," explained Pa. "His relatives took away the furniture some time ago, except for a few bits nobody wanted." The sitting-room contained two such objects—a hat-stand with lion's-paw feet, and a cabinet radio dating from the forties. A hideous gas fire squatted on the tiled hearth of what was in better days an open fireplace. The wallpaper was sallow with age, and damp had stained it in one corner. There was a rose-entwined card crookedly pinned to one wall that read Bless

This House. Dust-blotted windows blurred the bright day outside.

"Well," Pa went on, clearing his throat. "Of course you have to use your imagination . . . see the potential, I mean, Ralph, as you know how to do with a manuscript that may not look great at first glance. New plaster and paint in here, fitted carpets, some bright chintz—"

"Oh yes," said Nan eagerly. "It could look lovely."

We wandered out to the kitchen. A tap had been allowed to drip into the enamel sink, which was marked by a long stain of rust. A hole in the shabby linoleum caught me by one toe and made me stumble. The cupboard doors stood open haphazardly exposing torn shelf-paper patterned with roses. The one small window was almost completely overgrown with ivy.

"Now this really does challenge the imagination," said Ralph dryly.

"Of course the place badly needs doing up," Pa conceded. "But look, here's a nice larder that would make a utility room. And there's quite a decent-sized garden out there— looks like half an acre. I wouldn't be surprised if there weren't room to build out a little extension, maybe. Toolhouse as well. Plenty of room for veggies and all that."

Nan was peering out intently between the window's cobwebs. "Yes," she said. "We could grow herbs."

I thought I heard Ralph mutter something like "We could have our heads read," but no one else seemed to notice.

"They're only asking twenty-seven for it, you know," Pa said as he led the way upstairs. "And another four or five would do the place up, put in central heating and so on. That's a real bargain for these days, and when you consider it's only seven miles from Canterbury."

Boris flopped up the steep stairs after us. A small hall gave access to three dust-haunted bedrooms and a bathroom surprisingly fitted with a new, bright-blue toilet, sink, and tub.

"Oh!" said Nan. "Everything up here should be blue and white. Curtains and rugs on my loom."

"That would be nice," I put in, trying to help.

"It's not very big, of course," Pa went on, "but that's exactly why this place will be snapped up. Londoners wanting a weekend retreat. There's a great demand for these older cottages."

"Well, it may be a residence, but it's not much of a bijou," Ralph said. I caught his eye and looked away. Pa frowned. Boris, panting, wandered in and out among our legs, his claws clicking on the bare boards. "I know it needs a lot of work," Pa said, "but that's half the fun of it. For a starter home, anyhow, it seems to me it would just suit you two. Remember, you'll be up in London for the inside of every week, Ralph. It's quite big enough for a couple. Of course, later on you might want more space, but—well, it's only a suggestion, you know. Something else might turn up before May—though I doubt it. Anyhow, this could be my wedding present to you both, if you want to consider it."

"Oh, Pa!" said Nan. She turned to Ralph. His face softened as she took his arm and gazed at him eagerly with her light-blue eyes.

"Well, it's for you to say, my love," he told her. "Very generous of you, Monty. No doubt it would look very different if it were all done up—quite attractive and cosy, I daresay."

"I'm sure you agree about that, Polly," said Pa, fixing me with his eye.

"Well, if you want the truth, Pa, I really don't think—"

"It's lovely," said Nan. She looked around the little hall as if at a palace. "My first own home. Our own place. Lovely."

"Exactly," said Pa, looking at me.

I said nothing.

"Well, that's agreed, then, is it? The great thing is, the son wants to be rid of it at once—he's emigrating—so the red tape of the deal can be cut quite short. We'll have a surveyor round right away; get an estimate on the repairs and so on. Then I can make Dawson an offer, and we'll see how it goes from there."

Ralph smiled genially as Nan reached over to put a kiss on each of Pa's bearded cheeks. After a final look around downstairs, we went out to inspect the garden. Nan led the way and Pa, catching my hand, followed her out into the sunny air. Behind us, Boris must have managed to catch his tail somehow as the door closed, for he shot out after us with an anguished yelp.

"And what are the bridesmaids wearing, Polly?"

"Well, the children are all going to be decked out in Kate Greenaway outfits, so willy-nilly Olivia and I will have to be vaguely Victorian. I thought of something like this, maybe."

I flipped open a library copy of *Queen Victoria's Sketchbook* which I had brought over to the Vicarage to show Hermione. The young Queen in 1840 had made a quite attractive drawing of the maid-of-honour dresses to be worn at her own wedding. It showed a simpering miss in an off-the-shoulder wasp-waisted gown. A cluster of white roses caught up the wide skirt at one side. More roses were pinned at the side of the hair and on the breast in the centre of a lacy fichu.

"It's a bit saccharine, but what can you do. Nan's going for white satin with a lace veil and miles of train. I must say it surprises, me, rather. I'd have thought a quiet registry office in ordinary clothes would have been much more her style, even if it isn't Pa's."

"Acting out," murmured Hermione, wrinkling her short nose in a friendly way over the maid of honour. The dining-

room where we sat over tea had a wan, filtered light re-
fracted from a thin film of snow that freakishly that afternoon had painted everything outdoors with white rime. Only
the firs in the Vicarage garden looked natural; all the other
trees and shrubs in their new foliage had a somewhat embarrassed air. Richard had gone out to preside at a funeral. The
thought of a black mouth open in that cold white ground
sent a shiver through me. The sky was an odd, leaden, yellowish colour, and Hermione had forgotten to switch on any
lamps.

"Sometimes, you know, I feel very uneasy about that," I
said. "It's all very well, the fun and games of dressing up
for a party. But marriage ... that's real. Costumes ... I
don't know ... they make the whole thing into a sort of
charade." I stole a quick glance across the table at her, but
her face screwed itself into a mischievous grin.

"Oh well," she said. "Dress-up ceremonies do fill a need.
They give such a nice touch of fantasy to reality, or maybe
it's the other way around. Any case, regalia's always had
its fascination. What a pity, for instance, that Victorian
funerals have gone out of style. All that woeful drama, with
black plumes and weepers of crepe. Nowadays it's hardly
worth one's while to die, with mourners wearing any old
colour, no kid gloves, and no baked meats afterward."

"Yes, but surely one can go too far. Ralph laughed last
night till I thought he'd damage himself over a picture we
found of Dearest Albert, got up for his wedding in a British
field marshal's uniform, with white tights, and the Order of
the Garter on his manly leg. And yet a grey topper and ascot
tie with striped trousers is every bit as ridiculous, isn't it."

"On the other hand, did you know that Albert the Good
tried to insist that every one of his bride's twelve attendants
be of spotless reputation, and their *mothers as well*? Talk
about fantasy. They managed to talk him out of it, but still.
You see how completely appropriate for him to wear the
Order of the Garter. The costume is always suitable, one

way or another, my view."

"Me as a demure Victorian virgin? Come on."

"Are you so sure, Pol? There's a bit of a touch-me-not air about you, admit it."

A sudden, unwelcome recollection of my various rejections of Hamish, starting last Midsummer Eve, jumped into my mind. Surely I had reacted to all his moderate advances as if they were attempted rape. It was only poetic justice that he should have ended by rejecting me. There was even, to be honest, an element of class snobbery in my treatment of him, and what could be a more nineteenth-century adjunct to prudery than that? The snow outside had begun to melt and plop off the trees with a ridiculous noise like the derisive sound made by rude small boys. Sighing, I pushed my cup over for more tea.

"Anyhow, I saw some rather pretty light-blue stuff in town the other day — very virginal and suitable — and I bought enough for Olivia and me. She's taller than I am, but thank God we've got roughly the same build and colouring, so twin dresses won't look too ludicrous. The next problem is finding a dressmaker. I'd much rather not fag all the way to London for fittings—do you know anybody local who could do the job?"

"Of course I do," said Hermione, splashing tea into her own cup. "And so do you. Mavis Ironmould. Beercart Lane in Canterbury. She made your sister's dress for the *Comus* party. Getting on a bit these days is Mavis, but she's as clever as paint. Do you nicely, I should think."

"How could I have forgotten a name like that. Yes, she did a nice job on that dress. Could she cope with Nan's wedding-dress as well, do you think?"

"Why don't we call her up and ask. If she's willing, I'll drive you in to see her. I always like a chat with Mavis."

"Thanks, Hermione. You're on."

Mrs. Ironmould was a bent little woman of seventy-plus with

a chronic sniff and one shoulder higher than the other. She wore a black dress trimmed with jet and received us with an air of dignified gloom that suggested there was an invisible coffin in her front room. Nothing worse was actually there, though, than a row of aspidistras at the window that shed a bilious greenish light over the maroon carpet and maroon furniture with bony wooden elbows. The sewing-machine in the corner was genteelly shrouded in a blue plush cover. I was greatly diverted to recognize a print on the wall — none other than the half-dressed lady of the jumble sale. Peering closer at it, I saw it had a title: *Gone*.

"Well, then, how are you, Mavis," asked Hermione, flopping onto the sofa.

"I don't complain."

"That's the spirit."

"It's me feet, mostly. Bunions."

"You're looking very well."

"Ah. Threatened with an ulster, I've been. But that don't show."

"Just as well, isn't it. Now, as we told you on the phone, this young lady needs a bridesmaid's dress made up — where's your sketch, Polly?"

"I have it here. And the material."

Mavis took the parcel of stuff to the window to peer at it in the light that struggled in through her lace curtains. There was a long silence while she fingered the delicate fabric dubiously with her vein-knotted hand. An evil smell of dog emanated from an old beast in a basket near the electric fire. He opened a red-rimmed eye and growled at me; otherwise I might have thought he'd died some time ago.

"Not much body to it, is there," Mavis said. "Nor I don't know how it will drape, I'm sure. Still, there it is. Bought it now, haven't you." She sniffed. Study of the sketch appeared to depress her even further. "Bunchy, with them flowers," she muttered. "Well, we can try, I suppose, if that's what you fancy. People will ave their own ideas, say what you like."

"Yes, they will. Must make it difficult for you."

She gave me a glance from pin-sharp black eyes; but my little flash of combative spirit seemed to cheer her up faintly. Without further demur she got out a tape and measured me, sniffing. On a scrap of wrapping-paper she noted down my dimensions with the stump of a pencil.

"Never married yourself, did you, Mavis," Hermione asked while this was going on.

"Oh no. Call meself Mrs. because why not. But I never fancied matrimony. Besides I ad to look after me old mum, didn't I. Enough for anyone, that job was."

"Old Mrs. Ironmould lived to be over a hundred, Polly."

"Did she really," I said, politely repressing the comment "How terrible."

"That she did. Balmy as a seagull the last ten years she was, too. I'll just go and find me calendar so we can fix a date for the first fitting."

She disappeared with a final sniff into a back room. Hermione tossed down her copy of *Woman's Own* and went over to the dog-basket. I gazed for something to do at a large glass-framed box on the wall containing a macabre wreath made up of different-coloured locks of human hair.

"Them bits of air come from my great-grandmother's children," Mavis said, coming back with a calendar that had kittens on it. "Nine of them she ad, and only the one of them lived past twenty. March fifteenth do you? And if your sister likes to come with you, we'll measure er up. Though I *suppose* er shape asn't changed since the summer."

"No. No, it hasn't." I felt my face aching to stretch in a mad, appreciative grin.

"Poor old boy," said Hermione to the dog. "You really ought to have the poor brute put down, Mavis."

The old dog sighed as if in agreement.

"Oh, I couldn't do that," said Mavis. "Company, that's what e is. Only friend I ave left. Older than I am, Peter, dividing by seven." With a grim sort of pride she added, "Don't know what I shall do when e's gone, for somebody to talk to."

As soon as we were out in the wind-swept street, I seized Hermione's elbow in a sharp grip. "Why didn't you *warn* me? I thought I might have to lie down in there and die of sheer gloom."

"Oh, would you really call it gloom?" said Hermione. "I'm not sure I would. She gets such enormous pleasure out of it."

Every day now the postman climbed off his bicycle at our door and announced himself with a loud double knock. Wedding presents of every possible size and shape were handed in, and Nan received each and every one with a child's unclouded delight. Enchanted, she would hold up the parcels and gloat over the tissue wrappings and silver ribbon, but she could never bear to wait for the weekend to unwrap them with Ralph. Whether the gift was a tea-cosy or a microwave oven, she received it with the same glee and set it out proudly on the dining-room buffet, which had been cleared for display purposes. Toasters, corkscrews, bookends, crystal glasses, coffee-makers, cheese-boards rained in and overflowed with their cards onto many smaller tables. When not occupied with other chores, Hamish could be found inspecting and listing these items with a bemused expression on his enigmatic face.

All my waking hours as well as most of his now went into the logistics of planning the wedding rehearsal and the reception after the actual ceremony, to which over a hundred people were invited. (Lally, of course, serenely continued to do nothing at all.) The phone rang incessantly with tradesmen, well-wishers, and relatives all requiring attention. Pa had to go up to London repeatedly to deal with legal and financial matters whose details he did not discuss with me. Ralph's weekend visits were taken up with supervision of the cottage renovations, which of course were going ahead as slowly as possible, with many maddening hitches and delays. In different ways and degrees, most of us began to show the effects of mounting pressure. With me it took the form of chronic fatigue and occasional, unpredictable spurts of anger. Only Hamish maintained his usual tart, ironic manner and Lally her air of sweet, vague detachment.

"I'll be damn glad when all this nonsense is over," I said crossly to Hamish one evening as I bundled up a mass of gift wrapping for the rubbish-bin. "Look at the time, and Pa not back from town yet. He looks worn out. And it's months since he even thought about his novel, never mind worked on it. And those papers for Harvard haven't been touched for — No, this whole formal-wedding business is just a ridiculous waste of time and energy for everybody."

"For the likes of you and me, maybe. But not for Nan."

As we spoke the slow, regular thud of her loom could be heard from her workroom. Every day now she spent hours of absorbed and happy work on yards of handsome blue-and-white material later to become curtains and a bedspread for the cottage master-bedroom. Whatever the rest of us might privately feel, there was no doubt or anxiety of any kind in her mind, that was clear, and just to think of that calmed me now.

"Yes, bless her. She's really happy."

The front door opened and Ralph came in, shaking rain off his hat. The dogs rushed to greet him, Boris barking wildly, and he shoved them wearily away. "Get out of it, you two. Hullo, Polly. God, what a drag this trip down is on a Saturday. And I stopped off at the cottage to look at those fitted cabinets for the kitchen — would you believe they've sent the wrong kind? Sometimes I think this whole

country will slide into the sea out of sheer bloody ineffi-
ciency. I need a drink."

The sound of his voice brought Nan hurrying out to
throw her arms around his neck.

"Come and see the new presents," she said, tugging him
toward the dining-room. "James and Marguerite sent a
whole set of lovely blue china. It's so pretty. And what do
you think Richard—"

"Oh, not now, Nan. For God's sake let me sit down in
peace for a few minutes. Is Monty not back yet?" Smoothing back the immaculate silvering wings of his hair he
walked into the sitting-room and poured himself a whisky.

"He had some lawyer or other to see," I said. "Should
be home soon, though." I sat down. My legs were aching.
Lally, already attractively disposed on her velvet sofa for
the happy hour, raised her martini glass to Ralph with a
smile. She had tucked a scarf of red-and-gold Indian tissue
into the neck of her black dress, and the effect, with a new
bright lipstick, was highly becoming.

"My guess is, you know," said Ralph, sitting down heavily, "that the cottage is not going to be habitable before
July at the earliest. The latest is that Fisk tells me we'll
need planning permission, if you please, to put a patch of
hardstanding in the garden for the car. I mean it's simply
incredible, the bureaucratic complications every time you
turn around. No, I'd say July at the earliest. But I suppose
it's out of the question now to shove the wedding date on
a bit."

"Not unless you want to visit me regularly in the asy-
lum," Hamish said. "The invitations went out yesterday."

"Well, I didn't really expect it would be on." Ralph
shrugged and applied himself to his drink. Nan came in,
beaming, with the teapot and creamer of the new china held
high to show him, and he glanced at it dutifully.

"Yes, dear, very pretty. What's for dinner, or are we wait-

ing for Monty? I had no time for lunch—must say I'm empty
as a drum." On this hint, Nan at once slipped away to the
kitchen. "It's very awkward, you know," he went on, "dividing the time between here and town every week." He lifted
his chin to indicate he was addressing us in general rather
than anyone in particular, and swirled the whisky rather
fretfully in his glass. "Monty, of course, has other things on
his plate, and Hamish has more than enough to do here; but
somebody really needs to be on the spot full-time to oversee
the work on that cottage, or it's likely to go on for years.
As it is, though . . . I mean, Nan does her best and all that,
but when I tell her about those bloody cupboards, she is
going to say 'Oh dear', and that will be it for her, as far as
coping with anything goes. Oh well, I suppose the whole
mess will sort itself out somehow before we all die of exhaustion. Nan, did I tell you the bloody kitchen cabinets they
sent don't fit?"

She paused on her way toward him with a silver bowl
in one hand and a platter of cheese and ham slices in the
other. "Oh dear," she said. We all smiled at her fondly,
Ralph included.

"This lovely rose-bowl is from the Vicar and Hermione,"
she said. "See, they had our initials engraved on it. Look,
Ralph."

"Yes, yes. Very nice. Good ham, this."

"I told him two rings, please, and keep 'obey' in the
words. Was that all right?" She set the bowl on the man-
telpiece and stood back to admire it.

"Obey? Good Lord. That seems very antiquated. Unless
it's switched around so the husband promises. That would
be more like it—bring it right up to date."

There was an awkward little gap after this remark which
no one seemed able to fill up; but Nan, head on one side
admiring the bowl, did not seem to have heard it.

"And double rings?" she asked then, turning to him with
her wide smile.

He made a sharp gesture of irritation. "I hardly see the need for two of the damn things. Unless one's for my nose." We all saw the sudden, childish trembling of Nan's mouth before she turned aside to hide it. Ralph was not looking directly at Lally, but she slowly turned her head and gave him a steady glance. He returned it with a curious intentness as if, between these long-time partners, a signal of warning had been given and received. I got to my feet, but Ralph was already on his long legs, folding Nan in a contrite embrace.

"Forgive me, sweetheart. You know that was just a joke. Not even a good one. I got it wrong . . . too tired and edgy, that's all. You shall have ten rings if you want them. All right now? That's my darling." She emerged from his arms wet-eyed but smiling, and five minutes later seemed to have forgotten the whole incident. But Lally was very silent, almost sombre, for the rest of the evening, and so was I.

Tired as I was, I sat up that night for Pa. Everyone else trailed off to bed, leaving me alone with the ticking hall-clock and a pot of coffee on a warmer for company. When his key finally scratched at the door, it was after midnight.

"What on earth are you doing up, dear?" he said, tossing his coat across a chair. "That bloody train had signal trouble again. I had to wait over an hour at Ashford."

I got up stiffly, yawning. "Want some coffee?"

"All right." He flung himself into his armchair with a groan and thrust his legs out full length. "God, I'm tired." He did indeed look weary, and, in some indefinable but palpable way, rather depressed as well.

"It's too much, you know, Pa, all this to-and-froing. You look exhausted."

"Well, it's taken some doing, you know, to safeguard Nan's interests. 'During coverture' — how's that for a phrase. But her money's tied up now, all safe and sound.

They only need to send one or two things down here for my signature now; then everything will be finalized."

"That's a grim sort of word, isn't it. You know, Pa, I really wish—"

"What?"

"Well, that there were more time. I'm still not . . . at all comfortable about this."

"My dear, at the start there might have been some cause. But I should have thought that by now anybody could see what a thoroughly good idea this is. Ralph is unmistakably a happy man. And Nan is transformed. You're looking very peaked, Pol—you're overtired—that's all it is."

"Pa."

"Mm."

"Does it ever seem to you possible that Ralph might just back out of the whole thing at the last minute? Is that why you set such an early date for the wedding?"

"Now there it is," said Pa, sitting up to fix me with an irritable eye. "You're so worn out you've worked up an anxiety attack. Pure and simple case of nerves, my dear." After a pause he added casually between sips of coffee, "What triggered this off, anyhow?"

I told him about Ralph's comment on the rings, and Nan's tears.

"What!" he cried robustly. "Is that all? My dear Polly! You *have* lost your eye. The man's entitled to an occasional twinge of irritation, surely. He's only human. This is a big step for him. He's a high-strung fellow, you know. And it's a new role for him, the bridegroom. Of course he's under some strain—aren't we all. Obviously Nan has a case of bridal nerves herself. Nothing could be more natural. But if there's anything clearer in the world than his affection —even devotion—to Nan, I don't know what it is. And if he's well aware of all the advantages of this arrangement, surely that's all the better. Head and heart are both involved. Right? Now you go on up to bed, Polly, and get some sleep. It's easy to see you need it. Good night, my dear."

He looked fully alert now, bright-eyed and with a fresh colour in his cheeks. The vague air of depression that had hung about him earlier had completely vanished. Cheerfully he took me in his arm to the foot of the stairs. "Off you go, love. Sleep well."

"Good night, Pa."

He kissed me on the forehead and I went up to bed, where I did, in fact, sleep better than I had for weeks.

The April sun was so bright and warm that after tea it tempted us all out into the garden. Recent rain had washed clean a light southerly wind. The turf under our feet felt springy with life. In the borders primroses and lilies-of-the-valley breathed scent into the sunny air. "Eden before the fall, isn't it," I said to Lally. "Oh, absolutely," she said, and looked vaguely around before donning a large pair of dark glasses.

"One pound sterling says I can beat anyone here at croquet," said Pa, seizing a mallet.

"Done," said Ralph. "Be my partner, Hamish. We'll show him."

"And you'll be mine, Polly."

"Pa, you know I don't really understand the game. Not the way you play it, with all kinds of crazy complications."

"No problem," he said robustly. "Just do exactly what I tell you. Ready?—everybody choose a colour. Lall will be our referee."

With a smile Lally distributed herself gracefully on a long chair, first draping closer about her shoulders a blue-and-rose shawl that flattered her white skin and blue-shadowed eyes. She coaxed Darling to jump onto her lap and proceeded to stroke and murmur to him, casting only an occasional bored glance at the game. Nan, even less interested, wandered off in the direction of the orchard, where some of the fruit trees were just beginning to foam into blossom. Crackers had been missing for nearly a week, and as she walked away she called his ridiculous name repeatedly in a low, wistful voice.

Pa's style on the croquet court was elaborately designed not so much to outplay as to demoralize his opponents. He squatted to measure distances with the handle of his mallet. He stalked about to view the ball in play from every angle. He squinted through hoops with a cunning eye before deciding whether strategy favoured tapping his way through or making an aggressive attack on his opponent's ball. His smile was fiendish when he placed a foot on his own ball and with a triumphant crack sent his enemy off to the far edge of the lawn. Ralph was a keen player himself, who disliked losing almost as much as Pa did, so for a while the game was well fought, despite the less dedicated efforts of Hamish and me.

"*This* hoop next, Polly," Pa said, fuming. "Oh, what a ninny, missing that easy shot! Now look at the position you've put us in. You're not concentrating, girl."

"Why should I? It's only a game."

"Only a game! And what kind of attitude is that, I'd like to know."

"Quite right," Hamish put in. "All the world's a playing-field, you know. Or should know." He looked at me with his hard, unreadable blue eyes. "You remember *The Duchess of Malfi* — 'We are the stars' tennis-balls, struck and bandied / Which way please them.' Or if determinism isn't your bag, think of life as a chessboard, full of strategic games of logic like war and sex. Yes, by all means you should concentrate."

At this point Mrs. Pryde came to the window and with a scarlet-tipped talon beckoned me inside to answer the phone. It was Olivia calling from London, and she had so much to say, and so many questions to ask about the approaching wedding rehearsal, that by the time I went out to the garden again, Pa had lost all patience and haled Lally into the game in my place. She stood with the mallet gripped like a golf-club in her little hands, listening patiently to his instructions; but when he said, "Now!" she barely glanced at the ball before swinging at it. It rolled well to one side of the last pair of hoops. Ralph gleefully tapped his ball through to hit the goalpost with a smart crack.

"Bravo," cried Hamish. "Well done."

"Sheer blind luck," snorted Pa. He fumbled a pound note out of his wallet and stuffed it into Ralph's breast pocket. "As for you, Lall, that absurd dog of yours could have done a better job. Or was it," he added, moving closer to her, and lowering his voice, "just possibly deliberate sabotage?"

Lally flashed him a wicked little smile and redraped her pretty shawl. "Whatever makes you think I'd do a thing like that?" she murmured.

"I don't know exactly, but something does."

"Only men care about winning games," she said, widening her eyes at him. "Women are so much more *serious.*"

Smiling in spite of himself, he took her by the upper arm and gave her a mock shake. A sexual challenge that was almost visible seemed to leap in the air between them and I looked away, more than a little embarrassed. Had Ralph noticed it, I wondered. But I much preferred not to know the answer to that. Nan's reappearance at the bottom of the garden was such a welcome diversion that I went a few steps to meet her.

"No sign of him anywhere," she told me, opening sad, empty hands.

"Not to worry, Nan. He's just gone courting. He'll show up—cats always do."

The sun had disappeared behind a long rack of purple cloud that looked as solid as rock.

"That's right," Ralph said, slipping his arm around her. "Don't worry about it, love. Let's go in; it's getting damp out here now. And Mrs. Pryde had a word with your father at tea-time—she wants us in a bit early for dinner. I think the kitchen people are going to make us a presentation."

This turned out to be an accurate guess. Soon after the coffee was served, the char, the scullery-maid, and Mrs. Pryde bumped through the swing door with a large package. They formed up, clutching it communally, jostling each other and smiling broadly.

"We want you to ave this with our ever so good wishes," announced Mrs. Pryde, who had of course been elected spokesperson for the little group. She presented the box to Nan. With help from Ralph she stripped off the wrapping-paper on which pink wedding-bells rioted, and exposed a carton sealed shut with broad swathes of tape. It was several minutes before Ralph, hissing slightly under his breath, was able to reach his arms into the box and extricate a large electrical appliance flashing with chrome.

"Plug er in ere, sir," whispered the scullery-maid, and Ralph obeyed. After a preliminary buzz and crackle, blue and red mock flames began to play hectically around an artificial log. For a second or two we looked at it, lost for words.

"Thank you very, very much," Ralph finally said in a firm voice. "Most kind of you." He shook hands warmly with all three women. "A lovely gift. And very practical. It will keep us grand and warm next winter, won't it, dear."

Nan murmured agreement. The women gazed with proud satisfaction at their gift, which was now throwing a powerful smell of hot metal into the room.

"Nice, innit? We all chipped in," Mrs. Pryde said modestly. "Includin me daughter, which would be with us tonight if not pregnant. All contributed except Oldfisk, that is. No use expectin anythink from im. Not that e's mean, I'm not sayin that. Only awkward. Don't old with marryin and that, e told us. No use for it. Well, e's peculiar, and there it is. So was all is people. Fac is, is own parents never bothered with it, nor is grandparents neither, or so they say. Anyow, what e gets up to in that ut of is, where none of us as ever set a foot, nobody knows. E lives in them woods like some kind of mole, and I wouldn't mind bettin it's a proper sty, too, with nobody to clean the place up, not since is old mum died right after the war. And as for *er —* "

"Yes, thank you all so much," Pa intervened, since it seemed quite possible Mrs. P. might hold forth all night. The gathering then adjourned with smiles and good will on all sides, and soon after that I went up to bed.

Though I fell asleep quickly, something in the small hours —perhaps a creak or murmur from Lally's room next door —woke me suddenly. I lay there in the dark for some time, vaguely thinking in a disconnected way about the croquet game, Oldfisk's mother, Hamish's quotation, and the possible whereabouts of Crackers. The sounds in the sleeping house were faint and untraceable. A little squall of rain pattered on the window, then stopped. I tried to settle back to sleep, without success. Finally I sat up and groped for my slippers. Perhaps, I thought, a visit to the bathroom down the hall would have a tranquillizing effect. Opening my door noiselessly, I crept along the corridor, which was haunted by pale moonshine, and without a sound slipped into the loo.

Just as I turned to close the door, a movement down the hall caught my eye. A male figure was letting itself quietly out of Lally's room. He moved quickly to the top of the stairs and began to descend. My first thought was 'Pa! You naughty old man!' but before the figure disappeared from view I recognized Ralph's long, narrow back.

'And what in the name of heaven can I do about it?' I asked myself as I crept back to bed. 'Tell Pa? *Again?* He'll only wave the whole thing away, because he won't let anything stop this now — he won't want to know. And after all, maybe it doesn't mean anything. It might have been just a friendly little conference. Well, all right, that isn't too likely, not at three in the morning. But even if . . . I mean, that could be quite insignificant . . . just for old times' sake, something like that. In any case, it's nothing to do with me, is it? Nothing can be done about it, after all.'

The moon sank, the stars faded, the sun came up; and the only conclusion I could arrive at was, 'No, there can't. Not now.' So I said nothing about it to anybody.

The wedding rehearsal was only forty-eight hours away. If the roof of Seven Oaks could have been lifted, the scene would have resembled one of those ant-cities under glass, with all the occupants compulsively scurrying here and there, carrying things, scuttling past one another on errands, meeting and parting without communication. The cake, a towering, multi-storey affair, was delivered and carefully stored in the larder. Nan's wedding-dress came home and a whole wardrobe had to be cleared to accommodate its yards of skirt and train. The filmy veil, delivered separately in an enormous box, was draped, for want of a better place, over the loom in Nan's workroom, to keep it uncrushed. My own pale-blue gown had to be hurried back to Mrs. Ironmould for alteration because I'd lost weight since it was made. And Mrs. Pryde came in early one morning to lobby for inclusion in the wedding music of a song her daughter wanted to sing. Clearing her throat and checking that her top curlers were securely clamped, she warbled us a sample stanza:

> "Oh promise me that some day you and I
> Will take our love together to some sky,
> Where we can be alone and faith renew,
> And find the hollows where those flowers grew—
> Those first sweet violets of early spring—
> Which come in whispers, thrill us both, and sing
> Of love unspeakable that is to be,
> Oh promise me . . . "

"Oh yes, please," said Nan, ignoring my face. "That's pretty." She was clasping Crackers, who butted his head into her neck, purring loudly. He had turned up at last, thin and scruffy-coated, and she had been busy giving him a bath and treating his infected eye.

Leaving them to it, I hurried to answer the phone, which was ringing its head off in the little downstairs study. Hamish had somehow picked up a heavy cold, and by popular request had retired to bed to keep his germs from spreading. The Canterbury florist was on the line to ask would stephanotis do if he couldn't manage white rosebuds for the children's hair. I was just hanging up when Pa hurried in with a cablegram in his hands. Without bothering to close the door, he raised his voice above the char's chatter in the dining-room, where she was helping to pack up Nan's presents.

"What d'ye think of this, Pol!" he cried. "Remember that chap from Johns Hopkins who wanted me to give a lecture series in the States? Well, he's offering to organize a coast-to-coast reading tour this fall. Ten universities and four organizations hot on culture are committed already. A thousand dollars a night, and travel expenses. Marvellous publicity, too, of course. Won't that be a bit of a lark, eh?"

"You're not actually going to do it! Leave everything here and — what will — and quite apart from everything else, it would be hellishly strenuous, Pa."

"Of course it will be. It will also be very stimulating. Actual contact with readers—the questions they ask—it's all *productive*, you know. And another important thing— the support they give is deeply nourishing. Nobody realizes how isolated one is; how much one needs to hear from the reading public—actually to see them out there—"

"Well, I see all that, Pa, but I would have thought you'd prefer to get on with your new—" I began; but Pa was prowling around the room muttering, "Wisconsin. San Francisco. I've never been there."

As obbligato to this, the char's voice from the dining-room floated to us. "Ow look, Eileen. In' this ever so pretty." A faint crash followed. "You silly nit," another voice said crossly. "Well, go and get the Hoover, do."

"Oh yes, it's time I got around more," Pa was saying. "It's been a bit of a mistake, I'm afraid, this retreat into rural life. All this domesticity. A bit stifling. Family's all very well, Pol, but one needs . . . anyway, now things here have turned out as they have, there's no need any more for me to keep on this big house. Nan's taken care of now, and you're going back to London . . . I shall put Seven Oaks on the market as soon as the wedding's out of the way."

The whine of the vacuum cleaner rose briefly, then died away. "Footloose and fancy-free," pursued Pa, tilting up and down on the balls of his feet, "that's what I'm going to be. Travel. Change. No more responsibilities. What a shot in the old arm that will be, eh?" He performed a gay little chassé around the desk to make me smile. "I shall invite Hamish to come along with me as manager," he continued. "There's something wrong with him these days. Boredom, in all probability. The change will do him the world of good."

"But Pa, what about all that chat about a *mas* in Provence? Only a few weeks ago you—"

"Oh well, maybe some day. It's the west that beckons now—the new world." And he made an airy gesture that relegated the south of France to complete oblivion.

"Yes, but Pa, selling this place just like that—isn't it Lally's home now? Sorry if I seem confused, but surely you . . . that's the impression I had."

"My dear, Lally will be perfectly all right. She has a little income of her own, you know. Of course, she can stay on here for a bit—show the house and so on, if she likes—until it's sold. After that—well, she's not my responsibility, is she."

"Isn't she, Pa?" I asked with mounting indignation.

"Certainly not. She can go and live with her sister in Norfolk."

"She hates Norfolk. Come to that, she hates her sister."

"Well, that's not my problem."

"Now see here, Pa—"

A flick of movement in the gap of the open door caught my eye—a glimpse of blue and rose. Lally's shawl. She must have wandered into the dining-room, perhaps in search of a biscuit for Darling, and turned away again as soon as she noticed the two women there packing up the gifts. When I put my head out she was already disappearing gracefully from view. It seemed most improbable that she could have heard anything said in the office; nevertheless, I turned back to Pa to ask him sternly, "Have you discussed any of your plans with Lall? Because I think she damn well has a right to hear what they are, and the sooner the better."

"Oh, don't fuss yourself, child. Lally knows how to look after herself, never fear. Besides, my guess is that she's fed up to the eyes with country life herself by this time. I know her pretty well, Polly, after all these years. We understand each other. There's no call for anyone to worry about Lally."

I could not deny there was some truth in everything he said, and yet I had more to say to Pa, and opened my mouth to begin. But just then the phone rang again and, waving his telegram lightly in farewell, he slipped out of the room.

The evening of the rehearsal, Jill and her little sister climbed out of their father's car and joined us in the church porch. They wore narrow white frocks cut low at the ruffled neckline and bound under the armpits with broad sashes of blue satin. Fingerless lace mittens adorned their small hands. Slippers trimmed with blue rosettes could be glimpsed under the frilled hem of the dresses. They looked smugly aware of their own charm, but the same could not be said of Bill's youngest son, who looked truculently miserable.

He had obviously been inserted under protest into his pale-blue suit with its calf-length trousers and short jacket topped with a frilled collar of white linen. Under a tall white blue-banded hat with a curly brim, his eyes glared out, fiercely daring anybody to laugh. It had been decided to dress the children in their outfits tonight, so they would feel at ease in them before the actual wedding, and in Charley's case this was clearly a good idea, though I doubted whether he would ever be reconciled to the white socks and black slippers that completed his costume, or to the two-buttoned front flap of his Victorian trousers.

The rest of us stood in the porch or out under the green evening sky, exchanging small talk while we waited for Richard to arrive. Nan was in her old cords with a sweater knotted around her waist by the sleeves. She fidgeted restlessly to and fro, speaking to no one, until Ralph's car pulled up at the lych-gate.

"Here he is," said Pa, who had also been rather edgy and distrait all evening. "And here comes Richard as well. Now we can get on with it."

"Good evening, all," said the Vicar, making the rounds with a cordial handshake for everyone. He had evidently come straight from his garden and had to pause to knock clots of earth from his shoes before ushering us into the church.

As soon as Ralph joined us and took Nan's hand, a sort of calm dignity descended on her. She stood quietly beside our father at the end of the nave, her arm slipped through his, her eyes on the altar. Amid considerable wriggling and giggling, the young ones were marshalled into place at the head of the line, while Olivia and I took our places behind.

Richard strode up to the transept, gesturing to Ralph with his best man to come and stand at his elbow. Then, with the flourish of an orchestra conductor, he beckoned the bridal party forward. I paced toward him, keeping step with Olivia, in a stately fashion farcically out of keeping with my shabby old tweed skirt and wind-cheater. We reached the chancel, where, opening his worn prayer-book, but not looking at it, Richard began to skim through the Form of Solemnization of Matrimony.

Aside from a brief punch on the arm administered by Charley to Jill, who had put out her tongue at him, the children played their part with decorum. Everything went smoothly, even to the exchange of the rings, which was the one part of the affair, Ralph had confided to us repeatedly, that made him nervous as a cat.

There was a friendly sort of intimacy in the little church that gradually relaxed us all. When Nan sneezed explosively a general smile went round. Ralph scratched the back of his neck quite nonchalantly while Richard murmured on about the fruitful vine and the olive branches. Pa openly winked at me while he exhorted Nan to shun the plaiting of hair and wearing of gold, but to ornament herself with a meek and quiet spirit. But at the conclusion, as if to remind us where we were, Richard lifted his head and filled the whole church with the slow, clear words of a benediction: "The peace of God which passeth all understanding keep your hearts and minds in the knowledge and love of God, and the blessing of God Almighty be amongst you and remain with you always."

"Well, somebody has to cry at weddings," I muttered to Olivia, wiping my eyes.

We all piled into cars then and drove back to the house for a buffet meal. Hermione and Lally were waiting for us there, and greeted us with enthusiasm and a large jug of martinis. A faintly hilarious air about the two suggested they had already sampled it pretty freely, and we were not slow to follow their example. Soon the whole first floor of the house filled up with the convivial din of people enjoying themselves. Ralph fell into animated business chat with James. Richard helped himself largely to the lobster bisque and rolled his eyes at Nan in appreciation. Someone put on a tape, and the teasing rhythm of the tango threaded through the talk. The children tore around in pursuit of each other, sliding in their new slippers and agitating the dogs, until someone finally swept them off to bed.

Perhaps energized by the martinis, Lally drew Alan into a few steps of the tango, and after a moment he kicked the hall rugs aside so they could dip and glide with more abandon. She was wearing her low-cut black sheath edged with silk fringe, and it set off her still-trim figure and flushed cheeks very attractively. She managed to make the sinuous steps of the dance both languid and outrageously sexy. Ralph watched her with a faint smile. Richard, a forkful of chicken halfway to his mouth, stared at her, openly fascinated.

"A shameless kind of dance, isn't it?" Hermione said. "Like watching a couple of cobras mate. Reminds one how deadly serious and menacing sex actually is." Lally gave Alan a slit-eyed smile, as if she entirely agreed.

The headache that had nagged me intermittently all day was growing worse. I went upstairs and gave it some Aspirin to placate it, and on the way back met Nan coming up with a tray for Hamish, who was still nursing his cold in seclusion. She held the tray out to me invitingly, but I shook my head and continued on down. In the dining-room I looked about for Pa, but he had disappeared — someone said to take a phone call in the study. Ralph was telling Hermione about Crete, where he was taking Nan for their honeymoon. The music had switched to Boy George. Alan and Olivia were arguing about Northern Ireland. Eventually Lally announced benignly to the company at large that she was drunk, and, kissing everybody randomly within reach, she took herself off rather unsteadily to bed.

Soon after that the party broke up to allow everybody a good rest before the next day's festivities. Ralph, demurely observing the proprieties, drove off with the Vicar and Hermione, to spend his last bachelor night under a different roof from the bride. James and his wife adjourned to their hotel, and the rest of us scattered to our various beds.

For some time now — in fact, ever since Ralph's small-hours visit to the next room — I had taken a sleeping-pill to ensure an unbroken night, and I did so now. But some hours later, just after daybreak, I woke with a confused sense that someone in the house was crying. One of the children, perhaps, I thought. But even though I listened intently, the silence of the sleeping house was unbroken. Of course, it was nothing but the delusive tag-end of some dream or other, I told myself. There was not a sound from Lally's room. How could anyone imagine there would be, I told myself, grinning in the dark. She was no doubt dead to the world, and a good thing too. Poor old Lall, she was almost sure to have a wicked hangover when she did wake up.

At seven-thirty, three unshaven labourers arrived at the front door with the marquee. They had the disenchanted air of men who had been there before, and leaned against their van as if already exhausted.

"Pa!" I called. "Where do you want the tent? Will you come and cope?"

With his breakfast napkin still tucked into the front of his dressing-gown, Pa hurried to the door. Soon the whack of mallets and some very bad language rose from the misty, fragrant garden, where fitful gusts of wind and occasional spats of rain did their best to make life miserable for the working class.

"You must eat something, Polly," urged Pa, reseating himself at the table. "And see that Nan does too. We don't want anybody fainting in church. These scrambled eggs are excellent." To everyone's exasperation he had insisted on a full cooked breakfast which no one but himself had the time or inclination to eat. The hairdresser presented herself at eight — a cheerful, gum-chewing girl who, after wrapping herself in a violet nylon overall, set up her equipment in the upstairs bathroom and proceeded to wash and set the little girls' hair. Soon a pervasive smell of hair-spray drifted through the house. The florist's boxes arrived next, with the bride's bouquet and beribboned posies for her attendants. There was of course no room for it all in the fridge, so space had to be hurriedly made in the larder. Last-minute presents were delivered. The phone rang and rang. By nine-thirty Boris had barked himself hoarse, and I would have been glad to crawl back into bed.

The arrival at ten of the photographer, to survey the territory and take a few shots of the preparations, precipitated a crisis: Charley refused outright to be photographed in his Greenaway outfit. His brothers had been left behind in London expressly so they could not see him in this rig and torment him accordingly; but no one in the obtuse grown-up world had realized that this precaution would be wasted if pictures were taken of him in his pale blue and ruffles, to be put in the family album. In short, the rest of his entire life would be blighted. He made and repeated this point with passionate tears and some kicking. His mother, wringing her hands, was no use at all. "Pa, will you please do something about Charley," I said in desperation. "Kill him, if necessary. It's my turn with the hairdresser now. There's that wretched phone again—Hamish, will you—"

An hour later I emerged from the bathroom with my hair smoothed down over my ears from a demure centre part and pinned at the side with a cluster of flowers which released a cloying scent whenever I moved. I was fastening my dress, fumbling impatiently with its little hooks, when inarticulate roars from Pa's room brought me hurrying down to him with my bodice only half fastened.

"What on earth is it now?"

"My shoelace! It's broken off! Look at the damn thing! And I haven't got any more. Not a damn one. My best shoes! I can't wear brown laces. What the hell am I to do?"

"Try Hamish, Pa—he may have some. And cool down. You could always wear these black slip-ons, couldn't you?"

"They hurt my feet," he said pathetically. He was in his unbuttoned dress-shirt and waistcoat, with a towel still around his neck from shaving. Little threads of vein webbed the whites of his eyes and agitation made him breathe heavily.

"Now sit down for a minute, Pa, and take it easy. How did you get Charley to shut up?"

"Shameless bribery and corruption," he said with a faint smile.

"Ah."

"You look charming, Polly. Or will when you do yourself up."

"Thanks, Pa. I've got to fly now and help Nan dress. God, is that really the time?" But when I put my head into Nan's bedroom it was empty. Her workroom, too, was deserted, though the long veil had been taken away, I supposed for a last-minute pressing. I looked into the sitting-room where the little girls in their white frocks had been seated under strict orders to play with jigsaw puzzles. Their glossy hair, like mine, had been dressed down smoothly and bound at one side with a fillet of white flowers, and they looked angelic.

"Hullo, you two. Have you seen your Auntie Nan, Jill?"

"No. I'm hungry. I want some cake."

"Me too."

"Well, you can ask Mrs. Pryde for a biscuit, maybe, or an apple. Nothing sticky or messy."

"I want cake."

"You'll be sick, silly," said her sister, making a hideous face.

"Won't," said the other, her lip trembling ominously.

"Yes, you will."

"Dummy, I won't! I want cake."

"Me too. I want cake!"

I left them, suppressing an urge to knock their angelic heads together.

In the dining-room Olivia, picturesque in her Victorian finery, her dark hair beflowered like mine, stood at the window smoking a cigarette and looking out at the cloudy sky. It felt odd to look at anyone dressed exactly like myself, as if neither of us could be quite real. "Have you seen Nan?" I asked her rather breathlessly.

"Oh, she was around . . . carried her dress through. I think the rain's going to hold off."

"But where is she now? Surely not in the kitchen fussing over food. She has to get *dressed*."

No one was in the kitchen, however, except Eileen the scullery-maid, clamped into Walkman head-phones and swaying rhythmically as she washed up the breakfast things. I tried the little downstairs study next, and found Lally there, rather morosely huddled over a cup of black coffee. She was still in her dressing-gown, an embroidered silk affair from Hong Kong, and her hair had not yet been fluffed into its usual elaborate curls. It was carelessly brushed back and tied with a bit of ribbon. She looked very pale. It occurred to me that never in all the years I'd known her had I seen Lally without any make-up on. I was careful not to smile.

"It's getting a bit late, Lall — time to dress. Where's Nan, do you know?"

"No idea," muttered Lally.

"But this is ridiculous — does she know the time?"

"She never does."

"But — has she gone out, or what? Has Crackers gone

missing again? — It would be just like her to hare off looking for him, wedding or no wedding."

Lally lifted her face and looked at me. With a little shock
I saw that her eyelids were red and her colourless, soft
mouth was unsteady.

"Maybe there won't be a wedding," she said. And with
that, I recognized the authentic shape and ring of the crisis
I'd feared all along.

"What are you talking about, Lall?" I said through lips
that felt stiff.

"She came in here to ask me for something borrowed.
She actually asked *me* — and I said, 'Darling, the *bridegroom's* borrowed. Didn't you know?' Well, it's the truth,
isn't it? He'd never have looked at Nan if Monty hadn't
pinned all that money to her skirt. You know that. Ralph
doesn't give a damn about anybody, of course, but the point
is he doesn't give a damn about *her*. Everybody knows it.
Now she knows it too."

"Lally—"

"Yes, I told her the whole rather squalid story. So now
she knows. At least she stood here with her mouth open
while I told her. Of course, the woman's only half there,
so it's hard to tell, but I think she got the message. Yes,
I think she actually got it at last."

I looked at her. No words came. For a minute I could
neither think nor move. Around me the whole house was
full of Pa's voice calling, the phone ringing, children running,
Mrs. Pryde's cackling laugh. At last I found my legs and ran
out through the French doors, hoping I might catch Nan in
the flower-garden or beyond the brick wall where vegetables were pricking out between neatly pegged cords. A rake
and barrow stood on one of the paths, but no one was there.
Beyond the hedge stretched the orchard, white with blossom, and I hurried toward it, my mouth dry and heart
labouring. The grass was white with a snow of fallen petals.

Then something else white suddenly jumped into my frame of vision. With a sort of numb horror I saw a limp figure in voluminous white hanging from one of the apple trees. The wind lifted wide satin skirts and a long lace veil, and a drift of blossom blew around them. There was a moment when my eyes clouded with dizziness and I thought my knees would fold. I forced myself to go nearer, and then I saw that Pa's bearded, life-sized doll had been grotesquely stuffed into the wedding-gown and the whole thing strung up by the neck with a bit of cord from one of the higher boughs. The effect was black-comic, bizarre, and chilling beyond words. As if slyly chuckling, the wind fingered the yards of satin fabric and made it rustle. One of the dogs galloped up to me jovially and thrust his head under my hand. I looked numbly around, but there was no one at all in sight. Slowly, moving with stiff limbs, I went back to the house to tell my father.

The first person I met inside the French doors was Pa, now fully dressed in his cutaway coat with striped trousers and a camellia in his buttonhole. "Where have you—" he began. After one glance at my face, he drew me into the little study and closed the door quietly after us. Lally's empty cup was still on the desk, but nothing else of hers occupied the room except her gardenia scent.

I told him what had to be told. He listened, head a little thrown back, his face quite expressionless. Strangely, he remained perfectly calm. He did not even seem greatly surprised. After I'd finished, there was a brief silence. I noticed that both his shoes were done up with black laces, and thought, "Hamish must have had an extra pair," as if this were quite important. At last Pa lifted his shoulders in something almost like a shrug.

"So," he said, looking at his watch. "It's nearly noon. I'll phone the Vicarage right away and let them know. Hamish will have to get started at once dismantling everything here, and warning off as many guests as he can reach. If you see Olivia, get her to tell the mothers . . . they might as well pack up and take the kids back to London straight away—that will make for less confusion in the house. Are you all right? Want a nip of brandy or anything? Well, before anything else, if you can manage it, I want you to go out there and take down that—bring the wedding-dress in, before anyone sees it. There's going to be talk enough without that. All right? Sure? Can you do that?"

"Yes."

"Good girl. Go right away." He turned to pick up the phone with a perfectly steady hand and began to dial. I went back to the dining-room, which was momentarily deserted, and on the buffet found one of those corkscrews with a knife attached to it. Without waiting even to glance around for Olivia, I went out again with the cold metal object in my colder hand, and crossed the two gardens to the orchard. The sun had now come out in full radiance and the long gown shone as the wind lifted and billowed it. A few drops of rain had spangled the satin and it made my eyes dazzle in the bright light.

Without a ladder, cutting the mannequin down seemed at first impossible, but with the help of fierce determination and a few low-leaning boughs, I managed to clamber up high enough to saw at the rope with my knife. An amazing length of time seemed to elapse and my arm ached before the cord finally parted. After that, dragging down the voluminous gown with its train and veil was astonishingly difficult. Twigs and branches snared the fabric as I tugged at it. The wind blew and further entangled the lace veil, so that finally I had to tear it free. Petals and drops of rain from the tree showered coldly down on my Victorian coiffure and my bare neck and arms. My pale-blue skirts were damp and stained with moss by the time I finally managed to bundle the whole white mass into my arms and stumble back to the house with it.

I had no idea whether all this took five minutes or an hour, but when I re-entered the house it was obvious that the news had spread. In place of all the hustle and busy-ness, a sort of consternation hung in the quiet air. At the front door stood Bill's car, half loaded with luggage, its four doors gaping open. Beside it, young Charley, hands in jean pockets, kicked pebbles with a contented air. A taxi from Canterbury was also in the drive, its engine running, and I was just in time to glimpse Lally's trim leg vanishing into it. Down the drive it went, grew small, and disappeared.

Hamish appeared from somewhere and took the cumber-some soiled bundle out of my arms. Lifting one of the win-dow-seats he stuffed the whole thing inside and dropped the lid on it. From a crack at the side of the swing door, Mrs. Pryde's avid eye stared at us a moment, then vanished. To have the grotesque doll and all that heavy drapery lifted away from me and hidden was such a huge relief that my arms began to tremble. The trembling swept all through me and made my teeth chatter together.

"You sit down," Hamish's voice said loudly. He pushed me into a chair and disappeared. Some time later he was back with a decanter in his hand. He bent over me and folded my cold hand around a glass. He looked intently into my eyes. Then he lifted my chin and with the ball of his thumb very lightly chafed my cold lips. This created a stab of pleas-ure so keen it stopped the trembling at once. A vague, sur-prised sort of warmth began to spread all through my cold flesh.

"Now drink this," he said. The neat brandy burned my throat, but it cleared a little of the confusion out of my head.

"Hamish, we have to find Nan. I'm frightened."

"Don't worry. We'll find her."

"Where can she have gone?"

"Not to the Vicarage. Richard was the likeliest person, I thought. But we checked. She hasn't been there."

"The cottage, maybe."

"Yes. The phone's not in yet. I'll drive over there right away."

"Let me come. If she's there—"

"Change that dress first. Yes, you'd better come. She trusts you."

"Don't—" I began before my throat closed. But my tears froze before they could form. The whole situation was still like a shadow-play, dreamlike and numb, and the one thing to hope for was that it stay that way. Pa now appeared in the doorway, upright, calm, even debonair in his formal clothes. 'Well, at least he's all right so far,' I thought. 'We don't have to cope with him collapsing; not yet, at any rate.'

"We're going to the cottage now to see if Nan's there," Hamish told him. "After that we'll try the village . . . she knows people there—Bagshot, perhaps . . . Anyhow, someone may have seen her. Then Canterbury. If there's no sign of her before dark, I think you'll have to notify the police."

"Yes," said Pa calmly. It seemed that for him, too, none of this was quite real. But he turned away from us to look out in defeat at the bright day. "I never thought," he said in bewilderment, as if to himself, "that Nan would do a thing like this to me."

Darkness came and there was still no word of Nan. The house had by then emptied. Ralph waited at the Vicarage for news. Our phone was still. The servants had all scattered to their homes to discuss the whole thing at luxurious length. We three wandered from room to room swallowing cups of tea like medicine, pausing often to listen at doors and windows for any step or voice outside. Nothing was out there, though, but the wind.

At other times we sat in chairs and looked at each other.

"Did she have any money with her?"

"I don't know. Probably not."

"What was she wearing, do you know?"

"Those awful old cords—I think."

"Someone must have seen her."

"Nobody seems to."

"She can't simply have vanished into thin air."

"No."

"I suppose it is better for Ralph to stay over there with Richard, in case she—"

"Yes."

"I simply can't think what else she'd do but come back home."

"Has anybody seen Crackers today?"

"I don't know—why?"

Then we would get up and walk about again. The dogs pattered after us restlessly. Ivan whimpered from time to time until Pa said violently, "Shut that god-damn dog in the kitchen."

"It's nearly ten, Monty," Hamish said, after dragging Ivan away. "Will you call the police or do you want me to do it?"

"I'll do it." Heavily he moved off to the phone.

"You go up to bed, Polly," Hamish said.

The very thought of bed made me feel stunned with fatigue, and it was several minutes before I could find the energy to drag myself upstairs. Yet once in my room, where I mechanically undressed and brushed out my hair, I was suddenly restless again. I paced up and down in my dressing-gown, peering out often into the dark, where there was nothing to see but my own white face staring at me from the glass. The discarded flowers of my head-dress, wilted now, and hours ago dropped into the wastebasket, sent up a sweet, corrupt odour.

Dimly down below I heard a car pull up and an official voice rumble. The police would want full details, of course, and a photograph. Were there any pictures of Nan? And if there were, what would they show of her? The official voice rumbled again, then the front door closed after it, and the car drove off. The slow feet of Pa came upstairs and went into his room. Then the uneven, heavier tread of Hamish followed. The lights went out, all but one in the downstairs hall. The house was perfectly quiet. I kept on pacing up and down.

After a while I wrapped the skirts of my gown close and went down the stairs to the second floor. In the dark I opened Hamish's door, dropped my robe on the floor, and went to his bed. Even before he touched me the releasing tears were wet on my face.

The random things that happened next had some of the bizarre detachment from reality of a clock striking thirteen. One event followed another without causal connection or consequence of any kind.

Days went by and there was no news of Nan.

Pa developed an attack of gout (this time in both knees) that was so severe we had to ask Bagshot to call. He administered a shot of cortisone which gave instant relief, and before leaving to rattle away in his little car, he paused to say to me, "I was very sorry—very sorry indeed—to hear about Nan. Will you be sure to let me know if ever there's anything I can do to help." There was a new air of self-confidence about him which not only took most of the dither out of his conversation but made it possible for him to be genuinely kind. I thanked him and took away the thought that there must be more in post-office Gladys than met the eye.

The police circulated Nan's description but were unable to find any trace of her.

One afternoon the powerful and quite groundless conviction came to me that Richard knew where she was, and for some reason was unwilling to tell us. I went straight to the Vicarage to confront him. He was digging manure

into his rose beds and paused to listen to me with one foot
on the fork. His blue eyes opened wide and he shook his
head.

"My dear Polly," he said. "I wish I did know."

"I'm responsible for a lot of this, you realize," I told him.

"Yes, I do."

"At least you tell no soothing lies. This will never wash
off any of us, especially me."

"Maybe not. But there are times, you know, when guilt
can have a positive value. What you're feeling now is painful, even terrible, but it's not negative, d'ye see what I
mean? You were detached before — only half here. Half
committed. That isn't true now, is it."

"No. Not now."

"Why don't you go in and say hello to Hermione."

"Yes. I'll do that."

I pushed open the Vicarage front door and stepped inside. An eldritch shriek of laughter led me along the narrow
Edwardian hallway to the kitchen. There I found Hermione
swathed in a turban she had improvised out of a tea-towel.
A flour-daubed plastic apron depicting the Union Jack covered her portly front. She had just extracted a cake from
the oven. Even as I looked at it, the sponge sank further
in the middle and leaned to one side as if exhausted. It
smelled quite strongly of tarragon.

"Isn't it ghastly!" she cried, slapping it down on the table
and wiping her eyes with an oven mitt. "My own invention!
Horrible! Just shows you the dangers of creativity. Sit
down, dear."

Every available space seemed to be occupied with bags,
canisters, spoons, and bowls, as well as unrelated objects
like a handful of unposted letters, shampoo, a screwdriver,
and the black cat; but by dint of transferring a flour-
dredger to the table and the cat to my lap, I cleared a
stool for myself. Hermione briskly set a cracked teacup
half full of gin at my elbow.

"Tuck into that, Pol, you look as if you'd been brooding. Great mistake, that. Only leads to indigestion and self-righteousness. Well, the house seems quite empty now with Ralph gone, so I thought I'd do some baking. As you see, *not* a success; but it keeps me out of mischief." She gave me a comradely wink. "He was rather good company, Ralph. Men like that generally are, don't you find."

"If you mean men without a shadow, no," I said sourly.

"Indigestion and self-righteousness," repeated Hermione. "Not as attractive a couple as Irony and Pity."

I kicked the leg of my stool. After a moment I said, "Where did he go?—back to London? And never even bothered to say goodbye to us? Even for Ralph that's pretty cool."

"Your father was here yesterday. They had a long talk. Quite amicable, as far as I could tell from the keyhole. And after all, I don't suppose Ralph owes anybody an apology, does he."

"Nobody but God, maybe."

"Now there you go again, Pol, being severe. Young people are so pitilessly judgemental. Not of themselves, which would be right and proper, but of their elders. How can you know what the man thinks and feels after this fiasco?"

"What he thinks is maybe his own business. But would you say he feels anything—anything at all?"

Hermione considered this, rubbing the end of her nose thoughtfully. "The day it happened, he seemed quite . . . put out. After that, who could tell."

"Exactly. Put out. That would be all he's capable of."

"Don't be too sure. Nobody won in that affair, did they? Everybody, in fact, lost. Suffered, if you prefer."

I kicked my stool again. "But some of us a lot more than others. Because we had a lot more of ourselves invested."

"Not sure that's the same thing as a moral advantage. Anyway, who are we to measure what Ralph lost?"

Purring loudly, the cat turned itself around in my lap,

gave its tail two brisk licks, then fell asleep precipitately in mid-purr. I sipped my gin. Hermione broke off a bit of the cake, tasted it, and hastily opened the kitchen door to spit it out. A thrush immediately seized it and flew off with it in triumph.

"Nothing will happen to him," I said; "that's what gets to me. He'll just go on as usual, groomed and urbane, having malt whiskies at other people's expense, and charming publishers at book fairs."

"Haven't we all got a surface that's constructed for camouflage? And camouflage is a protective device, yes?"

I thought about this. 'Not with Hamish,' I thought of saying, then changed my mind.

"Lally will probably track him down and go back to him in the end," Hermione went on. "They belong together, after all. Think about that. Wouldn't you call that a form of poetic justice?"

Unwillingly I gave a snuffling little laugh. Whether it was the gin or the small warmth of the cat on my lap, or Hermione's crooked fortune-teller's turban from which tendrils of her red hair were escaping wildly in all directions, something eased and comforted me. I felt almost cheerful as I tilted up the teacup to drain its last drops. Hermione, on the other hand, stared in a hallucinated sort of way out at the sunny green garden where Richard could be seen delving, and muttered only half audibly, "This vegetable world ... all that coarse material ... if only we could see through it to those other presences, angels and archangels, patriarchs, prophets, apostles, the flower of Heaven and all the saints ... all of them made of air, nothing but air, and yet they're here all around us every day ... Now *there's* that pesky gas bill. How on earth did it get on the floor?"

Without attempting to answer, I stood up, said goodbye to Hermione with a kiss, and groped my way out along the dark corridor toward the front door, where I'd left my bicycle. As I came into the main hall, which was occupied by a patch of sunlight so brilliant it made me blink, I thought for the fraction of a second that I saw a little boy about six years old at the foot of the stairs. He seemed to be playing. An instant later he was gone.

There continued to be no news of Nan.

One morning Oldfisk failed to turn up for work. He had missed some days without anyone's noticing, because his work habits, like everything else about him, were eccentric. But this time he never reappeared.

I woke up cold as a stone with fear one morning about six, and, turning to Hamish, shook him awake. His arms came around me before his eyes opened.

"The pond," I said. "Why didn't I think of it before?— the pond. She liked the pond."

"Polly, take it easy. What pond?"

"She showed it to me once. Past the old railway. About a mile from here. Across that field with the cows."

"We'll get dressed and you'll show me where."

We slipped out of the house and walked across the fields. A fine, milky mist first veiled everything, then slowly lifted. The pond was there, sheltered by its leaning trees. The water was dark and deep, rippled by a fresh wind. On one of its muddy lips were footprints that might have been a woman's. Hamish turned me away from them. We drove after that to the Canterbury police station. Hamish went in alone. After a few minutes two men set off in a van with equipment in it for dragging.

No body was found in the pond.

Crackers disappeared again. This time he did not come back.

Around sunset one day I idled around the garden trying to fill in time by nipping deadheads off the early roses, and picking up stray bits of litter left by the workmen when they removed the marquee. They had made muddy wounds in the soft green turf with their work-boots and tent-pegs. I tried to smooth away these scars with my foot. The air felt empty. The house at my back was silent and vacant. Hamish had driven off on some errand or other, and the staff had all gone home for the day. Though there was a gusty, rather cold wind fitfully seething in the trees and tossing the taller flowers to and fro, everything seemed static, as if the earth had halted on its axis and time had forgotten how to move on.

Then my eye was caught by the sudden appearance over the top of the brick wall of a tall tongue of orange flame. It seemed to stand there silently and look at me like a messenger. A moment later a gush of black smoke rose with it, as well as a powerful reek of paraffin. It was too windy a day for such a big fire, and I went swiftly through the brick archway to remonstrate with Fisk, forgetting he'd not been seen for over a week.

It was Pa who stood in the kitchen-garden, rake in hand, his white hair dishevelled by the wind. He had heaped up a great pyre, on which was now burning the dirty white mass of the wedding-dress. On top of it all he had flung the life-sized doll, like some latter-day Guy Fawkes. As the flames licked this effigy in the shimmer of heat, it seemed to writhe horribly, and I could not look at it. Pa, however, stared steadily into the blaze. If he knew I was there, he gave no sign of it.

The smoke billowed up to stain the moody sky. He wiped the sleeve of his torn old sweater across his forehead, leaving a dark smudge there. I went close to him then and linked my arm through his, but he made no response.

In silence we watched the figure on the pyre crumple and shrink till it was wholly consumed. Finally, when nothing was left of it but a few black cinders fluttering upward on the wind, I said, "Man and Superman. You were right to burn it, Pa."

But he did not even glance at me before turning aside to a carton at his feet I had not noticed before. He bent, and, before I realized what he was doing, drew up a mass of typed pages and threw them recklessly on the fire. The flames leaped up again toward the yellow sky. I looked helplessly around for Hamish, but he was nowhere in sight.

"Pa! What are you doing? That's never your—"

Turning his head stiffly he looked at me, but made no answer before stooping to bring up another double handful of manuscript. On these pages I could see a web of close-packed hand-written interlinings and crossings-out. All the craftsman's struggles and striving were recorded there like a signature of authenticity.

"I am burning rubbish," he said.

"Oh Pa, don't talk nonsense. Your book — all that work—"

"Words. It's only words. The charlatan's tatty little box of tricks."

"No Pa, you're just being — if you're trying to punish yourself, stop it this minute."

He did not appear to hear me. "It's only patter. Double-talk. The spiel of the con man tricking attention away from what's really going on. Just a lot of make-believe. What is it but a gimmick. Look, folks, there's nothing here—look there, here's something of value. Just a box of tricks. And in this case, the trick doesn't even work." He threw more papers on the blaze. They curled and fluttered as if alive; one of them, tilted and flung up by an air current, drifted intact over the brick wall. I tried to pull back his arm as he bent to get more out of the box, but he shook my hand off indifferently.

"Please, Pa—this is just stupid. If it were all those letters and things for the archives—but not your book. That's

something else entirely . . . it's the best of you, can't you
get that much right at least?"

It seemed to me so important to make him understand
that I actually tried to wrest the papers out of his hands
before he could destroy any more of them. But he simply
went on calmly tossing the pages onto the fire as if I were
not there. It was obvious that he saw himself as Prospero,
breaking all his charms, drowning his book. No one could
alter that vision of himself, and reluctantly I realized that
no one should try. In the yellow gleam of the setting sun
his eyes were red with smoke or tears, and I had no more
to say to him. I stood there in silence till the box was empty
and the fire sank low. Then he raked it over with earth and
together we went into the house.

Then there was the morning when I had a strangely vivid
dream. In an entanglement of forest far from anywhere
stood a little hut almost hidden by tall grass and sunlit wild
vegetation. No one could be seen or heard, but smoke rose
from the chimney, and a faint singing hum hung in the air.
Even though I could not see her, I knew that Nan was
inside there, spinning at her wheel. I called her name and
Crackers looked out at me from the green undergrowth,
then disappeared. When I called once more, hut and woods
and all vanished, but I could still hear that faint, singing
hum.

Once more I woke Hamish, who patiently heard me out.
We got up, he put me into the car, and without saying anything to Pa, we set out in search of Fisk's hut. Two hours
of inquiry went by, stopping, questioning, and going on,
before we drew up by a group of grubby boys kicking a
tennis-ball from side to side of a rural lane.

"Oldfisk?" one of them said with a grin. He exchanged
a smirk with his friends. "E's bonkers, mister. So was is
dad. So's is girlfriend. *And* is cats and dogs. Well-known
fac. You can't want *im.*"

"Where's his house?" Hamish said, with no change of expression.

The boy's face became cunningly vacant. Hamish brought out his wallet and said casually, "Near here somewhere, isn't it? Want to show us where?"

Once more they exchanged glances. One of them pointed to the left, where an overgrown, abandoned road straggled into some woods. "Down along there," he said, his eyes fixed on the wallet.

"Right. Thanks." Hamish handed over a bill. The whole group instantly took to their heels, guffawing and punching each other as they went. We drove along the neglected roadway until it petered out. Evidence of motorcycle-club gatherings and sexual encounters littered the track. We went on foot farther into the copse. The path thinned and then vanished as the woods thickened. Still we went on, clambering over tangled fallen branches and pushing through shoulder-high bracken. The air felt close, hot, and dead. Flies sang around our heads. Brambles tore at our clothes and tall stinging-nettles burned our hands. At last through the foliage we spotted the dark roof of a hut, out of which poked a skewed metal chimney. No smoke came from it. There was no sound of any kind to be heard. As we pushed our way closer, we saw that the hovel was derelict, its windows smashed, the door pulled half off its hinges. Obviously no one had lived there for some time.

We stood there looking at it in silence. For the first time then I understood that I would never see Nan again.

Epilogue

I n autumn sunlight thick with dust and diesel fumes, I trotted along Oxford Street on my way home from work. A plastic shopping-bag containing shoe-polish, sherry, and a new egg-whisk swung from my hand. A lazy little breeze fluttered the London litter of sweet-wrappers, cigarette-ends, and bus tickets on the grimy pavement. Just as I paused to look at a pyramid of new novels in a bookstore window, a familiar figure dodged between clusters of shoppers and caught up with me. It was Walt the actor, sporting a broad and jaunty smile. He also wore a new up-curled RAF moustache which gave his freckled face the comic absurdity of a child wearing a pirate's eyepatch.

"Polly, my duck! What a nice surprise running into you! It's been ages—back in London now, are you?"

"Yes, ages. How are you, Walt?"

"Bursting with health, ta. Come on — you're not in a hurry, are you? Let's have a coffee and a nice little natter."

It would have been hard—in fact, impossible—to explain to Walt how much, without exactly being in a hurry, I wanted to get home to a commonplace three-room flat in Fulham occupied mostly by shabby books; so I let him seize my elbow and hustle me into a nearby milk bar. Here a number of weary housewives leaned on the counter easing their feet before facing the rush-hour battle to get home with their string bags of shopping. I set down my own plastic container of trivia with care on the grubby floor and joined the line-up.

"Two white, please," said Walt to a smock-clad attendant glazed with boredom. "Now let's catch up on the news, love. I was sorry to hear all that ... er ... about your sister. Very upsetting, it must have been. But she turned up safe and sound in the end, I'm sure."

"No, I'm afraid not."

He made a grimace of sympathy. "Really? What a pity. But that doesn't say she won't one day. I mean, after all, it hasn't been all that long ... "

"No, Walt, she'll never come back." My voice was so flat and final that his mask of condolence shifted slightly to allow curiosity to glance out. It was clear he was yearning to ask any number of questions, but there was no rational way I could explain even to myself why I knew this with such painful certainty about Nan, no matter how hard I tried to believe she was still somewhere—elsewhere—perhaps everywhere. Convictions of this kind are much too formless as well as too potent to drop into light dialogue with someone like Walt; so I said nothing more.

After wiping his moustache free of coffee foam, Walt cleared his throat. Then he went on, "And your poor pa. Boston, wasn't it, where he collapsed? Sheer exhaustion, of course. These Americans — they kill their celebrities with kindness, don't they."

"In this case, it would be better if they had."

Once more he turned on me a slightly startled eye.

"Surely that's coming on a bit strong, Pol."

"Is it? The stroke he had didn't finish him off—it just left him partly paralysed. Half dead. And for a man like Pa, that's—well."

"Oh, but they can do wonderful rehab now — " began Walt bravely.

"Sure. They patched him up enough to be flown home. That's to say, to a quite nice nursing-home near Dover, where we can get down to see him often. His mind's clear and he can speak quite plainly now."

"I remember what a performance he gave at that *Comus* affair," Walt went on, resolutely cheerful. "That was a fun evening, wasn't it? Really good theatre. The old boy gave it so much flash and go, and let's face it, Milton just doesn't often play that well. And of course all those wonderful novels of his ... everybody's looking forward madly to your pa's next."

Out of kindness, I let this pass without comment. For the last months, Ralph had as a matter of strategy been putting it about that Pa's new novel would soon be finished; but of course all of us, including Pa, knew better. Without even that illusion left, he spent his days in a wheelchair, his whole existence briskly and kindly manipulated by therapists, nurses, and orderlies. Poor Prospero, once so confident in his basic premise, "There's no harm done." I ached for him. Often he cried. Often he said in his blurred voice how much rather he'd be dead. My regular visits to Sunset Lodge were grim beyond words; but there was no point in trying to convey this kind of reality to anyone else, much less a happy citizen of the world of appearances like Walt.

"But let's hear about you, Polly," he went on brightly. Catching his own eye in the mirror over the counter, he adjusted one of his curly forelocks. "You're in work, I hope?"

"Well, of a sort. I read short stories for Auntie on Radio Four."

"Fabulous! I'm doing a film for ITV on the Battle of Britain. Jolly good show, what? And are you married, love, or still playing the field?"

I paused a moment. "Living with somebody." This was an exactly accurate statement, as far as it went; but once more I found it impossible to reveal anything more to Walt.

How could I have begun to explain that I was immersed now in a domestic life that looked from the outside stunningly banal, but on the inside was fraught with every possible variety of jealousy, quarrels, hilarity, and tears.

"Just my luck," Walt was saying with a lecherous upward twirl of his moustache. "I always seem to bump into you too late to do myself any good. Whatever became of that adorer of yours at the masked ball—the one with the red hair and the kilt—all masterful silence and dullness—or can't you remember?"

I smiled. "Oh, that one. He took a job as librarian at a girls' school."

"The perfect place for him. Thick glasses and a scholar's stoop. Not your scene at all, ducky."

My smile faded. Hamish wore contact lenses now, and a swimming course had toughened the muscles in his arms and legs with their pelt of red-gold hair. The fear of losing him was, in fact, central and ever-present. Those nubile little brats at St. Joan's used the school library with quite unneccessary frequency, and I resented them fiercely—an attitude that, to my extreme annoyance, seemed to give Hamish much quiet amusement.

"Well," said Walt, squeezing my hand lightly, "whatever you're up to these days with whoever-it-is, the set-up seems to agree with you. You're looking grand."

"So are you, Walt. Wizard, in fact. But now I've got to push—need to buy a sausage or two before the shops close. Great fun to see you. Thanks for the coffee. Remember me to everybody, and take care."

Briskly I seized my bag and started for the door while he was still fumbling with change. He called after me, "Will do. But hold on, Pol—let me have your tele—"

But I hurried away to lose myself in the home-bound crowd, not caring that haste made my limp more noticeable than usual. Much as I liked him, Walt was part of a raffish, role-playing world which I had no wish to rejoin. In so far as such a thing is possible, I was no longer acting any part whatever, either in public or in private. The face that met me in the mirror these days was simply my own. The prosaic supper sausages, an evening with my librarian with slippers toasting by a suburban gas-fire — these were my habitat now. As for personal drama, every twenty-eight days provided suspense, hope, and fear enough to fill any stage. Even though in my heart of hearts I suspected I was barren, there was always the outside chance of what Hermione once called the dangers of creativity.

I made off at a smart pace for the nearest Underground station, Walt and his moustache already fading from my mind. Overhead the sky streamed with a long cavalcade of clouds flowing in shapes that suggested a throng of extraterrestrial commuters formed out of molten light. Beautiful, bodiless, nameless, they flowed serenely across their airy element, and I braced myself against the push and jostle of impatient fellow-travellers a moment to look up at their brightness; but even as I did so, they dimmed and flowed away from me.